Long
D0982669

Longsword

Victoria Thorne

St. Martin's Press
New York

LCC: 81-23220
ISBN: 0-312-49679-6

First published in Great Britain by Corgi Books

First U.S. Edition
10 9 8 7 6 5 4 3 2 1

The girl gave a sudden cry of protest. The chief of the beggars had caught her arm and, as she reached for her dagger, the second of the men caught her free hand and twisted it up and away from her belt . . .

Gervase quickly threw back his cloak and drew his sword from where it had hung behind his right shoulder. Producing weapons from under their rags, the band of four turned to deal with the newcomer.

Gervase sent one man sprawling in the dust with a kick and a shrewd blow from the pommel of his sword, as a cudgel was raised to smite him . . . The second beggar had a dagger and, as he slashed at Gervase, so he found himself facing an incredibly long sword, snaking over the top of his hand to prick at his throat. The man howled, tripping over his own feet in an effort to avoid that wicked-looking blade. As the third beggar attempted to come up behind Gervase, the tall man sidestepped, throwing his sword from his left hand into his right to meet the leader who had a blade of his own in his hand . . . it was sent clattering as the man howled and doubled over, clutching at his elbow . . .

It was over.

Chapter One

The man broke out of the forest, and came to a halt. Across his path lay a dusty road, and beyond that rose the curtain walls and towers of a large castle. It was not at all what he had expected to see. He looked about him. He was a tall man, and despite his homespun cloak, there was an air of authority about him. A party of beggars were advancing towards him along the road.

"Give ye good day, sirrahs!" said the tall man. "What is the name of this place?"

"Castle Malling," said the leader of the beggars. The lone traveller turned and looked at the castle with renewed interest. The beggars had also halted, and were looking at him.

"Are you on the road, like us?" asked their leader. There was a protrusion under the traveller's cloak behind his right shoulder which betrayed the presence of a sword. The tall man started, and drew the hood of his cloak further forward over his head. The beggar persisted. "If you're down on your luck, you're in good company. Why not step along with us awhile? There's pickings in plenty, for those who can use a sword."

The lone traveller shook his head.

The beggar shrugged. "If you change your mind . . . . It's nigh on sunset, and we have an appointment with the Lady of Malling." The traveller lifted his head in surprise. "Oh, not that way!" the beggar assured him. "I meant only that she distributes alms at the gate at sunset. If you can feign illness, she might even give you a bed for the night." He began to adjust his arm in a bloodstained sling, while one of his fellows bandaged an eye, and a third practised a limp.

The traveller shook his head once more, and walked back along the road to where a spring tumbled down the bank. The beggars went on their way. Only when they were some distance off did the traveller push back the hood of his cloak and dash water over his face. His eyes were heavy-lidded from lack of sleep, and his dark red hair tousled. Though the cloak he wore was that of a peasant, the rest of his attire proclaimed him to be of noble birth. His linen shirt was of the finest weave, and the supple leather of his tunic and boots were fastened with gilded tassels. He drank, made the best toilet he could, and then sat down at the wayside to consider what he should do next.

He had been travelling since the middle of the previous night, without stopping to eat or drink. He had thought he would be far to the south of the forest by this time, and it was a blow to find that he had mistaken his way and arrived at Castle Malling instead.

The hue and cry would have begun at dawn – or perhaps later in the morning – it would have depended what time they had seen fit to send for the prisoner . . . and then dogs, men and horses would have set off in pursuit of the fugitive . . . .

Gervase Escot drew in his breath and put his head in his hands. Even now he could not believe it.

Six months ago; nay, even three . . . his uncle had been planning that Gervase should marry the Lady of Malling, and now he was a fugitive whose only chance lay in escaping abroad before the sheriffs caught up with him . . . for a theft he had not committed . . . .

They would not look for him in this direction. The dogs might well have followed him to the stream, but finding no trail on the far side would conclude, rightly, that he had intended to wade downstream till he could strike through the trees south-west to the downs, and the sea beyond. It must have been somewhere along the stream that he had missed the turn to the sea and safety.

His stomach contracted. There was a sick taste in his mouth. Food he must have, and a horse, yet he knew that he had only enough money in his wallet for a loaf of bread. How would it be if he were to join the crowd of beggars at the castle gate, and beg for bread from the woman who was to have been his wife?

The idea amused him. His mouth twisted, and his eyes, which were more yellow than hazel, narrowed. He was not a handsome man, though well-made, with a long, lean frame. His hands and feet were slender, his shoulders supple. His height alone would have made him noticeable in a crowd, but his auburn hair and narrow head, with its strongly-marked nose and chin, rendered him memorable. He had the ugly, humorous look of one who has battled long with life, and for the most part been the victor.

But not this time.

He groaned aloud. It was in his mind to curse the day he was born, but then he reflected that his mother must have done enough of that since, in bearing him, she had given up her own lease on life. Again his lips twisted. He rose to his feet and, adjusting the harness in which he carried his sword behind his shoulder, he pulled the hood over his head and took the path to the castle. He would not beg for food while he had a few pence left in his wallet, but he would take a look at the Lady of Malling before he went on his way.

The castle wall was built of granite blocks, with here and there a turret peering down on those who walked below.

The road bent to follow the curve of the wall, and presently a small postern gate came into view. Here a trestle table had been set up, in front of which stood a crowd of beggars, together with a plainly-dressed woman and two children. Gervase stepped into the shadow of the wall, and drew his hood further over his head. He thought it was lucky he had never been to Malling before, nor met its Lady.

A dark-haired girl of middling height came out of the postern, and looked around her. Then she withdrew, letting the gate bang to behind her. One of the beggars called after her to make haste, for they were hungry, and it was nigh on sundown.

Doubtless the girl – a waiting woman by the plain cut and drab colour of her gown – had gone to fetch her mistress, but women were notoriously bad at keeping to time, and the Lady of Malling might be some while yet.

Gervase straightened his shoulders, and pushed himself off the wall. He would not wait on the Lady of Malling.

What! Hang around to catch a glimpse of some woman who could mean nothing to him now?

His movement caught the eye of the leader of the beggars Gervase had encountered earlier. The four men were huddled together, talking in low voices and casting uneasy glances around. Gervase hesitated. The men were plotting something. No doubt he was imagining things, but he had gained the impression that they intended some villainy when they met the Lady of Malling. Yet what was that to him? Nothing.

The dark-haired girl hurried out of the postern once more, this time carrying a large basket piled with bread and scraps of meat. She called to someone behind her to hurry, for they were already past the hour. An elderly woman in the wimple and apron of a servant followed her, also bearing a basket, and entreating her mistress in a tone of despair: "Wait, my lady – it is not seemly, indeed it is not . . . !"

The girl lifted her basket onto the trestle with an effort, and smiled both at the elderly woman, and at the people waiting for alms. "Indeed it is, nurse!" she said. "Shall these poor folk go hungry because Anselm is busy and the others too proud to help me? Come, good people . . . here is some bread for you . . . and for you . . . What, man! That is a painful sore on your face; sit over there till I have finished, and I will dress it for you. . . ."

Gervase stood still. Was this in truth the Lady of Malling? Was this the famous beauty of whom he had heard so much? This squat, black-browed girl with a figure that hardly showed to advantage in a high-necked, long-sleeved, drab gown, and whose skin spoke of exposure to the weather? Was this the girl who had presided over the last tournament at York, and been acclaimed Queen of Beauty in countless ballads and poems?

Gervase laughed aloud. What folly! The girl was no more of a beauty than he was, and he knew that he was accounted an ugly man. He thought it was ever so, that rumour multiplied rumour until a girl who was well enough to look at – provided she be well-dowered – must ever be spoken of as a beauty. He was well out of the marriage, whatever else befell him.

The girl looked up from examining the child which the plainly-dressed woman was pushing forward. She had heard Gervase's laugh, and as she raised her eyes in enquiry, her own lips formed a smile. It was as if she were saying, Tell me why you laugh, and I will laugh, too.

Then eye met eye, and the tall man laughed no more. Neither did the girl. A frown formed on her brow, and she bent her head once more over the ailing child, while her cheek suffused with colour. He turned his back, biting his lip. He said to himself, "She is not a beauty . . . no, far from it! And yet her eyes are so deep and dark, and her smile so lovely . . . her face is too wide for beauty, her brow too low, but her features mirror every thought . . . skin like that should be soft to touch. Her hair is so pretty, curling so wildly . . . a pity to confine it in a net . . . she has a charm, an innocence . . . and yet a mind of her own . . . ."

At that point the girl gave a cry of protest, which brought Gervase round to face her. The beggars . . . he had thought as much! There was trouble afoot, with the girl objecting to their demand for a bed that night.

"No and no!" she said, stepping back, and emptying the last of the crusts onto the table. "You were this way last week, and your arm seemed well enough to me then . . . and your companions no worse . . . and surely it was your left arm, and not your right?"

"And what are poor discharged soldiers to do, then?" whined one.

"Work!" she cried, swinging one empty basket into the other.

"Give us alms, and we will go in peace," said the leader, edging towards her round the table. His eyes were on the purse that swung from her girdle. Gervase cursed under his breath. To draw attention to himself by going to her aid would be to court disaster . . . his description would be only too easily recognised . . . .

"Food ye have had in plenty," said the girl, giving the baskets to her nurse. "No more can I give ye, and no more will I!"

"Shelter there is for women and children, but not for poor wounded soldiers?"

The woman and her two children had been ushered through the postern gate into the castle, and so had the man with the sore on his face, but the girl now barred the door to the beggars with her own person.

"My lady, shall I call for help?" The servant cowered against the wall, frightened at the beggars' threatening looks. "I told you we should have waited . . . ."

"Get ye within, nurse. I am coming . . . ."

The chief of the beggars caught her arm, and as she reached for her dagger, the second of the men grabbed her free hand, and twisted it up and away from her belt.

Gervase threw back his cloak and drew his sword, left-handed, from where it hung behind his right shoulder. His long legs carried him easily over the ground, while the nurse cried out and ran within the castle. The rest of those who had sought alms fled, screaming, as the band of four turned to deal with the newcomer. From under their rags they produced an assortment of weapons and advanced on Gervase. The nurse ran out again, still screaming. She made darting runs to and from the postern gate like a distracted hen.

"One against four," shouted their leader. "And I have her purse already!"

It was a poor sort of fight. Gervase sent one man sprawling in the dust with a kick and a shrewd blow from the pommel of his sword, as a cudgel was raised to smite him . . . .

The second beggar had a dagger, and as he slashed at Gervase he found himself facing an incredibly long sword, snaking over the top of his hand to prick at his throat. The man howled, dropped his dagger, and tripped over his own feet in an effort to avoid the wicked-looking blade.

The third beggar attempted to come up behind Gervase, but even as he raised his crutch, the tall man sidestepped, throwing his sword from his left hand into his right, to meet the onslaught of their leader who had a blade of his own in his hand. This was sent clattering into the distance as the man howled, doubling over, clutching at his elbow . . . .

The nurse screamed. A half-dozen assorted servants and men-at-arms erupted from the postern. The four beggars gathered themselves together and fled, leaving a cudgel, a crutch and a sword behind to mark their passing.

It was over. The girl licked a trifle of blood from her hand. Her eyes were wide, seemingly more interested than afraid. She smiled at Gervase, revealing good teeth.

She said, "Thank you, messire. Such swordplay!" Her voice was as warm now as it had been matter-of-fact before.

"I doubt if my intervention was really necessary," replied Gervase, sheathing his sword.

"It was my folly that brought it about," said the girl. "I ought to have waited for Anselm, or called for help earlier. But no-one has ever offered me violence before . . . ." She stood upright, with care. She was, perhaps, more shaken by her adventure than she cared to acknowledge.

"And you knew I would intervene, if necessary," said Gervase. As the words left his mouth, he was astonished at himself for saying them . . . for even thinking them.

She did not evade the charge. "Yes," she said, with a simplicity that he guessed was characteristic of her. "I knew you would come to my aid if I needed help." The nurse was urging the girl within. The men-at-arms were returning with two of the beggars, and the girl's purse.

"My father will wish to thank you," she said. "Come within, messire . . . ?"

She waited for him to supply his name. He drew back. He could not possibly announce himself as Sir Gervase Escot of Ware, who had once been a suitor for her hand. He could not embarrass the Lord of Malling, or risk the sheriff's arrival while he was being entertained as became his station . . . .

"I am travelling in haste," he said. "I will seek a bed at the inn in the village."

The girl's face flamed with hurt pride. "Will you not allow us to repay . . . ?"

"Your pardon, lady. A bed for the night would be welcome, and something to eat and drink from the buttery, but I would not wish to trouble your father. . . ."

Still her eyes showed that his refusal had hurt her. He bent his head, the better to resist her silent pleading. She did not know what she was asking . . . .

The nurse intervened. "My lady, it would be wiser not to disturb your father with news of this . . . surely he will blame me for allowing you to come out unattended. No harm was done. Your purse has been recovered, and if this poor man . . . doubtless he knows his place, and would be overwhelmed by being taken into the hall when the company are at meat already . . . ."

"I do not think it is that," said the girl softly.

No, it is not that, said Gervase to himself. How quick of understanding was this girl! In another minute she would surely guess that he was a fugitive . . . .

"Will you accept a bed in the infirmary?" she asked him. "Will you share the fare provided for the men and women who lie there?"

He had no words to express his gratitude. She held out her hand; he took it, and bowed over it. It was broad in the palm, and capable. It was not the soft hand of a Queen of Beauty, yet it pleased Gervase. He wanted to carry her hand to his lips but he did not dare . . . and yet he did not know why. Perhaps because she did not seem to expect it?

"Your name, messire?"

He thought quickly. To give his own name would be to invite trouble, even if they had not yet heard, here in Malling, of the theft.

"William," he began and hesitated. His father's name had been William.

"I shall call you William Longsword," she said, as if she had not noticed his hesitation, though surely she had. "Your weapon is long enough to have spitted all four of those rascals at once!"

He smiled but made no reply. Inwardly he cursed himself for having drawn his sword, for was it not almost as notable as his red hair? He put up a hand to his hood, to find that it had flown back long since. Well, it was done. Any that passed that way would hear the tale of the red-headed man with the long sword, and he would be identified as clearly as if he had claimed himself Gervase Escot of Ware. It was done, and he was weary to the bone. The girl's face changed;

her face was so mobile it took the imprint of each passing thought.

She said, "You are tired. Come, follow me."

She led him, with the nurse jealously coming between them, through the postern into a courtyard ringed with the blank walls of granaries. A low arch led into another court in which a cheerful bustle surrounded the kitchens. The fragrant scent of roasting meats lingered on the air, and the aroma of home-brewed ale. A sharp turn led into a quiet cloister, greying over with shadows as the sun sank. A cresset was alight in one corner, and a servant – an ancient, toothless, bald-headed man – was hobbling about setting more torches aglow here and there. A candle and a fire gave warmth and light in one cell, but she stopped at another nearby, and there left him, saying she must attend to her patients. A candle and meats were forthcoming. There was clean linen on the bed, and fresh rushes on the floor. He would have fared worse, perhaps, in the inn. And he had saved his money.

He ate, drank, snuffed the candle, and fell on the bed to sleep.

One moment he was asleep, and the next aware of confused sounds and lights. He was on his feet in an instant, eyes wide, left hand reaching for his sword, wondering where he was.

"Look what ye've done now, ye lack-witted, clumsy . . . ." The ancient man who had brought his supper was passing by. The door had swung open. The ancient put his head in, seeing that Gervase was up, to reassure him. "'Tis nothing, messire. The boy knocked against your door in passing, being but new-woken, and the catch is not good . . . ."

Gervase relaxed his grip on his sword. A false alarm. He remembered now where he was. He stepped to the door to look up at the sky. Was it far off dawn? The night was still dark, but there was a faint glimmer in the east, over the roof of the cloister opposite, which told of the day to come. He had slept well. Perhaps it would be a good thing if he went on his way now, before the rest of the castle woke.

"He's gone for the Lady Beata," said the ancient, pleased to find someone awake and therefore, presumably, ready for a gossip in the middle of the night. Gervase wondered if the man ever slept. He seemed as fresh, or as jaded, as in the evening when he had ministered to Gervase.

"There's a poor traveller a-dying in the end cell, ye see, and she likes to be with them at the end, to take their last wishes if she can, and fold their hands over a sprig of rosemary. Then in the morning she says a mass for their souls. She does it for everyone, rich or poor. There's many a man come a few extra miles on his journey to die here – as did that poor creature – knowing as she'd say a mass for him, poor sinner though he be . . . ."

Gervase thought it was unlikely that any such death-bed would fall to his lot. He found himself wishing, with a fervour that surprised him, that the projected marriage had still been possible.

"She comes." The ancient turned to watch the nurse pass through the far side of the cloisters, treading at the heels of a dark-cloaked figure. A gangling boy bore a torch to the cresset, and set it alight. His duty done, he went yawning back to his pallet.

"Where's your hurry?" asked the ancient, as Gervase began to buckle on his sword-belt. "The portcullis won't be lifted till dawn. I thought you were to be presented to Lord Henry? –"

"I am journeying in haste. Perhaps the postern gate is open?"

The ancient shook his head. Gervase sat down on the bed, bidding himself show no sign of impatience. He was securely locked in, as securely as if he had still been in the inner store at Ware, though this time there would be no men arriving in the middle of the night to try to murder him. . . .

"I must be off in the dawn," he said.

The aged man doddered away, and Gervase fell to watching the flickering light in the cell opposite. It was in his mind to walk out into the cloister until he could see into that cell, so that he could watch her minister to the dying man.

But he did not, for surely a man had a right to privacy when he was dying . . . and if she were to catch him spying on her . . . . "Beata," he said to himself. "Bay-ah-ta . . . a lovely name . . . ." He bit his lip, and buried his face in his hands. He must think! A man fleeing from justice does not think clearly. He had an hour or so before dawn . . . he must use it to consider, as dispassionately as he could, what had happened and what he should do about it.

The accusation of theft . . . his own indignant protestation of innocence . . . his uncle looking sick, turning from him, casting him off.

Ah, the pain of that moment when his uncle had turned away from him . . . after so many years of loyalty and hard work . . . it was as if those years had never been, as if he had spent his life for nothing . . . .

"Let him be branded as a thief!" Now who had spoken the words first? His uncle's new wife? Or her loving cousin, Sir Bertrand, that attentive relative of hers, who was always at her elbow?

Branded! Gervase supposed he must have protested. He could only remember staring at them in disbelief. True, his uncle's ring had been found in his wallet, but how it had got there, he had no idea. Or at least, he had some idea of how the trick had been worked, but it was impossible to accuse his uncle's beloved wife of theft, or of bearing false witness against him. How clever the woman had been, turning Ralph Escot from his nephew with such accusations and half-truths as could not be disproved, only denied!

It was Sir Bertrand who had helped the stricken old man away, and Sir Bertrand who had presided over that travesty of a court case. It was Sir Bertrand who had given orders for Gervase to be locked in the innermost of the stone-built store-rooms, to await punishment. But was it Sir Bertrand who had come to that room in the middle of the night, carrying a rope with a noose at the end of it? Gervase shook his head. No, neither of the two men who had come to kill him had been as big as Sir Bertrand. The light had been bad, but . . . he concentrated, shutting his eyes . . . yes, he knew now who the two men were . . . there had been one servant from Sir Bertrand's retinue, and one from his aunt's.

If it had not been for the head groom, Gervase would have been dead by now. But that stalwart soul, who had taught him to ride when he was a child, had overheard enough to send him to the store-room window to warn Gervase and to slide Gervase's sword through the bars, that he might be armed against treachery.

Gervase groaned. What was he to do? His uncle had believed him guilty, and disowned him. For twenty-seven years he had been his uncle's heir, and though the young man and the old had often quarrelled, yet their quarrels had never been serious until Lord Escot had taken it into his head to marry. His new wife was an attractive widow, cousin to that Sir Bertrand de Bors who held land near Ware. Then all changed for Gervase. He saw now that he ought to have left Ware when Lady Escot arrived. But at first her words had been honeyed, and Gervase, though he had not liked her, had conceived it his duty to stay, for was he not his uncle's reeve and bailiff and steward, all rolled into one? Then Lady Escot had announced that she was to bear a child, and his uncle's eyes had begun to avoid his nephew's, and then . . . the accusation of theft, backed up by false witness . . . the woman declaring she had heard Gervase boast of his intention to keep the ring . . . that he had said such things about his uncle as could not be forgiven, especially by an old man . . . .

If Gervase had stayed, he would have been killed. He had been disowned, but that, apparently, had not been enough for Lady Escot. And he had no redress, for he had no proof, no money, no influence. He had nothing but his sword and the clothes on his back. Well, let it be so. He yawned. He would go out into the world and seek a new master – one who would reward his services with gold rather than blows. Chance had directed him away from the sea, and he would go where chance led him. Overseas he could have taken service in some army or other, earned his livelihood as a paid soldier . . . he had had experience of such work. He yawned again. To the devil with armies and battles and wounds . . . give him a quiet life, any day! Had he not tired long since of war?

So he would seek his livelihood by other means. He would not go abroad, but continue walking westward. If his uncle sent sheriffs after him, they would surely go south, expecting him to cross the Channel. He would be far safer going west . . . .

Before he knew it, he was asleep again, and only woke when the ancient shook his arm. Sunlight was filling the bare cell with warmth.

". . . and there was I thinking ye meant to be off at first light, and here it is an hour past dawn, and the Lady at Mass already . . . ."

Gervase started up. It had been in his mind to attend Mass with the Lady, and the knowledge that she was already gone to church gave him a feeling of loss. Yet what was he about, thinking of going to Mass, with the sun high in the sky, and the road before him?

" . . . but she looked in on you before she went, and told me that if you really did wish to be off without greeting her father–and it seemed to surprise her, I may say, that ye should be so scornful of our hospitality–she said I must see ye fed, and set ye on your way, and that if your road took you to Bristol, would ye act as escort to the poor lady with the two children whom she took in yester eve? One of them, to my mind, is sickening for something serious, but the poor mother is so determined to be away . . . ."

Bristol. The west. Gervase nodded. Chance was undoubtedly working in his favour. Who would think of connecting a lone fugitive with a man escorting a poor but respectable family to Bristol?

Yet though he told himself that all was going well, he was filled with a feeling of depression that he could not shake off. He looked across the cloister, but the door of the dead man's cell was closed. He felt as if he, too, had been shut out. Beata, he thought. The name meant happiness, or blessedness. A good name for her. He wished her well. He wished . . . . He shrugged. He must be on his way.

Chapter Two

The glossy leaves of summer had changed colour and were beginning to fall from the trees before Gervase came to Malling again. This time he did not stride down the road with all the confidence of youth and health. Gone were the long sword, the rough but serviceable cloak, fine linen, tunic and boots; instead, he crept along on feet wrapped in bloodstained bindings, and his emaciated body was clothed only in a tattered tunic and loincloth. Gone was the long stride and proud carriage; he leaned on a staff cut from the hedgerow, and the sun and the rain alike beat on his bare head.

He paused within sight of the castle, more to rest than because he was too early to join the poor people at the postern gate. He looked at the stream, and debated within himself whether he had the strength to get up off the ground again, if he stooped to slake his thirst. He doubted he had. He forced himself to move forward, then wavered and nearly fell. The last rays of the sun were gilding the walls of the castle, and caught at his face. He winced, and shielded his eyes. Face, hands and arms – even his legs – were swollen and red.

Twenty paces more, he said to himself. Then another twenty . . . she will not refuse to take in a dying man. I can go in peace, knowing that she will close my eyes . . . if only she is not afraid of my disease . . . if only . . . .

Ten paces, and he had to lean against the wall to rest. His forehead burned. He groaned and tried to cool it against the stone of the wall. The brightness of the sun had gone. Now he shivered, as his fever mounted. It would be very easy just to slip down and die, but then she would never say a mass for him, poor sinner that he was.

Gervase took another step, and felt the sky blacken above him. He clung to his staff, shutting his swollen evelids. On, he muttered. Only a little way now. How many days was it since he had started back to Malling? Eight? He had lost count. Another few steps, and the postern was in sight . . . or did his eyes deceive him? She would not recognise him, of course. Who would? But that did not matter. It was better so. If only she were not afraid of the disease . . . .

There were two men-at-arms behind her at the postern gate, and the nurse . . . the nurse's apron was blinding white . . . the girl was not looking his way, but talking to a youth with a twisted leg . . . suppose she did not see him, after all? Suppose the soldiers turned him away – soldiers posted there because of the beggars' attack on her, no doubt. The irony of it . . . .

He was there. He reached the trestle and put one hand on it, leaning on it and on his staff. The nurse was thrusting some bread at him, and remarking that he was nearly too late. The girl was turning away, having finished with her task for the evening. She had not seen him. Her hair was flying out from under its confining net, strong curls of glossy black, each with a mind of its own . . . she was trying to tuck them back in, and they were resisting her . . . .

"Take it, do!" said the nurse, poking the crust at him once more.

The girl looked round, her eyes widened, and her hands stilled.

"Longsword!" she cried. She ran round the trestle. She had her arm round Gervase, and was supporting him, his staff dropping away . . . he felt tears burn his cheeks. His throat swelled. He could not speak.

He heard the nurse cry out, and the girl say something about that being nonsense, and then she was giving orders, sharp and clear, and the two men-at-arms were coming forward, lifting him onto the trestle top, and carrying him through into the castle. For a few paces she walked beside him, with her hand in his, and then she withdrew her hand and he, striving to turn his head to see what had happened to her, lost consciousness, and went into the fiery hell that awaits those who contract smallpox.

She was bending over him, between him and the candle, and her head was haloed by its light. He was in such a fever . . . a red hell . . . .

The walls were plastered and whitewashed. The bed was hard and hot . . . .

The ancient man hovered, mumbling. His name was Anselm. The girl called him that. Water, more water. Ah . . . .

She was there again, on the other side of the bed, and now there was no nimbus of candlelight about her. She was frowning, biting her lip, bathing his face. He tried to smile up at her. His lips framed the words, "You knew me," but though he strove to speak, she did not seem able to hear him.

How many days? It was taking him a long time to die. He had not thought it would take so long. He had thought it would be all over quickly . . . all he had ever done had ended in failure . . . such an unsatisfactory life, best ended . . . . But perhaps it was an illusion that he was taking a long time to die? Perhaps they were still living through that first night, the night of his coming to the castle? He tried to ask the ancient Anselm, but his lips were too swollen, and one of his eyes completely closed.

It could not be the same day, for the girl was wearing different clothes. Her everyday dress was a plain affair of dark purplish-brown, but this was of sage green, with a pattern of gold threads. Then he saw it was not a different dress, but a green cloak cast over her shift, with the rays of the candle shooting gold across it here and there.

He tried to smile at her. He wanted to tell her that he had never seen anyone so beautiful. She sat on the stool beside his bed with one of her characteristically abrupt movements, and took his hand in hers . . . .

Then she was gone, and the candle was there again. It fretted him that she was not between him and the candle, to shield his eyes from the brightness. Then his sight blurred. Later – how much later? The sonorous words; he had known their meaning once, but now they echoed in his head like waves on the seashore. Then he realised that the girl's nails were digging into the palm of his hand, and the priest was asking him if he repented of his sins . . . .

Gervase tried to say that he was innocent of the theft of the ring, but the priest would not wait, taking his mumblings for assent. Gervase was shriven, and anointed, and received the Last Sacrament; and all this time he was aware of what was happening, although it seemed to be happening not to him, but to someone else.

It seemed to distress the girl that he was dying. She wept, and turned her shoulder on Anselm when that ancient came to enquire whether the corpse was not yet ready for his shroud. It worried Gervase that she wept. He could not understand why she should. He was happy enough to go, and he tried to tell her so.

". . . you shall not die!" said the girl. It was night, and she was wearing her cloak over her shift, with her hair loose about her shoulders. Such wonderful hair, curling and waving, running riot around her neck and over her brow, but not long enough . . . surely she did not cut it?

He found he could open both his eyes. Not much, but a little. The swellings on his mouth had abated, too. Perhaps he could even talk, if he tried hard enough.

He made an effort to moisten his lips and she, quick to help, held a goblet of wine to his mouth. He said, "It is better this way . . . close my eyes . . . a sprig of rosemary between my hands . . . ." He was surprised he could say so much, and even more surprised that she had heard and understood him.

"No," she said. "You must not die. You are too young. There is so much for you to do . . . ."

He moved his head in negation.

"Yes, there is," she said, nervously insistent. "Such skill with the sword . . . ."

"I sold my sword – to innkeeper – at Mere. The child – the boy – fell sick. Then the mother. I saw it was smallpox. She would not rest. Husband dead . . . wanted to take children to her father in Bristol. No money. She said to leave them . . . but I could not. So I sold everything, little by little . . . . only it was no good. The little girl lived longest . . . almost got there. I sold my tunic to give her burial and took their things on to the grandfather . . . but he did not care. He saw I was sickening, too . . . he turned me away . . . afraid of the infection . . . why are you not afraid? . . . . I thought you would bury me, if you were not afraid . . ."

She struck her hands together. "If only I had known! It is all my fault, for I guessed the child was sick. I will repay you, I will! I will send for your sword . . . you will live to fight again . . . ."

"Longsword is dead. When I sold my sword, I knew what I was doing. Tired of fighting . . . glad to be done with it . . ."

She put both hands to her forehead, pressing on the temples. "Oh, I am so stupid! I ought to be able to think of the right words . . . ."

Then the nurse came, and took the girl away. He had wanted to say goodbye to her, to thank her . . . but she was gone, and he had not said the words. A wave of fatigue hit him, and he nearly went under. If he went under, he would die. Why, then, was he holding back?

"He's still alive!" The girl sounded exultant.

He opened his eyes and smiled up at her. He wanted to tell her then, how grateful he was . . . but she was gone again. The day lay before him, long and dreary, and he knew that the waves of fatigue would come back, and that one of them might be so big that he would have to relinquish his hold on life. When he saw her next, he would tell her that he was too tired to go on . . . .

But the days passed, and though she came to his bedside in the night twice more, with her hair loose and her cloak around her shoulders, yet he did not die.

He stretched himself in the narrow bed, and without opening his eyes thought of that other bed of his, at Ware. That was a wide bed with an embroidered coverlet on it, with fine linen sheets, and wool blankets. There was a carved wooden screen he could pull round from behind the bedhead, if the wind turned to the north and the chimney smoked, or the draught came round the shutters on the windows. By his bedside there was a stand, on which his man would set water and towels morning and night, and beyond that again the big carved chest against the arras in which lay, carefully folded with sprigs of lavender, his linen shirts, his best tunic of blue-green damask, and the workaday ones of fine wool and leather. A cupboard on the wall held a mirror and a razor. A larger chest beside the door held his chainmail tunic, together with the helmet he had carried to the wars in France, and to tourneys . . . and his spurs . . . and the shield with the sign of the Escots blazoned on it, azure blue on black . . . .

At the foot of his bed, on a square of rush matting, would lie his two dogs, curled up in sleep, ready for the click of his fingers. Where were they now? Would someone look after them for him?

He sighed and turned himself on his side.

What should he do with himself this coming day? As Sir Gervase Escot of Ware he had had a number of alternatives. If his uncle were fit, and in a good temper, they would go hunting in the winter-time, and ride out to see to the farms in summer. Or they might hold court in the hall, and there Gervase would as likely as not be left to dispense justice by himself, for his uncle had less and less patience for disentangling court cases as he advanced in years and girth. Or they might get out the dice in the evenings, or the cards, or entertain passing travellers – a minstrel, perhaps – a neighbouring lord. His uncle would probably get drunk whether he did any of the other things first or not. Gervase enjoyed the wines of Gascony, but he did not at all relish the loss of control which drunkenness brought in its train. He was a man who liked to be in control of whatever situation he happened to find himself.

Now, lying in the bed at Malling, he put his hands to his head, remembering everything that had happened to him in the past few months . . . and kept his hands there, passing them over his face and head. He had been clean-shaven and long-haired when he had fallen ill. Now he had a beard and his hair had been shorn to allow the sores on his head to be cleansed every day. His skin was still raw in places, and one eyelid would never rise to the old extent again. He feared his face was badly marked, and then laughed, soundlessly, for what on earth did it matter if he were marked or no? He had never been a handsome man, and yet . . . he sighed . . . he had not been vain, but he had known himself attractive to women, and had taken a certain pleasure in that. Now he supposed he must be content if only he did not frighten children away with his ugly face and ginger beard. His hair was still auburn in colour, but he knew his beard was bright red, for Anselm frequently chuckled over the fact that his newly-grown beard was so much lighter than the hair on his head.

He opened his eyes and pushed and pulled himself into a sitting position. His arms trembled with the effort he had made. He laughed again, and again no sound escaped him. That he should be reduced to this! A child had more strength than he. His eyes went beyond the end of the bed to the bare wall opposite, and then up to the corner of the wall and ceiling above. In that corner, where joists of ancient wood ran, some long-dead craftsman had carved a crude winged figure holding a cross. The cross was held in front of the figure at such an angle that anyone who looked up from the bed might suppose that the cross was being held out to him.

Gervase looked, as he had looked a hundred times before. He tilted his head back against the plaster wall behind him, the better to study that cross. Was it meant for him? The angel seemed to say that it was. Yet Gervase saw that he could reject it or not, just as he chose.

He, Gervase Escot, who had died and been born again, could now decide of his own free will to devote the rest of his life to good works. Or not. It was clear to him that he had come to a crossroads in his life . . . cross roads . . . to a cross in the road . . . .

The girl had seemed sure that he would live to fight again, but he doubted it . . . the fighting part, anyway. He had done with wars, with dirt and disease and all that senseless expenditure of energy. Then what remained to him? He had had some idea, a long time ago . . . when he first left Escot . . . .

Without a sword, without clothes . . . without skills, except for fighting.

"So what do you want me to do?" he asked the angel.

The angel didn't reply. How could it? It was a carved figure, merely; a crude figure of wood with awkward wings. He wondered how that old-time carver had thought the angel would ever fold those wings. They were such large wings, and so very, very stiff. Not much of the angel could be seen, in fact, what with the cross, and its wings, and a rather uneven halo.

"Well," said Gervase to the angel, "perhaps good looks aren't as important here in the infirmary, as they might be outside . . . ."

And then he laughed aloud. And stopped, for he thought he had heard someone call for help. He looked suspiciously up at the angel, but naturally enough, the angel hadn't moved. The call came again, imperative, somewhat desperate.

Gervase sat up straight and looked out through the open door into the cloister, and beyond that into the green garth beyond. It was late in the afternoon, and it was raining. There was no-one about. It was the one time of day, in fact, when Anselm, who appeared to nurse anything up to a score of people with sporadic help from a young lad, was not present. Anselm always went to the buttery after his noon meal, and thence to the chapel. Gervase suspected that he went there to have an uninterrupted sleep, which was rarely allowed him at night. Usually the young lad was about somewhere, but this time he seemed conspicuous by his absence. The Lady Beata and her nurse would not reappear until they had distributed alms at the gate at sunset, and as it happened, there were very few occupants of the beds in the infirmary at the moment.

Gervase waited for someone to come. There was a big ward with a dozen beds in it at the far end of the cloister, to which most travellers were taken if they fell sick en route. Someone would come from there . . . or one of the women might hear, from the big room on the far side of the cloisters. The cells were reserved for those members of the castle who might fall ill and need attention. The cry had come from the cell next to Gervase. He did not know the name of its occupant, but he guessed that he was of some importance in the household, by the amount of time and trouble the Lady Beata took with him. The calls for help were repeated at frequent intervals. The man began to sound frantic.

Ah well, thought Gervase; no-one can expect me to do anything about it.

Oh, no? said the angel. Or rather, Gervase thought that was what the angel said. Conscience, he said to himself.

Perhaps the man's fallen out of bed.

Quite probably, from the sound of it.

Well, I can't lift him back again.

No? said the angel.

Gervase swore. He passed from swearing in English to French, and thence to Latin. Latin is a good language in which to swear. He swung his legs out of bed and stood up. The stone floor struck cold through the rushes. He winced. He was naked, and he had no clothes. More, the angel had not taken it into account that he had no strength in his legs. He sat on the bed. The angel prodded him off. He had got out of bed yesterday, hadn't he? And walked as far as the door? No! He snarled at the angel. He had not walked as far as the door. With the Lady Beata on one side of him, and the loutish boy on the other he had been dragged, feet trailing, to the door and back again. He had not walked.

He couldn't.

The angel shrugged. It was remarkable how his shoulders went up and down, when he was, after all, only a wooden figure.

Gervase pulled at the edge of the sheet on his bed. If the sheet came off easily, he would be able to cast it around him until he could get to the door and call for help. If the sheet stuck, then he would be justified in getting back into bed and forgetting all about the matter. The sheet came off easily. Gervase pulled it round his shoulders and, steadying himself with one hand against the wall, he shuffled to the doorway. The rain hissed down, pounding on the grass, sending spraylets far into the cloister, almost as far as Gervase. He could see no-one, hear nothing. Except for the sick man's cries, which were becoming more urgent and more weak with every passing minute.

"Malediction!" said Gervase to the angel. He turned with care to the right, steadying himself as before against the wall. The next cell was larger than his, with skins on the floor, and a fire in the hearth. The bed was not only furnished with linen sheets, but also a brocade coverlet; more, a thick curtain depended from a rod above the bedhead. An elderly man was sitting up in bed, beating with twisted and swollen hands at the bedclothes and curtain, set alight by an overturned candle.

"Help!" cried the elderly man.

"I'm here," said Gervase. There was no time to run for help – even if he were capable of running, which he was not. He pulled off the sheet which covered his nakedness, and threw it over the flames. Then he dragged on the coverlet, pulling it down over the burning material, and smothered the flames. He ended up on the floor, the flames out, the stink of burned cloth in his face, laughing weakly at his predicament. He lay on the floor . . . the old man lay on the bed . . . neither could move without help, and no help was forthcoming.

"Brother Fire, harm me not!" said Gervase, harking back to the preachings of St Francis of Assisi.

"Must you make a jest of everything?" demanded the man in the bed. Anger and fear brought colour to his thin cheeks. "Can you not see I am helpless? My leg . . . I am so swaddled about with clothing . . . Get up, sirrah! Cover your nakedness, if you please!"

Gervase rose to his knees, but his trembling legs would not support him, and he rested there, leaning against the bed, fighting off a sick dizziness which threatened to smother him . . . .

"Get off me, sirrah! Can you not see I am in pain? Where is Anselm? And the boy?"

Gervase took a deep breath, and the faint feeling receded. The old man was suffering from shock. He'd had a near escape from death. There was bound to be a reaction. If there were any wine to be had . . . .

Nearby was a chest, upon which stood a bowl of fruit, a flagon of wine and some goblets. Gervase lunged for the chest, poured wine for the old man, and gave it to him. His hands were so misshapen with rheumatism that he had to use both of them to hold the cup, and he trembled so much he spilt some of the precious liquid on his fine white beard. He must indeed be a person of some consequence, for a furred cloak had been thrown over his shoulders to keep him warm. A confidential secretary, perhaps? He had none of the look of a man who labours in the vineyard, but much of the air of authority which pertains to the owner thereof. A writing stand and portable desk stood nearby, on which were set out parchment, ink-horn and quills. On a peg on the wall hung a scholar's black gown, made of the finest wool.

"Cover yourself, pray!" said the old man, gesturing to the black robe. "And give yourself some wine, too. You deserve it."

Gervase looked at the robe, and then down at his shivering nakedness. He thought a scholar's robe would sit ill on his tall frame. Yet he was chilled, and the cloth of the robe would be warm. A linen shift hung beneath it; again, the quality was not such as he had been used to in the past, but it was a world removed from the rags in which he had returned to Malling. Should he cavil at wearing good linen again, because he had once worn something finer? The robe had a deep square yoke, from which the body of the gown fell to his calves in heavy pleats. The long full sleeves were slit up to the elbows, to allow the forearms freedom. He put on shift and robe, and at once his teeth stopped chattering; he felt as if he had taken a step of some importance.

The man on the bed inclined his head to Gervase and said, "I'm Hamo, steward of Malling, and confidential man of business to Lord Henry. You must be the discharged soldier from the next cell. You shall be rewarded for your prompt action, when my lady comes." He spoke with the kindly condescension of a servant high in favour with the nobility.

Gervase bowed his head, and kept his amusement to

himself. Yet surely Hamo was in the right of it, and a landless knight without a sword was worth far less than a trusted clerk.

"I was reaching for my desk," continued Hamo, "but my hands are no longer as nimble as they were once . . . though certainly Anselm left that candle too near the edge. My lord expects a report from me at the end of each week: a confidential report, not to be trusted to my junior clerks."

Gervase looked at the crippled hands, and wondered how the old man ever managed to hold the pen nowadays. He was a gallant old gentleman, this Hamo, with a lively eye and a shelf of books nearby to show that he had more than the rudiments of education in him.

"I'll pen it for you, if you like," offered Gervase. "That was a nasty shock you had. If you will trust me to do it for you?"

"You can write?" His incredulity was not flattering.

"I learned as a child, and then, when I was laid up with a broken leg in France, I improved my penmanship, lacking better employment for my time. The monks who cared for me were kind enough to say I could be trusted with simple tasks in that direction."

Knight and steward eyed one another. Finally Hamo gave a sharp nod, at which Gervase drew the desk towards him, and picked up the quill in his left hand.

"That is the devil's hand," objected Hamo. "No letters of mine will be written with the left hand."

"The monks said it did not matter which hand I wrote with, provided the task was done with God in mind. I write very ill with my right hand; if you wish, I will prove it to you."

Hamo raised his eybrows, but began to dictate his report. Presently Gervase's hand began to tremble, and he had to stop a while to rest. Finally the letter was finished, and handed to Hamo for checking. Gervase sank to the floor, and let his head fall back against the wall. His mind was not on the letter, but on the impossibility of walking back, unaided, to his own room.

Presently Hamo looked up from the letter. "Passably

written," he said. Then he frowned. Gervase had fallen asleep, sprawled against the wall, the quill still in his hand.

Hamo's eyes narrowed. "Left-handed," he said to himself. "Red-haired, left-handed, educated . . . and something of a swordsman. Now I wonder . . . ."

Chapter Three

The girl had brought him a dog to nurse back to health. The dog had been gored in an encounter with a wild boar, and Crispin, Beata's brother, had ordered Flash to be destroyed, because in his pain the dog had snapped at Crispin.

"Flash is a favourite of my father's," said the girl. "It seemed wrong to me to destroy the dog if a little rest and good care would set him to rights. Crispin is so hasty, sometimes. My father is away for six weeks, and knows only that the dog was gored. He doesn't know that Crispin has ordered Flash to be destroyed. My father would care for the dog himself, if he were here . . . he loves so few things or people . . . I would save the dog for him, if I could."

Flash licked Gervase's hand, and he smiled. The dog's right hind leg had been badly torn, but the wound was clean, and the animal looked interested in his surroundings. Beata crouched on the floor beside Flash, her hands clasped on her knees, her attention on the dog. She said, "If my brother discovered that I had disobeyed his orders and brought the dog to you, there would be trouble. Flash must be kept out of his sight . . . must remain here in the cloisters, until my father is returned."

Gervase was pleased to be allowed to do something for her. And in any case, the dog's bright eyes were already giving him his reward. He scooped him up, balanced himself on unsteady legs and bore Flash to a dark corner by his bed.

A letter lay, half-written, on the writing stand, which had now found its way into his own cell.

"I interrupted you in your work," she said, tucking a strand of wavy hair back into its net. "I'm sorry. Hamo is full of praise for you . . . ."

"Not to my face . . . ." He grimaced, easing the heavy collar of his gown over his right shoulder. He was still weak, and there was a place on his back where the skin had not healed properly.

"That is his way," she said, with amused indulgence. "But a kinder mortal never existed. Why, he took the trouble to teach me how to read and write when I was small, and now and then he will even lend me one of his precious books. He said you learned to write in France?"

"My leg was mauled in a skirmish before a besieged town gate, some four years back. I was left to recover at a priory where the monks divided their time between farming and copying manuscripts. I had learned the rudiments of the art in childhood, but my uncle had never encouraged such pursuits, so . . . I liked it there."

"With the monks? You?" She was incredulous.

"Is that so strange? I was tired of war, and thought it a better thing to sow the land with barley than with blood. I was nigh on throwing my sword away and taking the cloth at one time."

"That would have been a great waste of your talents!"

"What talents? A talent for killing men efficiently? I have no other."

She waved her hands in the air. "But you have! Hamo says you understand how estates are administered almost as well as he does . . . and there is your kindness . . . your giving of yourself to others, as you did to that sick family I foisted on you . . . ."

He laughed, but coloured up, flattered despite himself. He busied himself cutting a quill down to a point, while she took up her seat on his bed, her arms round her knees, and her chin tilted. He recognised the symptoms; she was feeling aggressive about something. Whatever it was, he was more than pleased to listen. Her eyes were critical, studying him.

He turned his head away. He wore the full costume of the scholar now, and though he privately thought he cut a ridiculous figure, did not appear so to anyone else. A coif of white linen covered his tell-tale hair, but he had kept his beard, which was so much lighter in colour than his hair. The beard made his long chin seem broader, subtly altering the shape of his head. What with that beard, and his pockmarks, he thought it unlikely anyone who had known him before would recognise him now.

"What thought you of the monks?" she asked.

"I thought much of their penmanship, and little of their piety."

"That is a harsh judgment." Was she angry?

"It was the truth. I thought you wanted that rather than conventional platitudes."

She was silent awhile, frowning at him. "You have no vocation, I think. What made you consider joining those you despise?"

"I was abandoned, penniless, in a foreign land, and they were kind to me. I had quarrelled with my uncle for the forty-fifth time – or may be it was the forty-sixth. I was sick of war; my uncle thought of nothing else. It seemed that I had been husbanding his resources for nine months of the year, only to have him squander the lot in a campaign every summer."

"It is not impossible to win fortunes in war. My father did, and my brother has not done so badly, either."

"My uncle was born without judgment. If he has to choose between two roads, he will make the wrong choice, always."

"And you were his counsellor?"

"For my sins. I think I first tried to stop him doing something foolish when I was eight, and he was thirty-eight . . . that was the year my father died, and I was taken to live with my uncle. For the following eighteen years I continued in my folly, trying to correct his folly, and it ended in folly, as I ought to have known that it would." The quill snapped beneath his fingers, and he set the pieces aside to start on another. 'It is also folly to put pressure on something that will not withstand it."

"You speak in riddles."

He had not meant that she should understand him. She sat perched on his bed like a child, unselfconscious, innocent, offering him friendship and, perhaps, more than friendship. He wanted to ask her why her nurse did not accompany her when she visited him in the afternoons, but he did not. Her visits were the highlights of his life. She wanted to be told everything, to know everything that he had seen, or done, or heard about. Her mind was quick, her knowledge of life limited. She seemed to have lived as cloistered as a nun, as neglected as a bastard child. Yet she was the Lady Beata of Malling, and herein was a riddle which he could not read.

She said, "Why did you not stay with the monks, then?"

"My uncle was foolish enough to get himself taken prisoner, and sent for me to return to England and raise his ransom. And so I did." He sighed. "He was so badly shaken that he agreed we should go no more campaigning, but stay on the estates and build up our resources, which had been sadly depleted, what with the ransom, and so many years of campaigning. We had three years at home; two of the harvests were excellent, and one was fair . . . and I thought in my folly that with age he had outgrown folly."

He looked at her again, to see if she had divined his secret, but she was frowning at the wall, twisting at a curl over her ear. He had told her his name was William of Leys, and that his uncle had had a small estate in the west country. She had seemed to accept this without question. But surely she must suspect that his tale bore a resemblance to that of her one-time suitor Gervase Escot of Ware? He had told her the truth in every other detail. He did not know whether he wanted her to guess or no. When she was with him he led the talk that way, and courted danger by telling her every day a little more here, a little more there . . . surely she must guess! But then, if she did guess, what would happen? Would he not be thrown out of Eden? Would there not be a dungeon and fetters for him, while messages were sent to Ware, or to the local sheriffs, that they had found the escaped criminal?

"And then?" she said. "What folly did your uncle commit to drive you from him this summer?"

"He married. He wed a youngish woman, who was

perhaps not as young as she made out. A woman with calculating eyes, and thin fingers. A woman with a most attentive male cousin ever at her elbow. My uncle lavished presents on his new wife, and still she asked for more. She whispered in his ear, and he began to frown on me. Her cousin found fault with everything I did about the estates. My uncle said no word in my defence. If I had been wise, I should have gone there and then, but I thought . . . I hoped . . . I had been his heir so long . . . and then she became pregnant . . . ." He paused and looked sideways at the girl.

She snapped her fingers. "The child was not her husband's?"

"It seemed unlikely, since he had been with many of the bond-women about the place, and never sired a child before. Yes, I thought it; and many another said it. My aunt heard the gossip and was furious. She arranged to have me accused of stealing a ring, a valuable ring which my uncle always wore, and of which he thought a great deal. It was said that I had boasted of finding the ring, and intended to keep it to pay my uncle out for his marriage. I was searched, and the ring was found in my wallet, though I swear I had not touched it. It might have been only my word against that of a servant, but that servant also bore witness that I had jested behind my uncle's back, saying that he was incapable even of consummating the marriage, let alone siring a child. There was just enough truth in what she said to wound my uncle. He said . . . oh, many things; about ingratitude, and . . . that he disinherited me, and so on. He allowed my aunt's cousin to put me on trial. And what a trial! It was a mockery! I protested in vain. I foresaw a bleak future . . . but worse was to come.

"The sentence of the court was that I was to be branded on the cheek as a thief. I was thrown into a cell for the night to await punishment . . . two men came to visit me in my cell, carrying a coil of rope . . . to make it look as though I had hanged myself . . . and so I fled."

Her questions were shrewd. He told her he would have fared better if she had been the judge in charge of his trial, and then he changed the subject. Re-opening the wounds of the past was a painful matter.

"When were you made a knight? What happened on your first campaign in France? How many cattle do you slaughter each winter? Have you ever been to London . . . taken part in a tourney?"

She wanted to know everything about him, and he in turn learned something of her active, useful life from her comments. She came each afternoon when her nurse was asleep, and Anselm in the chapel. At last came the question he had been dreading. "What of women?"

He looked at her, and she looked back at him, and neither could tell what the other was thinking. He had determined at first to tell her nothing of Anne and then he had thought to tell her a little – and now he was tongue-tied.

She said, "Surely your uncle arranged for you to be initiated by some trustworthy bond-woman? Crispin was; I think he was never so happy as in that year . . . and then he had to marry Joan, and . . . ." She sighed, and shook her head, implying that the marriage had not turned out well.

"Yes, there was a woman, a bond-woman called Anne. She was fair, and had a lovely laugh, and she was kind."

"Yes?" she prompted. "You loved her very much?"

"Yes and no. She was my comfort and joy for many years. She was older than me, and taught me . . . what a man should know. But she was unlettered, superstitious, an ignorant, and when I tried to tell her how I hated war, and about the waste that it creates of good land, she did not listen. She never paid attention when I tried to talk to her about serious matters." Would Beata understand the compliment he was implying to her, who did listen? "But Anne was faithful to me and I to her, so long as it lasted. She bore me a child, a boy . . . but he died of a fever when he was eighteen months old. My uncle married her to one of the huntsmen when I was away one time – he always did such things in my absence. She said it was for the best, after all, since she wanted more children, children who would be legitimate. I suppose it *was* for the best, but it rankled for a long time."

Your uncle should have arranged a marriage for you." She nodded with an assumption of worldly wisdom that sat oddly on her.

He wanted to say that Ralph Escot had done so, and that the marriage had been arranged with her, but he could not. He had a mighty desire to tell her the truth, but though the words hammered in his brain, he could not do so. She would turn from him in disgust, perhaps, or call the men-at-arms to have him thrown out of the castle . . . or if she believed his story, she might simply be so embarrassed that she would come to sit with him no more. At least this way, as her humble servant, he could see her and talk to her, and have her smile on him.

"What is it?" She put her head on one side like an inquisitive bird.

"I . . . the word is devotion," he said. He had not meant to say that. He had not known that that was what he felt towards her. But now the word was out. He watched the colour go from her face, but her eyes did not drop from his, nor her hand cease to play with a wayward curl. That was the trouble with her. She was quick enough to have caught his meaning, yet too little schooled in the ways of men to turn the compliment aside. And there was another paradox, that the Queen of Beauty should be unable to flirt with a man. He always experienced a sense of shock when he thought of her as Queen of Beauty.

Why did she not, as other women would, turn his words aside as a pretty phrase, meaning nothing? Ah, but she was not like that, and one half of him rejoiced in her lack of sophistication, while the other half writhed with embarrassment. What, was he, too, embarrassed? Was his tongue not readier than most? Why then did he not diminish his avowal with some light phrase? He bowed his head. He had spoken the words, and they should remain, undiminished, meaning exactly what they said. She moved, and he was alert once more.

She swung her feet off the bed and sat upright, her hands pressed down on the bed one on either side of her. Her head was bent, so that he was not able to read her expression. A fever seized him lest she had not understood him . . . and yet he knew that she had.

She went to stand in the doorway, looking out to where the rain pattered down on the grass in the middle of the garth.

She said, "Thank you." It was not at all what he had expected her to say. She turned to him, smiling – and yet her smile was not the carefree thing of an hour ago. Something trembled in her eye, at her lip: this smile was of joy and grief together. She said, "I did not know until you came – until you talked to me, and taught me – I see I was just a child, taking each day as it came, without thought of the future, accepting the rules laid down for me by others. I doubt you will find it easy to understand what you have done for me, you who have always been in the world and a part of the world. I have never left this castle, except twice in my life to ride to a manor of ours which lies two days' journey away. I have no-one to talk to but Hamo and Telfer, who is Master of the Hall . . . he attends to the running of the castle, you know . . . and they have their duties and little time to spare for an ignorant girl like me. My family are happy that I should occupy myself with the affairs of the infirmary, and of the home farm, and the giving of alms, for these things are considered suitable for such a one as I. But for the rest, I am not of the slightest importance to anybody. Occasionally a man or woman whom I have nursed back to health has expressed gratitude; and they meant it, and remembered me, perhaps for as long as they were in sight of the castle. But you . . . ." She fell silent, but he did not speak.

He did not understand her. Perhaps she had not realised he loved her? Did her innocence give her such protective armour that words of love meant nothing to her? He could well imagine that she must drive her suitors mad, if she turned away their declarations so lightly.

"It was not only that you came back," she said, "but that you departed as you did, taking on you the burden of that poor woman and her children. I do not think there was another man whom I would have dared ask to escort them, knowing as I did that the child was sick."

"I believe you were angry that I departed without seeing your father. Perhaps you understand now. I thought there would be pursuit . . . my motives in agreeing to escort that woman were not entirely . . . ."

"Think what it cost you!"

"I would do the same again."

"Yes, I know." She gave him a glowing look. "And then you returned."

"The wonder is that you knew me!"

"Of course I knew you! How could I mistake you?" He thought she had been about to add something else, but if so, she decided against it. He contemplated his penniless, friendless state, and wondered that he had dared even to hint at his love. Her marriage to him had come to naught, but soon now her father would arrange another . . . probably had already arranged another . . . the thought left a bad taste in his mouth.

She said, in a soft, dreamy voice, "I suppose you will leave us soon."

He flinched. He had not thought of going. He supposed he would have to do so. There was pain in the thought of leaving her, such pain as he had not thought it possible to bear without crying out. She moved close to him, setting her hand on his sleeve, looking up into his face.

"I will give you money with which to redeem your sword, and you may choose what clothing you wish from the store; chainmail too, if you wish. You are a knight, and as a knight you shall go from us."

"A knight without a sword. I have done with killing," he said, and his voice was as harsh as hers was soft.

"It is best you go – and what else can you do?"

"I would prefer to stay and serve you. Hamo will give me a clerk's position, I think."

"Ah, you do not know, then. I wondered. Then I thought that it could not make any difference to you . . . and then I thought someone else would surely tell you, so that I need not . . . . " She put her hand on the neck of her gown, pressing at her throat. Her eyes flickered away from his, and then returned. "My mother nearly died when she gave birth to twin daughters . . . ."

"You have a sister? Then it is she who is known as the Queen of Beauty?"

"You know of that, and not of . . . ? No, I can see you know nothing of it. Yes, Elaine and I were born at one birth, nineteen years ago come Christmas. As I say, they despaired of my mother's life, and so my father swore that if she lived, he would dedicate the child – if it was a girl – to the church. Elaine was the eldest but even as a baby she was beautiful, and I was not. So he chose me."

He fell back a pace. "You, to take vows? To become a nun?"

"Say no more, " she said. "I beg you, say no more!"

"You have no vocation! You were meant to be a wife and mother, to oversee the affairs of a busy household, not to spend endless hours in prayer."

"I know it, " she said, in a curiously dry voice. He had been about to protest further, but something in her tone stopped him, some note of authority, something he had not expected from her. She said, "I have no choice in the matter. It was settled for me at birth. At Christmas I am to go to the nuns at Reading, unless perchance my father has another relapse and needs me for a little longer. I was supposed to have gone on my eighteenth birthday, but he was ill . . . ."

"No child can be forced to take vows nowadays."

"I know that. Every year from the time I was old enough to repeat the words, I have been led to the altar on my birthday, my hair has been cut short, and I have given the required promise. I gave it again on my eighteenth birthday when it had been planned that I should leave . . . only the promise was waived by the bishop until such time as my father had recovered from a low fever . . . but he is better now, and unless something else happens, I must go this Christmas. That is why you must go, and go soon."

She had understood, then. She had understood that he loved her, and accepted his love, and was thankful for it. He was numbed with the drop from hope to despair. She opened her mouth as if she would say more, checked herself yet again, looked at him with a tender yet anxious glance, and disappeared. He sank onto the bed and put his head in his hands.

She had not been near him for two days. Gervase helped the dog out into the cloisters, where the warm sun belied the date on the calendar. The rain had gone, the clammy cold had gone, and the sky–what he could see of it–was as blue and as free of cloud as a man could wish. Gervase sank onto a convenient bench and closed his eyes. He hoped the warmth of the sun would help him in more ways than one. The chill of his unheated cell seemed to have seeped through to his bones.

She had not been near him since the day she had told him she was destined for the nunnery. Perhaps it was as well. She had passed his cell three or four times today, to see how Hamo did . . . did he not know her step by now, and every inflection of her voice as she talked with the old man?

Well, this was just one more battle he could not win. There were other women in the world . . . he checked himself on a sigh. No, there were no other women like her. He thought of the women he had known. He had seen many noble and beautiful women in his time, and he knew that none of them could hold a candle to her. He knew it, and the knowledge was a dead weight inside his breast.

He moved restlessly on the bench. Flash whined, and thrust his nose into Gervase's, hand. He pulled on the dog's ears, and the creature moved to sit on Gervase's feet – a trick he had developed of late, to attract attention.

If she had not been destined for the cloister . . . but that line of thought was painful.

What was he to do? She said he must leave, and he supposed he ought to do so. Should he redeem his sword – seek a living as a mercenary? No, he had turned his back on that life. Everyone at Malling assumed he was a discharged soldier, and unable to give the true explanation, Gervase had allowed the tale to pass. It was true that every year he had been duty bound to don armour and follow his uncle into the field, yet Gervase had always thought of this as a very small part of his life. For the rest, he had been absorbed in the care of his uncle's fields and farms.

Well, all that was gone, and it was no use thinking about it.

What remained to him? A clerk's position? He could

probably perform such duties, but the pay was poor, the prospects nil, and the work tedious.

Could he seek a position as a bailiff? That would indeed be better. Yet who would employ a man with no name, and no influence?

Someone tugged at the sleeve of his gown, and he looked up to see a boy of about nine years old, with a great rent in his tunic, and a broken toy in his hand. By his fine-drawn, not to say tearful appearance, and the good quality of his clothing, Gervase guessed the lad to be one of the pages about the castle. The boy held out his cup and ball, which should have been joined together with a leather thong, and was in two separate parts.

"The Lady Beata said you would mend this for me."

Gervase felt as if she had laid her warm, capable hands on his heart. She had not forgotten him! The page was young, and his nose needed wiping. Doubtless he had but newly come to the castle, and was still homesick. Gervase remembered only too well what it was like to be young and far from home. He also remembered – just in time – not to address the boy as an equal.

He said, "Let us see what we can do. What is your name, young master?"

Chapter Four

He had not yet left the cloister, but already he knew a great deal about the castle and its inhabitants. Pages, serving-men, clerks: as they passed through the cloisters on business, or visiting their friends, they stopped to pass the time of day with him. Telfer, the Master of the Hall, gave him a kindly word now and then on his way to sit with Hamo; Telfer was a stoutly-built man with thinning hair spread with care over a large-domed head. Gervase was surprised that such an important man as Telfer, with all the cares of running the castle on his shoulders, should stop to pass the time of day with a penniless invalid, but he supposed that Hamo had put in a good word for him.

As his health improved, and the emaciated look began to pass from his face, he found himself taking an interest in what went on around him, even though he knew that soon he must leave Malling. There were tantalising glimpses of quarrels in high places, glimpsed in the reports and letters he wrote for Hamo . . . his little friend the page told him tales of the Lady Joan and her son . . . convalescent men crept out of their cells and became expansive in the presence of a good listener.

He learned that Henry de la Boxe, Lord of Malling, had been a widower for seven years, and had apparently no intention of marrying again. He was a hard man with a reserved manner, who spent half his time in litigation and the other half consulting physicians about cures . . . not that he was a sick man, said his men, but he was interested in such things. Lord Henry was seldom seen at Malling, but his son and heir Christopher – commonly known as Crispin – usually resided there.

Voices were lowered and glances were cast over shoulders when the men spoke of Crispin, for his temper was sharp and his hand heavy. Crispin had two aims in life, and in both things his father opposed him. Crispin wanted control of at least some of the Malling estates, and he wanted to divorce his wife Joan. On neither question would Lord Henry give in to his son, and therefore the Malling men were divided in their loyalty, some holding to the old lord whose temper, though cold, was inclined to justice, and others gathering to the rising sun of the heir, saying that the old man could not last much longer, anyway. As far as Gervase could tell, Beata held to her father's side, as witness her bringing the dog to him; an action which now took on the light of courage amounting to foolhardiness. The servants hissed and shook their heads when they saw Gervase fondling the dog, and said that if my lord Crispin but knew . . . !

Between these two parties, the old and the new, there existed another powerful group in the castle, and Gervase spent more time thinking about this group than about both the others put together. Great estates do not govern themselves; farms do not produce a harvest without direction, nor do servants produce horses, linen or food as required without someone to oversee them. In the beginning Gervase had wondered at the attention rendered to that elderly and irascible old man Hamo, but now he wondered no longer. The great castle, with its many courts, storehouses, stable and gardens, its keep and towers and quarters for the men-at-arms, might be administered by Telfer, but the lands whose revenues supported the castle were administered by Hamo. To Gervase, Hamo seemed like a giant spider, sitting in the centre of the web of Malling, twitching a line here, spinning an extra length there, sending out reports and receiving them.

In her own way, Beata was also something of a spider, though her territory was confined, within the greater web woven by Hamo, to the infirmary, the home farm and the giving of alms at the gate. She did undertake other duties within the household itself – duties which ought by rights to have been carried out by Crispin's wife Joan – but these seemed spasmodic rather than routine. Only it was surprising how often someone would say, "I will ask the Lady Beata about . . . " whatever it was.

Neither Beata nor Hamo were responsible for the maintenance of law and order about the castle, though Telfer had some privileges in that direction, but a certain Captain Varons came frequently to see Hamo, and expressed his concern for the old man's health with such friendliness that Gervase deduced Varons to be at one with Hamo in all matters of importance.

This same Captain Varons would pass Gervase by without speaking to him, yet when he had gone Gervase would rub his forehead, and frown. He thought he had seen Varons somewhere before, but could not for the life of him recall where. Varons was not a man whom one could easily forget, for he had a thatch of hair so thick it would seem no rain could ever penetrate it; this thatch was prematurely grey, while his moustache was still black. He was a well-set up man, with an eye that missed little – or so said the servants.

And then there was Jaclin. Jaclin was, not to put too fine a point on it, a nuisance. He was a nuisance to himself, and a nuisance to everyone around him. He was reputed to be the natural son of a distant connection of Lord Henry's, and liked to speak of his cousin Crispin – though not within Crispin's hearing. Jaclin was aggressive but clumsy; handsome but slovenly in dress and deportment. He was somewhat younger than Crispin, and though he had received a smattering of education, was neither warrior enough to earn a fortune for himself in the lists, nor intelligent enough to make himself useful in matters of business. Lord Henry found the lad so irritating that he had refused to take him with him to London, and Crispin openly despised his base-born cousin, and laughed aloud when it was suggested that Jaclin accompany Crispin when next he went to a tourney. So Jaclin, like Beata, stayed at home, and unlike Beata, found nothing to do but drink, and bully whatever servants were unluckly enough to cross his path.

It was not long before he also tried to bully Gervase.

Gervase was busy carving a new top for the son of one of the men-at-arms when someone kicked him on the ankle.

"You, there! Cutpurse! Pigsmeat! Are you the scarecrow with whom my cousin Beata has been spending so much of her time?" Gervase raised his eyes without setting his work aside, and recognised Jaclin from what he had heard about him. Thick curly hair, like and yet unlike Beata's, hung around the lad's ears and over his left eye. His eye was restless, bold and overbright. His colour was high, his jaw set for a fight. "To your feet, scum!"

Holding onto his temper, Gervase did as he was bid. Now Gervase was a tall man, and topped Jaclin by some two inches, even though the youth had the advantage of him in weight.

Jaclin surveyed Gervase with disfavour. "Not much of the soldier about you, is there, scarecrow! Well, what have you to say for yourself?"

Gervase noted the well-shaped hands and muscular power of Jaclin's shoulders and legs; also the nails bitten to the quick, and the stains on the costly surcoat. "The Lady Beata was kind to me when I was sick, and I shall forever be grateful to her."

"She spends too much of her time here." It was a challenge which Gervase did not dare take up. The lad suspected something; not much, perhaps – but he was not thick-witted, whatever else he was. Gervase felt a stir of sympathy for Jaclin, remembering his own years of patient endurance before he had been old enough, or skilled enough, to have been treated as an equal by his uncle. Jaclin was still young enough to learn; a pity he was too old and too well-connected to be beaten for his bad manners.

"They say you used to own a long sword, a very good extra-long sword," said Jaclin, with an air of doubt. "You don't look as if you could handle a long sword, or any other sort of weapon, for that matter. I doubt not you stole it somewhere . . . eh?"

Gervase stiffened, but returned no answer.

"Well, it's all one. I have a fancy for a really good sword, and I have sent for it. My cousin Crispin has been away at the tourney – did you know that? When he returns, I shall arrange for him to watch me trounce some of the squires here, and then he will have to take me with him when he goes on campaign next year. I wish you to show me the trick you have of throwing the sword from one hand to the other. With that, and a sword that is longer than anyone else's, I shall be unbeatable."

Gervase felt bile hit the back of his mouth. He trembled, and saw that Jaclin noticed. The youth laughed. "What – do you turn ashen at the thought of my shaking a sword at you? You are all alike, you gutless rats . . . ."

"Your pardon," said Gervase, and his deep voice and cold look held Jaclin in mid-sentence. "I had hoped to redeem my sword for myself. The Lady Beata promised . . . ."

The youth's lower lip came out. "Trust a woman to interfere . . . but she's too late. I told Varons two days since that I wanted the sword, and gave him the money for it. It should be here by nightfall, or tomorrow at the latest; what do you say to that?"

Gervase said nothing, but stared past Jaclin into the gathering twilight. He could not understand why the thought of his sword passing into Jaclin's hands distressed him – had he not parted with it of his own accord? Yet it hurt.

"So," said Jaclin, "I want you to be in the tiltyard tomorrow an hour after dawn for my first practice."

"I am hardly fit yet to . . . ."

"I don't expect you to stand up to me. As if you could!" He laughed, but his eyes were watchful, waiting to see if Gervase dared to give him the lie. Gervase wet his lips. He guessed that Jaclin's prowess was not as great as he boasted, but to say so would be disastrous.

"There's a groat for ye." Jaclin tossed the coin in the air and let it fall. Then, still laughing, he left the cloister.

Gervase shuddered. His hands were so stiff from the effort he had made to control himself, that at first he could not uncurl them. He let the coin lie.

"Master William!" Gervase started. Would he ever get used to being called Master William? He put his knife and the half-completed top into his purse, and went into the end cell to see how the old man did. Hamo was sitting up, all hunched shoulders and knotted hands. Gervase thought he looked more like a king spider every day. A spider calling a fly into his web.

"Well, and what did you make of our noble kinsman, Jaclin?"

"He says he has sent for my sword. Who told him about it?"

"Nurse, I suppose. She thought your routing four unarmed beggars a tale worthy to tell her cronies. Doubtless everyone in the castle has heard of your prowess by now."

"The beggars were not unarmed," said Gervase, taking his customary seat at the reading desk, and looking to see what papers he was to copy, or letters to write. "Is it true that Captain Varons has sent for the sword? Can you not drop a word in his ear?"

"I?" The old man exhibited pious horror at the notion. "How would a word from me . . . ?"

"It would be more than enough, if you wished it. The Lady Beata promised . . . ."

"Ah, but what power has she here?" The thrust wounded Gervase, as it was meant to do. He tried to give no sign of distress, but knew that Hamo had learned somehow – but how? The girl had not been near Gervase for days – of his love, and of the hopelessness of it.

"A soldier without a sword," mused Hamo, turning up his eyes. "Eh, dear Lord! A soldier without a sword is like a crab without its shell . . . ."

"Or a craftsman without tools," said Gervase. "Luckily a quill costs nothing to make, save a little time. I can always take up a new craft . . . ."

"You should not interrupt an old man. I was going to say that a soldier without a sword is like a knight without a name, or a home, or kin that will recognise him."

Gervase stroked his beard with the feather of the quill in his hand, and considered the old man. The threat was there, in the air, all about them, even though Hamo had not put it into words. What was King Spider up to now? Did he know something, or merely suspect it? And if so . . . Gervase was too useful to him to be given over to the officers of the law . . . or was he? So Gervase peaked his eyebrows in enquiry, and Hamo allowed himself a chuckle of amusement.

"Well, well," said Hamo. "Let us leave it at that for the moment. You want your sword back, though I can't imagine why. Sheer contrariness, I wouldn't wonder. Just because Jaclin wants it. You have no money, and the clothes on your back are there at my whim – not that you haven't earned them – I'll say that for you, you're no idler . . . ."

Gervase waited, stroking his beard the while. The old man had been trying to say something to him for days, but had either been interrupted by visitors, or changed his mind at the last minute. Often now he dropped asleep in the middle of a conversation. Gervase was afraid that Hamo was failing fast.

"My hands," said Hamo, holding them up. "I want you to be my hands."

"I am willing, in so far as I am able. You know that."
"And my eyes and my ears," said Hamo. "And my brain."
There was a long silence. Gervase sat back, throwing the quill onto the desk before him. He folded his arms and surveyed the old man with a mixture of anger and dismay.
"No," said Gervase.
"You are always so hasty, you young men," said Hamo, at once assuming an air of senility. "We will speak of this again, when you have had time to think about it . . . you have worn me out with your nonsense, now . . . . " He closed his eyes and composed himself for sleep.

Later that day, he called Gervase in to him again.
He said, without preamble, "Well, have you taken time to consider the advantages of the position?"
"I considered the disadvantages of refusing you," Gervase replied. "Are you threatening me with imprisonment, or what?"
"I?" The bright eyes twinkled at him, but the old man still pretended he did not understand. "Now how could I threaten you with anything?"
"Old man," said Gervase at his most grim. "You know why I must leave Malling. A few days more, a week at the outside, and I shall be strong enough to take to the roads again. If I have earned my keep here . . . if my sword is lost to me for good, then I will earn my living as a clerk . . . . "
"Your sword is certainly lost to you for the time being. But why trudge the roads seeking another patron when there is one waiting for you here? Do you not feel that you owe me some return for my interest in you? Is the game not deep enough for you?"
"What game?"
"The game of power," said Hamo. "What else can be of interest to a man of your talents? You were a soldier once but you sold your sword. Therefore I deduce that you had no further use for it. Perhaps killing had come too easily to you, perhaps you had killed once too often . . . . "
Gervase acknowledged the hit with a grimace. Yes, it had been far too easy.

"What then remains for a man of your talents, but to serve the land?"

Now what did the old man know of that? Had Beata been talking to him?

"Yes," said Hamo. "There is your true bent; there and in the giving of justice in the courts. You seem to understand both sides of the business well. And so I offer you the post of steward to Malling."

The knowledge in Hamo's mind overshadowed their conversation. The old man was really saying, "Be my assistant, and I will keep your secret".

"No," Gervase shook his head. "It will not do. I am not thinking so much of myself now, as of others. It is wisest I go, and go soon. You must do as you think best about that other matter."

A little colour came into Hamo's pale cheeks. "I must apologise. My good friend Master Telfer warned me not to threaten you, and I see he was right. You understand that he and Captain Varons are joined with me in making this proposal?"

Gervase rose, without haste but showing that he intended to finish the conversation. "I told you, it is not fear of the past which makes me leave."

"Now I should have thought you would be anxious to stay . . . to prove your devotion."

Gervase's lips thinned. "If you know that," he said, his voice harsh, "then you know why I must go."

"On the contrary, I see no reason why you should, and perhaps – who knows? – it has been deferred a year already . . . . " Gervase started. "You had not thought of that, had you?" said the voice of the tempter.

"That you should even consider such a thing . . . !"

"What thing?" The voice was creamy with satisfaction. The bait had been well and truly taken, and both men knew it. "Sit down again; you are as restless as a small boy. Let us consider the advantages of the position. It is true that, lacking a family of my own, I have made the proper administration of Malling my life's work, yet I think many a man finishes his life without having left so great a mark on the world as I will have done, when I die. More, I am a rich man, owning land given me by a grateful master. You laboured long and hard in the past, to be rewarded with kicks and blows. My Lord Henry understands the value of a good servant . . . are not Master Telfer and Captain Varons proof of that? More, my Lord Henry is kind enough to call me 'friend', and to be troubled that I am still at work when I should be ending my days peacefully sleeping by the fire. I have already written to him, saying that I believe I have found a suitable replacement . . . . " He indicated a letter on the stand beside him, which had certainly not been penned by Gervase.

"Is there no man in Malling anxious to assume your mantle?"

"None. Or rather, none on whom both Lord Henry and his son would agree."

"And there is an objection to your plan. Would not Lord Crispin dismiss anyone Lord Henry appoints?"

"Crispin is young," said Hamo, and very wilful Swaun you . . . " He seemed about to say more on the subject. Then, abruptly, he dozed off. He was doing this frequently nowadays. Gervase made up the fire, and waited. Presently the old man opened his eyes again and resumed the conversation as if there had been no pause in it. "Crispin. The lad must always seek to test the limits of authority. He will test you, be sure of that. I do not think he will find you wanting. If you bend before his wrath, then he will despise you, and treat you accordingly, though I do not think you are the type to bend easily . . . . " The old man chuckled. "No, we are all three agreed on it – Varons, Telfer and I – you are the man for Malling. You look at the land, and turn over in your mind what acreage can be sown next year; you look at the sheep, and consider discounts and costs; you inspect barns, and give orders for their repair before they need rebuilding. You are a careful man with other men's money, you are ambitious, and you will work hard in the hope of retiring with a manor of your own eventually."

"How can you know me so well?"

Hamo made an impatient gesture. "Fool! Do you think

Lord Henry would ally his daughter to a man of whom he knew nothing? I made exhaustive enquiries at Ware when it was thought you would wed the Lady Elaine, and I was pleased with what I discovered."

"If you know so much, then you know why I left Ware . . . . "

"You should have left earlier! Could you not see which way the wind was blowing? You were as foolishly fond of your uncle as he is of his new wife . . . don't interrupt! Of course I didn't believe that stupid tale about a stolen ring. I doubt if anyone in his senses did. I'll tell you another tale I didn't believe . . . that you were found making love to your new aunt, just before you 'stole' the ring!"

Gervase's face turned a dark red. With an obvious effort he swallowed a hasty retort.

Hamo laughed until he coughed, and had to be given some wine. "If you could see your face! Eh, but it makes me laugh to think . . . did she try it on, the other way round? Eh? Is that why she's so vicious in speaking of you? Is that why you had to be not only disgraced, but also driven away?"

Gervase set his teeth.

"No-one ever believes that the woman can make advances, sometimes. . . ." Hamo settled himself deeper in his pillows. "So that was it . . . I did wonder. You can't go back, you know. No matter how your uncle pines for you . . . yes, he does talk of you now and then, mourning your loss . . . but then his lady wife gives him a kiss, and he forgets all about you."

"If I could only clear my name . . . ."

"Well, you can't. Put it out of your mind. Mud sticks, and without proof – and who can obtain that sort of proof? – you are without redress. No, you must continue to be Master William of Leys, and to hide that dark red hair of yours under a cap. Keep your beard, guard your tongue, forget about your sword, and entrench yourself as chief clerk here before Sir Bertrand comes . . . ."

"Sir Bertrand! Sir Bertrand de Bors? My aunt's cousin, the man who brought the charge of theft against me, and who . . . ."

"Who engineered your downfall, no doubt. Not that you can prove it, of course. Yes, he will be coming here, sooner or later. What, man! Do you ache to be at his throat? And what good would that do you, or Malling? The man comes as prospective husband for the Lady Elaine, and you had better forget all about being Sir Gervase Escot of Ware, and sink yourself in the personality of Master William of Leys. When the time is ripe, you can tell your story to Lord Henry if you wish . . . though if you take my advice, you will let the tale grow old before you refer to it. Lord Henry is under some obligation to Sir Bertrand, in connection with that court case we were discussing the other day, about the boundary of the Derbyshire estate."

"Did Lord Henry ask you to enquire as to Sir Bertrand's character?"

"He did, I did, and nothing good I found to tell, except that the man is brave, wealthy and fond of his cousin. I have advised against the match, yet I think it will go forward, for the reason I have stated. Besides, it is more than time that the Lady Elaine were wed. You are well out of that by the way . . . ."

Gervase winced. Beata, as a nun – every time he thought of her as a nun, it hurt. "I cannot stay, Hamo. She asked me to go."

Hamo said, "She might not have realised how much you would appreciate the proposition I have outlined to you. Of course you are devoted to her. Who is not? I daresay the castle will survive the spectacle of you making a fool of yourself over her. Or did you think, perhaps, that she asked you to go for her sake?" His incredulity and amusement grated on Gervase. He hardened his jaw.

"I promised," he said.

The old man shrugged. "Oh, if you are thinking only of yourself . . . doubtless when I tell her what an opening you have missed, she will add her word to mine."

"I do not believe she would . . . ."

"You think too highly of yourself. What is it to her, what you do? Only she will have some thought for the estates. If she goes at Christmas she will at least have the satisfaction of leaving Malling in good hands. And if she does not go . . . ."

There was a whisper of cloth against the lintel, and she was standing there, looking at him, with her hand to her throat. She paused a moment, then moved past him to Hamo's bedside, without looking at Gervase again. They had not come face to face for some days – he was not usually with Hamo at this hour – she obviously had not expected to see him there. . . .

"I was trying to persuade him to stay on," said Hamo, growing irritable as she sought to set his bedclothes to rights. "I thought he might make a good steward, take the burden off me . . . when you are gone, and your brother left to his own devices . . . Crispin needs a strong man at his elbow . . . ."

"When I am gone!" She repeated the words with a degree of wildness that made Gervase frown. "Why, are you so anxious to be rid of me?"

"I was only thinking of the future – of his future, too. He is so conceited, this long lad here, that he boasted you feared his remaining . . . ."

"Now that I did not say," Gervase protested; but she turned further from him, her hand on Hamo's forehead.

"Would not a man of his talents be appreciated here, when you are gone?" asked Hamo, peering out at Gervase from under Beata's hand, with a wicked grin on his face.

"Of course," she said. She turned her head and smiled in Gervase's direction, but although her eyes were brilliant, they did not rest on him, but passed over his shoulder. "Of course you must stay. I am sure you will do well."

Then she was gone.

There was a long silence. Gervase looked up from contemplation of his hands, to see that the old man was spent, leaning back with his eyes closed, but not asleep. His breathing rasped in the quiet of the cell. When Gervase put some wine to Hamo's lips, he refused it, trying to brush the goblet aside with hands that had lost all their strength.

"You . . . will stay? You are . . . needed here . . . ."

The eyes filmed over before Gervase could say yea or nay. The lips moved again, and Gervase bent close to hear the words. "You . . . used me up . . . with your nonsense . . . send . . . for that fool of a priest . . . ."

The mouth hung open, the breathing ceased, and then restarted. Gervase went for Anselm, and the priest.

In the early morning Hamo stirred on his bed, and opened his eyes. He did not see the anxious faces watching about his bed . . . his eye passed through Beata . . . and Telfer . . . and Varons . . . and Gervase . . . and seemed to seek out the new-risen sun, which was striking at the roof of the chapel opposite. Then Beata, with her hair loose about her, and her mantle slipping off her shoulders, laid him back on the pillow, closed his eyes, and folded his hands over a sprig of rosemary.

Chapter Five

The early Mass had finished, and the priest departed, but still Gervase knelt in the shadow of a pillar, and still the girl knelt before the altar. It was the second day after Hamo's funeral, and though many at Malling had attended Mass on the day he was buried, today their minds were on the return of Crispin and Elaine to the castle.

The girl had shed no tears this morning. She had attempted to cover her unruly curls with a white veil, but the heavy locks dragged at the light material. She rose to her feet, pulling at the veil. She stamped her foot. The back of her neck, the square set of her shoulders expressed something more active than sorrow.

"What, do you watch me still from the shadows? Come out!" She did not look at him, even now. He rose and went to stand where he could see her face, and still she looked at the altar, and not at him.

"You think I weep for him? I do not. I weep for myself. Does that shock you?"

He shook his head.

She said, "I tell you that I could curse him, now, here in chapel . . . he knew very well that I needed him now, more than ever . . . ." Her fingers twisted and tore at her belt. "I hope he hears me now, and I hope he suffers." She glanced at him, and glanced away. "You thought I was so holy, didn't you? You thought I came here to pray, and to meditate. I tell you I come here to scream and curse . . . ."

She caught her breath, and bowed her head, but still she did not weep.

So that was how it was with her! Gervase stroked his beard and wondered why she did not take her grief and resentment to the priest. And then he thought of the fat complacency of this particular castle chaplain, and understood that she could look for no help there . . . only conventional words of solace . . . and her trouble lay too deep for them. . . .

She said, "If you tell me to seek resignation in the love of Our Lord, I will scream!"

No, he thought; she has tried the priest, and he has failed her.

He said, "Yes. He's left us in a mess, hasn't he?"

At once the tension left her body. She put her hands over her eyes, sighed, shook her head, and busied herself once more with her veil. He thought she looked worn out. There were dark marks round her eyes, and her mouth had a tendency to tremble when she did not hold it firm.

She said, "I cannot go through with it. Yet there is no way out. No, I cannot do it."

He said, "I cannot go through with it, either. Yet I see no way out of it. And so I will do it."

"Ah, you reverse my meaning. You say we can do what we have to do? I used to think like that, once. Now I do not."

"You are tired . . . ."

"And you are not? Did you not watch beside him until he died, and did you not watch the following night beside his body? And are you so far restored to health that you did not feel every hour of those watches as a year off your life?"

He did not answer that he had loved Hamo; she knew it.

She sighed again. "Well, today is another day. I have to ride out to the farm, and then make my rounds in the infirmary. If I could rest, then . . . but I cannot, for my sister and brother are returned. Elaine will wish me to spend some time with her, and the priest wants . . . ." She laughed, a hard laugh. "He wants me to hand over Hamo's legacy to the church. Did you know that Hamo had left his all to me? The money I shall distribute in alms at the gate, but the manor . . . . No, and no. Doubtless the priest will have some more hard things to say about my lack of piety . . . did you not know that I was devoid of Christian charity? Oh, but I am. I will not give those acres of rich meadowland to the church. I do not know yet what I will do with them, but they are mine to give or withhold, and surely I will withhold them if it seems to me right to do so. Telfer is to have two of Hamo's books, and the others I will take for myself . . . until Christmas, that is. His clothes are for you, and his desk and other furniture. His room in the keep is also yours . . . you must have a page show you where it is, and you must sleep there from now on."

"Are you sure you want me to stay?"

"No, I am not sure, but that was what he wished, and so . . . . Come or go, what difference should it make to me?" She gave him a look of defiance.

"No difference, if you would have it so." He looked back at her, holding her eye in his.

"Why then, do we discuss it? Oh, I want to hurt someone . . . something . . . ." She clutched at her hair, and now tears came. He made a movement towards her and she fled, the door of the chapel banging closed at her heels.

"Christ preserve us!" said Gervase, in heartfelt prayer.

He went out into the chill morning. The dog had been waiting outside the chapel for him. Gervase bent and fondled Flash's ears. What now?

Jaclin strode up, arms akimbo, surveying Gervase. "Well pigsmeat! Back on your legs again? No longer needed to nurse the old man? No excuse now, have you, for refusing to serve me? See my new sword?" He gestured to where a long blade in a well-remembered scabbard hung at his side. Gervase looked and his eyelids contracted with the effort not to show how keenly he felt his loss. He told himself that he had parted with the sword of his own free will, yet was that strictly true? Had he not been feverish at that time? Or was his distress due to the fact that he felt Jaclin unworthy of such a good weapon?

"Your pardon," said a liveried servant, bowing low to Jaclin, "but the clerk is required instantly in the keep."

Jaclin grabbed a handful of Gervase's gown, and drew him near. Eye to eye they stood, while Jaclin exposed his teeth, and his colour deepened.

"You'll show me that trick now . . . scum that you are!"

"And be dismissed the castle within the hour, because I refused a summons to the keep?"

Jaclin's gaze lost its intensity, and he loosed his hold. "Well, go then. Crawl to my cousin Crispin, as Hamo did. Crawl, snake; down on your belly and crawl. And when you have finished crawling you may creep to the tiltyard and if there is any manhood left in you, I will make you eat it!"

Gervase bowed, and turned to follow the servant.

The man waited till they were crossing the courtyard, and out of Jaclin's hearing, before venturing on a comment. "It is Master Telfer that sent for you . . . not my Lord Crispin. But I thought you would not wish to go with Master Jaclin, anyway."

"I thank thee. I am hardly fit enough yet to tangle with him. Back, Flash! You must not come with me today." The dog seated himself, wagging his tail. "Back home, I say!" Gervase indicated the door to the cloisters. The dog whined, flattened his ears, and slowly withdrew the way they had come, turning to look back after Gervase many times until he finally disappeared from sight.

The servant shook his head at Gervase. "If my Lord Crispin sees that dog . . . he has a hasty temper . . . .

Telfer was sitting at a table in a pleasant room high up in the keep. The glazed window overlooked a walled garden, and the panelled walls were painted in a cheerful design of red and green. There was no fireplace here – doubtless that was why the old man had been taken down to the infirmary, where the end cell could be heated. Not many bedrooms, even in a well-maintained castle, could boast of a fireplace.

However, there were cushions on the settle, and skins had been laid over the rushes on the floor. A smaller room led off this – more of an alcove than a room – in which were a bed, a chest, and a stand for washing things. A comfortable chair, together with a footstool, stood by the window, and beyond that a cupboard on the wall contained books and rolls of paper. A great press behind the door was also filled with papers, and beyond lay an oak chest with a massive lock, the lid of which now lay open so that they might see the contents. The servant bowed and left the room.

Telfer stared at Gervase, and Gervase stared back. There was about this encounter something of the wary assessment of two gladiators in the ring. Neither could be sure of the other's goodwill or intentions.

Telfer spoke first. "This is your domain. Those are the tools of your trade. They are bringing up Hamo's writing desk and other effects now. Here are your keys. Guard them with your life. The manorial rolls, the proofs of Malling's ownership, are in that chest. Any monies you collect should also be kept there. You will see there is no money there now; of this we will speak later."

In silence Gervase took the proffered bunch of keys and attached it to his belt.

"Next door to this you will find two clerks, junior to you. They are to be trusted so far but no further. They are limited in experience though one of them, Hamo said, might be considered promising. The affairs of Malling are administered from these rooms, and you will hold yourself available at all times for those who wish to speak to you on such matters. Theoretically, you are responsible only to Lord Henry, but in practice you must also consider the demands of his son. I will give you what assistance is in my power, and the clerks will explain to you what is usually done."

"I doubt I shall be found wanting."

"You administered three manors for your uncle in satisfactory fashion; here you have twelve manors, and various other pieces of land . . . property in London . . . market rights . . . leases . . . you have dealt with all such things before; only the scale is different."

"You know, then? About Ware?"

"Your first appearance here was so closely followed by enquiries for a man of your age and appearance, that we could not help but guess. Pedlars, minstrels, travellers all brought the same tale to Ware. It was believed you had escaped to France; we did not contradict the story. There was one marvellous rumor about the devil helping you to escape from a locked and barred room . . . ." Telfer smiled with evident amusement. "And another about a scorned woman, who trumped up a charge of theft against you . . . a charge which you could not refute without accusing her of having tried to seduce you . . . ." And now Telfer was grave again. "That was how the ring got into your purse, wasn't it? Lady Escot put it there?"

"I do not think so," said Gervase, and his voice was heavy. "Who else knows of it?"

"We thought it best not to discuss it with anyone. Only Hamo and I knew . . . and now it is only you and me."

"Varons?"

Telfer shook his head. "He might have thought it necessary to arrest you, and hold you for trial. He has a touching faith in Lord Henry's ability as a judge. But in this matter I agreed with Hamo that a man is not likely to be believed if he accuses a woman of making advances to him, and that we had best leave the matter alone. We both consider it our good fortune that you were forced to leave Ware, and that you have no prospects. Hamo was going to tell you – if he had time – about how he came to serve Malling. He was the younger son of a knight who beggared himself by going on a crusade. His widow ceded his lands to Lord Henry, to pay her husband's debts. The elder brother was taken on as esquire – he was killed at Lord Henry's side, fighting in France – and Hamo became steward of Malling. He said you knew how to serve a difficult master. Lord Henry is easy to serve, and by the time he comes to the end of his life, you will have learned how to deal with his son."

"All this – or much of it – Hamo had already told me. It makes sense, and yet I still hanker for Ware."

"That is natural enough. But consider; your uncle dotes

on his wife, and has gone so far as to make a new will in her favour. You cannot clear your name. Put the past behind you, and take what we offer."

"And if I find I cannot put the past behind me?"

"You will be paid a salary as is usual, each quarter day. By Christmas you should have earned enough to buy yourself clothes and another sword, if you still wish to leave. A word of warning. Three bailiffs owe you allegiance; one to take your orders for the manors in the immediate vicinity of the castle; one for the manors that lie in Kent, Sussex and on the outskirts of London, and a third who is responsible for the sheep-farming in the Midlands. The latter two are honest men, long in our employ, and have rendered their accounts promptly. You will find them easy to deal with. But the man who has recently been appointed to oversee the reeves – the village foremen – here . . . he is a different matter. He is one who hangs on my Lord Crispin's sleeve and whispers in his ear. His accounts are always late, and frequently have to be queried. That chest," and he pointed to the oak chest, "should contain monies collected from the manors hereabouts for which Rocca is responsible, but though he promised Hamo to pay the Michaelmas dues in to me, he has not yet done so . . . and October is far advanced. I take little interest in the affairs of the manors – as you can imagine, I have more than enough to do victualling and maintaining the castle itself – yet I have heard rumours about this man Rocca which make me uneasy. Hamo has been ailing for nigh on a year. It is many months since he was able to ride out and see for himself what was going on. It fretted him that he had to rely on reports from a man whom he suspected – rightly or wrongly – of cheating him."

"What did he suspect?"

"That Rocca was extracting more than his due from the peasants, and rendering less than his due to my lord. The balance has gone . . . who knows where? In bribing those whose duty it was to observe Rocca's doings? On Rocca's back? In the building of a new house for Rocca?"

"You wish me to challenge his accounts?"

"If it can be done discreetly, yes. Yet the situation is not as straightforward as one might wish. Rocca is my Lord Crispin's candidate, and he has my lord's ear at all times. To attack outright might be dangerous, until my Lord Henry confirms your appointment."

Gervase thought of Jaclin's jeer "Crawl to Crispin". . . .

Telfer smiled, and it was the sleek smile of one glad to pass responsibility to another for what could prove to be a dangerous matter. He said, "My own poor quarters lie directly above this. I am accustomed to passing an hour in Hamo's company after the evening meal every night. I trust you will make me welcome in the same way." It was a command, and not an invitation. "By the by, my Lord Crispin is returned, as you may have heard. He expects you to wait on him in the green solar above the Great Hall at noon."

He was gone. Gervase gazed around him, thinking that his lines had fallen in pleasant places. A servant came in, bowing, with hot water and clean towels. Gervase stripped to the waist, washed, and took down a hand mirror to inspect his face. He had not seen his image since he had been taken ill, and though he had prepared himself for a shock, he was still horrified to see how much his appearance had altered. His skin was pock-marked, and the jut of his beard broadened the lower part of his face so that he looked less of a soldier than a scholar. His hair had grown somewhat, but lay close to his head, flattened by the linen coif and close-fitting black scholar's cap, which covered his head from forehead to the nape of his neck. One eyelid was now heavier than the other. His cheeks were sallow and thin, his lips bloodless. He looked years older than he had done the day he first stumbled on Malling.

He looked down at his body. It was as lean as ever, but the muscles did not respond to his call as they had done once. He doubted that he would be able to carry his long sword for any length of time now, never mind wield it in battle. He pulled on a clean shirt from the pile in the chest in his bedroom, and wandered back into the main room. He stopped, staring out of the window, then stepped to one side, lest someone see him from the garden.

A party of richly-dressed young men and women was making its way through the walks between the espaliered fruit trees. In their midst, the centre of attention, came a beautiful young girl, with a gaily-dressed nobleman hovering at her shoulder. They were all laughing, and the sound of their laughter was bitter to the ears of Gervase. A while ago he had been satisfied with his lot, but now he was filled with envy. Once he would have walked among those women as of right, and they would have hung on his arm as that girl now hung on the arm of the dandified creature in the furred tunic. And no-one would have thrust him to the rear, as Jaclin was being thrust at this moment.

The beautiful girl swayed and bent her slender figure like a dancer, managing a spangled scarf with skill as she flirted with the gallant beside her. She had long silky hair of a shimmering gold, that slipped and slithered over her breasts in artful manner as she lifted and dropped her shoulders . . . such art was there! Such artfulness to conceal art! Gervase accorded her his reluctant admiration. She turned, and turning bent her body, so disposing of her skirt that the silken overgown slid apart to reveal a clinging robe beneath, a robe of material so fine that it seemed to the onlooker that if he only looked hard enough, and at the right angle, he would see through it . . . and did not.

She drooped long lashes over her cheeks, while glancing up and sideways at the young man. Her laugh was as joyful as her smile. She clapped her hands, gathered her skirts – with artful abandon – and made as if to run away from her gallant.

He, poor fool seeing nothing of the art but much of the beauty, tried to catch her in his arms . . . whereat all the rest of the company laughed and clapped their hands . . . except only for Jaclin, glowering in the background, trying to hitch his new sword higher lest it catch in his heels . . . .

Then another party entered the garden, and at once the beautiful girl abandoned her lover and flew to the newcomers, to hang on the arm of a fair-headed man in a black silk tunic. Her lover hung back, awkwardly bowing. The fair-haired man took the beauty away with him, holding her firmly by the arm, and sending her admirer a look of such contempt that the poor youth turned away, biting his lip.

Now the garden was empty, but for a couple of women making their way across it with baskets in their hands . . . poorly-dressed, chatting among themselves . . . a boy with a barrow, an ancient crone scolding him from the doorway.

"The Queen of Beauty?" Gervase asked himself. "Was that the girl I was supposed to marry?" Receiving no answer, he checked the whereabouts of the sun in the sky, resumed his outer clothing and went in search of his new master.

The green solar was large and full of light. It occupied the whole second floor of a tower which had been built adjacent to the ancient keep, some fifty years ago. Four windows let light through the thickness of the wall, and these were both glazed and hung with shutters. There were skins on the tiled floor, and embroidered hangings on the wall on either side of the great fireplace. A group of men and women, including the lovelorn swain of the garden, hung about the fire, chatting to each other while watching the fair-haired man, who walked before the windows with his sister.

Gervase took up his stand inside the door, and waited for his new master to notice him. He watched Lord Crispin, as did the rest of the company . . . aye, and as did the servants, who were busying themselves with mending the fire, and handing round wine and nuts to the guests.

Crispin was a big-boned man of some twenty-four summers. His hair curled with that self-will seen in Beata's locks, but he was as fair as she was dark. His black silk tunic was embroidered all over with a red-gold thread, and the neckline was studded with precious stones. He carried a pair of heavily-embroidered gloves in his right hand, and beat them on his left to emphasise the points he was making. He wore an enormous sapphire set in a heavy gold ring on his right forefinger. There was a scar on his left cheek which darkened when he was angered, and faded when he was in a good humour.

Gervase, studying him, felt that he had seen such men in

France; they were brave because they lacked imagination, cunning enough in matters concerning their own advancement, and usually carried their wine well. They were not over-intelligent. This man was handsome, but he had the over-full lower lip of one who liked his own way. Something in the movement of eyelid and lip hinted at petulance. Gervase remembered Jaclin saying "Crawl to Crispin" . . . He began to wonder if it were too late for him to withdraw.

The Lady Elaine bent her head to listen to her brother. Her attitude was that of a child caught out in a misdemeanour. She bit her lip, her colour came and went. She played with her hair, shrugging expressive shoulders. But she made no verbal comment on what he said. Presently she left him, and called some of the women to her. A page was bidden play a tune on his lute, and she began, slowly at first, and then with gathering enjoyment, to practise some dance steps with her women. Her admirer turned to scowl at the fire, and his companions drew away from him. Gervase looked for Jaclin, but he was not there. Beata . . .? Ah, no. She had ridden out to the home farm on business. Question: did her farm now come under his direction, or no?

Crispin threw himself down in a chair, and snapped his fingers for a servant to bring him some wine. Now he will call me to him, thought Gervase; but Crispin did not. Instead his eye rested on the awkward figure of a thick-set woman in a red silk dress, who was dandling a child on her knee. The woman rose and went timidly to Crispin, dragging the child after her. Gervase thought this woman must be the Lady Joan, Crispin's older and somewhat neglected wife, who had brought him a fat estate but – if gossip did not lie – no other joy in bed or out of it. The child was heavily-built and stared about him with an air of incomprehension, with his fist in his mouth. He had been born deaf and dumb, and Gervase had been told that Crispin would fain put his wife aside, since she had given him no other child but this. To his credit, Crispin now set the boy on his knee, and tried to coax a smile from him . . . but the child, lumpish and dull, sucked on his hand and would not respond.

Joan began to talk, or scold, rather. Crispin's face changed, the scar on his cheek darkening. He thrust the child from him, and gestured the woman away. Then he threw himself back in his chair, and rapped on its arm, frowning.

Now: thought Gervase. But it was not to be. There was a blur of reddish-purple, and a man in an extravagantly-cut and furred gown of murrey cloth came to lean over Crispin's chair, with his hand before his mouth, bending to whisper in his lord's ear. Crispin smiled. His eye passed over the group at the fire and went beyond it to where Gervase stood, with his arms folded, leaning against the wall. Gervase was sure that the newcomer had spoken of him, and that what the man had said was calculated to turn Crispin from him. There was something unfriendly in the newcomer's eye as he looked at Gervase . . . spiteful, almost . . . the layers of fat around his eyes creasing as he smirked and whispered.

Rocca: thought Gervase. And it looks as if he's bent on discrediting me before I can discredit him. There was nothing Gervase could do about it. He must wait. And chafing, he waited.

Two clerks were summoned by a page, and laid documents on a table close to Crispin's chair. The man in the murrey gown bent over Crispin, bowing, as he submitted documents for Crispin's approval. Now and then he cast a look of triumph over his shoulder at Gervase.

So, thought Gervase; the ambitious bailiff does not content himself with what he has, but seeks to displace me as man of business.

Crispin was frowning, throwing a letter down onto the table. Rocca caught up the letter, looking it over with agonised concentration. The two clerks had their heads together, and those same heads were turning to where Gervase stood, while their fingers smoothed away smiles.

Aha, thought Gervase; so Rocca does not have the backing of the two clerks! Now what is wrong with that letter, I wonder?

At long last Crispin flicked his fingers at Gervase, who crossed the room to stand before his new lord. The dancers paused as he passed by, and the group round the fire turned to see how he would be received. Gervase bowed to Crispin. The offending letter lay on the table before him. It appeared to be written in a fair hand. The penmanship was that of the younger of the two clerks. Gervase was familiar with it from the work he had done for Hamo.

"You are the new clerk, William of Leys?" Crispin's fingers tapped on the arm of his chair, and his foot twitched as if he would like to kick somebody or something. "My sister, Lady Beata, tells me it was Hamo's dying wish that you take his place in our household. I do not, myself, see the necessity for bringing in someone from outside, who cannot know our ways, and who owes no loyalty to me . . . to our house. What say you to that?"

Gervase weighed his words with care. "My lord, Hamo was good enough to say that I possessed certain skills which fitted me for the position . . . and I am a penniless man." He would have said more but on a sudden stopped, with his eyes on the letter before him. The words were clearly penned, so clearly that he might read them from where he stood.

". . . with Sir Bertrand de Bors . . . ."

His enemy's name was written there.

"That is all very well," said Crispin, his foot beating the floor in time with his hand. "Yet I had my own candidate in mind . . . a man whom I can trust."

Yet you have not dared to appoint him, thought Gervase, bringing his mind back to Crispin with an effort. You have not dared to usurp your father's prerogative to appoint a new steward, although you would very much like to do so . . . what offended you about that letter? If only I knew that . . . .

"I could give you a trial as my secretary, I suppose . . . if it was clearly understood that in all matters Rocca here acts as my deputy, and that where he gives orders, they have my authority. You understand that?"

Gervase looked at Rocca, and the bailiff looked back, smiling, bowing, perspiring. Gervase thought that this was not at all what Hamo and Telfer had intended.

"You understand, dimwit!"

Gervase bowed.

"I would not do even this much for you," said Crispin, "if it were not that Rocca lacks the ability to dictate letters properly. Though I must say you do not inspire confidence in me, either. Of all the hangdog . . . yes, what is it, Rocca?" Rocca leaned over Crispin's shoulder, and whispered something in his lord's ear, at which Crispin burst out laughing. Gervase felt his face burn, and stiffened his back, keeping his eyes full on Crispin. That noble lord had the grace to look shamefaced for a moment, and then, shrugging conscience away, remembered that Gervase was only a clerk, and had no right to take exception to being laughed at by his betters. He glowered at Gervase, and his scar became dark. He gestured to the letter, and Gervase picked it up.

The tidings it contained were enough to bring sweat to his brow, yet he held the letter steady. "It is well enough written," he said, "but the style of address in the case of my lord bishop is incorrect. . . ."

The hand ceased to tap, and the foot stilled. "Very well," said Crispin, in a voice which plainly indicated he did not think it well at all. "I see you know something of the work. Have the letter rewritten, for I wish it despatched today. For the rest, Rocca will instruct you . . . aye, and give you a lesson in how you should comport yourself in the presence of the nobility. . . ." Rocca bent over Crispin's shoulder once more. Crispin listened, his brow contracting. His foot began to twitch again. His shoulder thrust Rocca aside. "Yes," he said to Gervase. "And you will also give Rocca quittance of monies he has disbursed to me . . . the Michaelmas rents . . . it is all in order."

Gervase understood at once that it was not in order. A protest rose to his lips, and was stifled. This was something for Lord Henry to deal with; a clerk who had made a bad beginning with his lord could not possibly raise the matter.

And at that inauspicious moment, with Crispin already disposed to find fault with Gervase, Flash slipped through the door, unregarded by the sentry, and made his way across the solar to Gervase. Flash's tail announced his pleasure at finding Gervase once more. He nosed at Gervase's heels, sneezed, sat down to scratch, and looked around him with evident enjoyment at being out and about in company again.

Crispin drew in his breath. The scar glowed on his cheek. "I ordered that dog destroyed! Who has dared. . . .?"

Flash responded to the angry voice with a sharp bark, and then sat on Gervase's feet, betraying the hand that had nursed him.

Gervase smiled a thin-lipped, one-sided smile. The dog could not have made the matter more clear if he had tried. "Flash was brought to me to nurse back to health," he said. "I believe he was a favourite of Lord Henry's?"

If he had thought to earn protection by invoking Lord Henry's name, he was mistaken.

"Were you not told I had given orders that he be destroyed?"

Gervase sighed. "Yes, I was so told, but . . . ."

"You admit you deliberately disobeyed my orders?"

Should Gervase mention the Lady Beata's part in this matter? He stroked his beard and was silent. The girl had known she was running a risk, but he would not betray her.

The younger of the two clerks, a fresh-faced young man, stammered something about the Lady Beata. Gervase gave him a cold glance, and the clerk stopped. The dancers had also stopped. The Lady Elaine had come to perch on the edge of the table, her pretty face alight with curiosity. The bailiff smirked in the background, and rubbed his hands.

"Varons!" The captain stepped forward, his hands fidgeting with his sword-belt. "Take that rogue of a clerk out and give him fifty lashes! Apparently he does not understand who is master here!"

Varons hesitated. "My lord, he is new risen from sick-bed, and might not survive fifty lashes. He is a valuable man, my lord."

"He will be even more valuable when he has learned his lesson. . . . Oh, very well! Have it your own way. Set him in the stocks till nightfall!"

Chapter Six

Gervase said to himself, "This is not happening to me . . . !"

The Lady Elaine was looking at him with detached curiosity, playing with a tress of her long hair. Everyone else was shrugging, and turning away. Rocca was smiling. The two clerks were busying themselves, gathering up papers from the table. Crispin called for more wine, and Varons touched Gervase on the shoulder and gestured to the door. Gervase went with him, the dog by his side.

"Flash," said Gervase, as they descended to the courtyard. "Will you look to the dog?"

"How can I?" Varons spoke softly, out of the side of his mouth.

"Someone could take him out to the home farm, the one under Lady Beata's supervision . . . ?"

Verons nodded. He called to a passing servant, and gave the dog into his care with a few quick words. Gervase walked across, unaccompanied, to where the stocks were situated at the side of the courtyard. The main well of the castle was nearby, and women were constantly coming to it to fetch water. No doubt an unpopular person sitting in the stocks would be liberally baptised with "carelessly" thrown water.

Varons returned with his sergeant, who carried a great hoop of keys.

"I regret this," said Varons, indicating that Gervase seat himself on the ground, and set his ankles in the appropriate semi-circular shapes cut in the lower timber of the stocks.

"No more than I do," replied Gervase with equal courtesy. He set his hands on the earth on either side of him, as Varons lowered the top timber onto his legs, and the sergeant locked the two baulks into position.

Then Gervase was alone, and an object of amusement and

speculation for all those who had time on their hands, or business which took them through the courtyard. He crossed his arms on his breast, and at once the backs of his knees protested. His feet were too far off the ground for him to sit upright in comfort. He might lie flat on his back, but this posture did not appeal to him, as being undignified, and positively inciting the throwing of water, rotten apples and other refuse. He sat and considered his options, which were few. He could play the clown for those who watched . . . but no, he was too angry. He could pretend he had sat in the stocks countless times before . . . pretend to ignore his humiliation – for it was humiliating – he felt as if he were being seared with the shame of it.

He himself had condemned men to this punishment now, for stealing, for adultery, for various minor offences such as drunkenness . . . he had never thought of what it might be like to be put in the stocks himself. It was like . . . he tried to find a word for it. . . .

"What you in there for?" asked a voice above him. It was the young page whose toy he had mended. The lad was eating an apple, and accompanied by one of his fellows.

"For offending my Lord Crispin."

The lad munched on his apple and then, struck by a generous thought, offered it to Gervase. Gervase realised that his mouth was parched. A half-eaten apple seemed the most welcome gift the boy could give him. He took the apple, bowed his thanks, and proceeded to finish it. The boy nodded, satisfied, and went off to play.

There was a whip of cloth over his legs, and the Lady Beata was bending over him, holding back her hair, which had – of course – come away from its net.

"What do you do here? Was it the dog? Crispin was angry?" She struck her hands together, her colour high.

"He does not know you were concerned."

"Did you think I would let you carry the blame? He will not harm me . . . he dare not!" Yet she did not seem certain of her immunity. "I will go to him straight away, and tell him you acted under my orders. . . ."

"That will not get me released. The real reason why I am

here is because he did not like the look in my eye. He merely used the dog as an excuse to have me punished. By the way, did you know Rocca wants to be steward?"

"Rocca!" Again she struck her hands together. "That man . . . I come across his snail's track everywhere!" She clasped her hands, head bent, eyes going from side to side. "Doubtless you did handle him badly . . . he is worried about . . . never mind! He likes to be flattered . . . if you had gone down on your knees and begged forgiveness . . . but I might have known you would not!"

Gervase laughed. Again the girl struck her hands together and cried, "You are a fool!"

"Granted!"

"I can promise nothing. . . . "

"I expect nothing."

"I suppose you defied him to his face, told him you would do it again?"

"I did not actually say so, but I daresay he understood that well enough."

"Of all the stiff-necked . . . ." She gave a scream, strangled in her throat, but expressive of her frustration. "Men!"

She swung round and ran off towards the stairs that led up into the keep, then stopped and ran back, unpinning her cloak. She laid the cloak behind him on the ground. "It will be more comfortable for you if you lie back . . . ." She beckoned a passing servant to her, and gave orders for bread and ale to be brought to Master William.

"I thank you," said Gervase. "Listen; do not trouble yourself to plead my cause with your brother. Is it not enough that I should be made uncomfortable for a few hours, without your . . . ."

"Does your back ache already? I wish I knew what to do."

"Forget about me. Ego te absolvo . . . ." He used the church's formula for the forgiveness of sins.

"And am I therefore absolved? I think not." Yet she shrank a little as she glanced over her shoulder at the keep. "I will go to him straight away. No-one will harm you if they realise I am protecting you."

"Try to weep before him, say it was all a misunderstanding, that you thought he meant another dog to be destroyed, and not Flash . . . devise some formula to save his face."

"I would do it so badly. I have never begged for anything."

"'Of all the stiff-necked women!'"

She laughed, despite her anxiety.

"Remember that I am a 'valuable man'. . . ." She frowned at this, so he frowned back at her. "Yes, I have it on the best authority that I am a valuable man, worth, I daresay, quite as much as a good hunting dog or a falcon. Besides which, your brother has a letter he wishes despatched today, and he will need my services to dictate it. Which reminds me, would you have the younger of the two clerks sent here to me?"

"Thomas. A reliable lad, and Hamo thought he might one day take over from him. . . ."

"Master Thomas has already taken a hand in the game, if I mistake not."

"Has he? What game? You talk like Hamo. I wish I understood what was going on . . . but I am wasting time. I will go to him, now."

She walked slowly but with gathering determination towards the keep. Gervase eased his aching back by lying down. Almost at once booted feet thumped by his head, and a tankard appeared on the earth beside him. When he leaned on one elbow to see which servant had brought him sustenance, there was no-one nearby . . . but neither was anyone laughing at him any longer.

Two neatly-shod feet came into view, supporting the fresh, guileless-looking clerk, Thomas. Gervase eyed him with a sour smile.

"I do not know whether to thank you for your attempted intervention with my Lord Crispin or no," he said. The young man bowed, but did not comment. Gervase stroked his beard. "That letter . . . you penned it?"

"At Master Rocca's dictation." The lad was innocence personified.

"Did he know you were digging pitfalls for him, when he

dictated it? My guess is that you know very well the proper form of address for a bishop, but left it out for some reason of your own. . . ."

"Master William!"

". . . such as disliking Rocca a trifle more than you disliked my being appointed over your head?"

"As to that . . . ." Thomas paused, choosing his words with care. "Hamo told me you had the experience which I lack, that I could learn much from you. . . ."

"You are ambitious? That is a good fault." He sighed, and eased his aching back, biting his lip. "Well, it is best we clear the air between us. May I take it that you have already rewritten the offending letter?"

Colour stained the young man's cheeks. "It seemed to me . . . my lord might not release you before sunset . . . though he does sometimes turn round and remit punishments. However, I thought it not to be relied upon, and so . . . ."

"You saw your chance to leap into my shoes? Well, I do not blame you for that, but you must make up your mind whose man you are." The lad hesitated. "Let me ask you this," said Gervase. "Are you cunning enough yet to expose Rocca, while retaining Lord Crispin's ear?"

"Not yet," said the young clerk, looking uneasily around. Did he suspect their conversation was overheard? Had he so much respect for Rocca? "Look you here, Master William; I will serve you to the best of my ability if you will bring down Rocca, and recommend me for your post when you leave. Or, if you stay, if you will recommend me for another, equally good post."

"Agreed. And now, we have work to do, for all that I am temporarily in a poor position for writing. I will take a look at that letter you have rewritten, and then I will give you my keys, that you may fetch the manorial rolls with which Rocca is concerned. I may be laid on my back, but that is no reason for us to waste time . . . ."

High up in the new tower, above the solar in which Gervase had been received by Crispin, lay the bedchamber occupied by the twin daughters of Lord Henry. Chests containing an assortment of costly clothing lay around the chamber in some disarray, for the Lady Elaine had changed her mind several times about the gown she proposed to wear that evening. One plain chest and a peg on the wall accommodated the Lady Beata's clothing, and perhaps nothing illustrated the difference between the two sisters so much as their manner of preparing for the main meal of the day.

The Lady Elaine was devotedly served by two tiring-women, perfectionists in the art of presenting beauty. For nigh on an hour she had been sitting on a stool while the women pulled on and off coloured silk stockings, tied garters, pampered her skin with lotions and tried the effect of certain beribboned garlands on her hair.

Beata came in with a rush, tearing off the net which had made such a poor job of controlling her locks, shook back her hair, pulled a comb through it with her teeth set against the pain of dealing with tangles, and looped her girdle more closely around her waist. As she turned to the light, Elaine saw that Beata's left cheek was swollen and red.

"Enough," said the Lady Elaine, waving her women away. "I wish to speak with my sister. Beata, where have you been? Nurse has been looking all over for you, and I wanted you . . . ."

"With the priest," said Beata, picking up a hand-mirror and putting it to a use different from that for which it was intended. It was cool against the heat of her bruised cheek.

"So he did hit you. Let me see . . . I have a lotion here." Elaine was not unintelligent, and she loved her sister despite – or perhaps because of – the fact that they were so unlike. "There, now . . . if you wish to cry . . . ."

Beata tossed her head. "I am not going to cry. Nothing and nobody can make me cry. Father Anthony scolded me, but little I care for him. Or for anything that my brother says or does! I am going to write to my father, to tell him what is in my mind, and no-one is going to stop me. Surely Father will listen to me . . . ."

Elaine blinked at her sister. Beata straightened her

shoulders, and turned to Elaine with a brilliant smile. "Well, and what have you found to do on your first day back at Malling? I was at the farm in the morning, you know . . . ."

Elaine was easily reassured that all was now well with her sister. Was she not anxious to make a confidence herself? "Well, it was all agreed, as you know, that I should marry young Gerald . . . ."

"Gerald? You go too fast for me. The last time you were here there was some other man spoken of for you . . . Gervase something?"

"Escot. Yes. They tell me he was very ugly, so I am glad I am not going to marry him now."

"Some ugly men are such delightful company that you forget their appearance . . . or come to think they have an air of distinction better than good looks . . . ."

"Do you think so? Well, anyway, Father told me ages ago that the man was not to be thought of any more, because his uncle had married and was like to produce an heir, which made this Gervase Escot of little importance . . . and I was glad because Father seemed to think that Gerald would do well enough as my husband. Gerald is not so very rich, of course, but his family is good."

"He is a pretty lad, and loves you well."

"Yes, I think he does." She stated her opinion dispassionately. "I thought it would be not so bad to be married to him . . . ."

"You would rule him, of course."

Elaine smiled, and then sobered. "But now Crispin says that Gerald is not to be thought of, either. He has received fresh instructions from Father, about another match, and Gerald is to be discouraged." She sighed, but as one regretting the loss of a pretty trifle, rather than of a lover.

"Well . . . poor Gerald," said Beata, her attention wandering. "But you have had a-many lovers and by this time . . . who is to be the next, pray?"

"Someone called Sir Bertrand de Bors. I do not like him." She said this with the gentle distaste of one refusing a dish at supper. "He is always pulling on my arm, or trying to touch my neck."

"You have met him? Well, at least that makes a change. Of all the men proposed for your hand so far, you have had first-hand knowledge of only two."

"There was that Scots knight . . . ." Elaine began to tell off her lovers on her fingers. "But then there was some trouble on the border and his castle was burned to the ground. Then Gerald for a little, and after him Sir John from London, so great in his self-esteem I thought he would burst his tunic. Then there was Sir Gervase Escot – though him I never saw – and now Sir Bertrand."

"Well, what is this new man like? Hamo would have known . . . ." Beata sighed.

"Ah, dear Hamo." The regret was as lightly expressed as for the loss of Gerald. "Well, Sir Bertrand is a connection of the Escots. They say he is rich. He has gained many prizes in tourneys of recent years, though I do not think he has been at war – not in France, anyway. He bore my ribbons in the tournament at York recently, and carried everything before him. He is so big that . . . ." She gestured widely with her hands. "And so tall, and his hands have hairs on their backs. I don't think," she said in considering fashion, "that he is as rich as Sir John was, but he is related to our sister-in-law Joan, and half the nobility in the Sussex area, and he was able to help Father in some litigation or other. I don't understand what it was all about, though he did try to tell me. When he looks at me he makes me feel uncomfortable . . . and he leans on me when he sits next me at table."

There was no response to this confession, so Elaine looked up to see her sister gazing at her with apparent attention, while tearing her veil into shreds.

"Beata! What on earth is the matter with you?"

"Nothing. Or rather, everything. Elaine, what am I going to do?"

Elaine stared at her sister without comprehension. "Do? Why? Is there anything you want to do that you cannot? Are you worried about Father Anthony scolding you or Crispin being out of temper?"

"That! That is nothing! No, I meant . . . what am I going to do with the rest of my life?"

"In the convent, you mean? You go at Christmas, don't you? Ah, I shall miss you. Crispin says Father wants me to be married at Christmas. Then we shall both be gone . . . ."

"Yes, in the convent. What am I to do with myself? Sit and embroider, sit and listen to the gospels being read at me? Kneel and pray? Kneel and sing? Sit and pray? Walk slowly around the cloister with my eyes on the ground? Talk softly within permitted hours, and eat to the sound of yet more readings from the gospels?"

"It is a good life, surely." There was gentle rebuke in Elaine's voice.

"For some, maybe. But for me? Think, Elaine! Think of what I am . . . and think of that life. For once in your life, Elaine, think! And help me! Am I not busy from morning to night, working with my hands and my head and every part of me? Is there a minute of my day in which I am safe from interruption for some question of the household, or of the infirmary? What of the constant cares of the farm, and its produce? Of the charity at the gates? Of all the hundred and one things I do during the day . . . am I to stop short, and do nothing for the rest of my life?"

"To pray is a holy work . . . a lifetime's work . . . ."

"So Father Anthony says. I do not believe it."

"Blasphemy!" whispered Elaine, her eyes going to the door. Suppose someone should overhear . . . !

"Commonsense! Prayer is all very well, but it is not enough. I can sit in the chapel and think with pity of the poor people at the gates waiting to be fed, and I can call down blessing on their heads but that will not put bread into their mouths, will it? A poor man's sores need to be tended, a starving child to be given food . . . 'feed my lambs' . . . prayer is nothing . . . you have to use your head and your hands to get anything done."

"But without prayer . . . you pray twice a day . . . you go to Mass. Beata, what has come over you? This is most unlike . . . ."

"I have feared the future for years, and thrust the thought of it from me. Every time someone reminded me that I was destined for the church, I would experience a sense of shock, and then I would think that something would prevent it from happening! Why, last year my departure was postponed . . . why not this years also? Why should I ever go? For weeks at a time I have been able to forget, except when my hair grows long enough to remind me that every twelvemonth it will be cut short again, to remind all men that I am not a woman . . . just a thing destined to be sold to the church to redeem my father's vow . . . his pride, rather . . . !"

"Beata, I must not listen to . . . ."

"You will! Elaine, I think I am going mad!"

Again Elaine's eyes went to the door, but this time in the hope that someone might come and help her. She asked, "Have you spoken of this to Father Anthony?"

"I have tried, but he dismisses my words as the foolishness of a girl who is fed over well. I am told to fast, to make a novena of prayers. I have done neither. I need my strength to carry out the work I do here among the sick and the poor. I need every minute of my day, not to spend in prayer, but in nursing the sick, or in so arranging matters on the farm that I have money for charity. I have no time for prayers as you think of time for prayers. I sit down and try to pray, and the thought of some sick child, or of some task left undone comes into my mind, and the more I try to dismiss it, the more uneasy I become. Sometimes I force myself to sit still for almost half an hour, and when I get up, I fly from the chapel as if on wings, and there are always a hundred more things to be attended to, because I have stolen that half hour from my true work. . . ." She had finished. Head bent, and hands lax, she dropped onto the bed and sat there, quite still. She did not weep, but shivered and then set her teeth.

Elaine fidgeted with her hair, and with the neck of her gown. She put a pleat in her skirt, and then smoothed it out again. Twice she opened her mouth to speak, and twice closed it again.

At last, "You asked me for help, but what can I do?"

Beata lifted her head. Her eyes were ringed with shadows, and she looked ill. She put out her hand, and it trembled. Elaine took her sister's hand, and patted it, making little noises of a reassuring nature, as if she thought her sister were sick in her body, and not in her mind.

"Would you help me distribute alms at the gate at sunset every night? Would you come with me round the infirmary, and see what has to be done there? If I am to go at Christmas, someone must be found to take my place . . . ." She gave a hard sob, a dry sound, quickly stifled. "I know what you will say; you are leaving at Christmas, too, and therefore cannot help me. Yet there must be someone, somewhere in the castle. . . . There is a man who might . . . the affairs of the farm would be safe in his hands, and he could be trusted to see the money went to charity, and not into my father's coffers . . . ."

"The new secretary? The one Crispin put in the stocks? He made a bad beginning, but . . . ."

"Perhaps Hamo was wrong to think Master William had been sent here to help us . . . perhaps he will not stay. Perhaps it would be better if he went."

"Oh, no," said Elaine, yawning. "Crispin likes him now. He was angry to hear his orders had been disobeyed, and he thought the new clerk held his head too high for a servant, but when Crispin went to see how he did in the stocks, Master William was studying the manorial rolls, lying flat on his back, reading . . . ." She laughed at the remembrance. "With the two other clerks fussing around, writing notes at Master William's dictation! Crispin threw back his head and laughed, and so did we all. Then Crispin bade Captain Varons release Master William, and said he would give him a purse of silver coins to ease his back."

"I wish I had been there," said Beata, convulsively clasping and unclasping her hands about her upper arms. "I had been sent to be scolded by Father Anthony. Could he stand unaided?"

Elaine did not make the mistake of thinking her sister's query was for the priest. "Not at first, but Crispin took one of his arms, and the younger of the two clerks took the other, and then Master William bowed his thanks to Crispin. Crispin told him not to be such a fool again, and that was that." Now she, too, fell to fidgeting. "I wish Sir Bertrand were not coming. I wish it were not he. I wish . . . ."

"For Gerald?"

"Perhaps." She sighed. "for no-one special, but Gerald would do, I suppose. Crispin says Father will hold a tourney here at Christmas to celebrate our double wedding, you to the church, me to Sir Bertrand . . . ."

"Horrible!" said Beata. "If I must be sent out of sight, let it be with the minimum of ceremony . . . let me creep away, unnoticed. To celebrate a forced marriage, to expect me to smile and enjoy . . . no, I could not!"

"Ah, but you will!" said Elaine, putting her arms round Beata. "You must help me, and I will help you, and we will go smiling to our bridegrooms. I shall need your supporting arm when I met him again. I must confess I am a little afraid of this Sir Bertrand . . . ."

"You will enslave him, as you do all your other lovers."

"I do not think so."

Beata put her head on her sister's shoulder, and they clasped one another, seeking comfort. And though neither found the reassurance they sought, yet they found some ease in having opened their hearts to each other.

Chapter Seven

Gervase went looking for the Lady Beata, and found her in the cloisters of the infirmary. She drew him into one of the unoccupied rooms, telling Anselm to go on ahead, and that she would be with him in a minute.

"I am a little stiff," he admitted, acknowledging her enquiry as to his health. "But a ride out to the nearest manors will clear that. What I wanted to ask you was about . . . ."

"Rocca," she said. "Yes. I will tell you what I know, but it is not much. He was appointed bailiff on the death of his father – who was bailiff here for some twenty years, and who was a good man withal. Rocca was appointed on Crispin's recommendation some two years ago, even though Hamo opposed him at the time. At first there seemed little reason to suppose the appointment a bad one. The returns from the farms hereabouts increased slightly. The harvest was good that first year. However, this year we had a dreadful storm which flattened the crops just when they should have been harvested. You would have expected the yields from the peasants to have dropped because of the storm, but they didn't. My father, of course, was pleased. But I have noticed as I ride to and from the Glebe Farm that a certain air of neglect . . . I do not know that I can give you anything by way of evidence . . . ."

"You think he squeezed the peasants to give the same high return this Michaelmas as if there had been a good harvest. You think he did it to curry favour with your father – or your brother?"

"Yes. Also, there have been tales of villeins fleeing our lands, which never was the case before, and each one that goes reduces the rent roll . . . and I know Rocca boasts of having put down seditious talk among the peasants with severity. I may be wrong, but I think he confuses 'grumbling' with 'sedition', in order that none dare speak against him, or petition my father for leniency. There are whispers among my folk at the Glebe Farm about Rocca, but they will not talk freely, even to me. They seem to think Rocca all-powerful. He is supposed to have been promised the management of the Glebe Farm, in addition to those he already has, when I go into the convent. I do not think my father has given him this promise, but Crispin might have done so. This worries me; the Glebe was part of my great-grandmother's dowry and the profits have always been devoted by the women of our family to charitable purposes. I suppose Crispin will say that he will gladly set aside an equal amount from the ordinary revenues, to be spent on charity, but it is not the same thing as having control of the finances myself . . . and I suppose he could also say that there will be no-one to administer the affairs of the Glebe properly when I am gone, and that Rocca will have to do it in my stead. Joan will not do it, nor Elaine . . . if they can tell wheat from barley I should be surprised . . . or add a column of figures, or bully the miller, who will be honest only so long as he is in fear of my tongue . . . ." She caught herself up, and went out into the cloister, tying a veil over her hair, and fastening her cloak.

"Well, that is enough of my troubles. I must ride out to the Glebe today, for my reeve's eldest son is sick, and I promised to send him over some medicine last night, but then . . . something happened to prevent me. If I go straight away . . . there is a poor woman came in last night; she is still in labour this morning, and the midwife in the throes of another case . . . . "

"Your hair is beautiful," he said, following her, and speaking low. Her hands stilled, and her colour rose. Her eyelids drooped, yet she spoke no word to reprove him for his impertinence.

"Ah, there is Jaclin . . ." She turned from him, speaking sharply. "He is waiting for you, no doubt. I wish he had a feeling for the land. I am never so happy as when I ride out and about, but he . . . if only he could even read and write! But he is all for the tourney, and war. I suppose he has heard that Father intends to hold a tourney here at Christmas." He exclaimed something. "Yes," she said. "Jaclin intends to blood your sword prettily . . . that is exactly how he talks about it, as if it were a magic weapon, to ensure his conquering all in the lists . . . . "

"He is a fool."

"Treat him gently, for my sake, if not for his own. He longs to be a great warrior, to have my father notice him, to be of importance in the world."

"Hola, Master William! Why were you not in the tilt-yard this morning? Did I not tell you I wished to practise?" Jaclin grinned. "I hear you need to be chastised before you will obey orders – is that so?" He grasped Gervase's upper arm, and shook him. "Is . . . that . . . really . . . so?"

"Enough, Jaclin!" said Beata. "We ride out on business now. When Master William has an hour to spare . . . . "

"Will you not ride with me?" said Gervase to Jaclin. "We could practise in some private glade away from the eyes of the curious . . . and your knowledge of the country would help me to a better understanding of my duties."

Jaclin smiled. Preening himself, he led the way to the stables, where the Lady Beata's horse was already saddled up, and a sorry-looking mule waited nearby for Gervase.

"You cannot ride that!" said Beata, to Gervase. "It was Hamo's, but it is so long since he rode out . . . he was ailing for over a year."

Gervase put one long leg over the mule. The soles of both feet touched the ground. He looked around, collecting the attention of the grooms.

"Have you nothing a trifle higher off the ground?" he enquired, with no sign of ill-temper.

The head groom, laughing, allowed he might be able to supply something more in keeping with Gervase's height.

"Something good," said Jaclin, fussing over the girths of his own horse. "He rides out with me, and I don't want him falling behind."

The head groom, after enquiring if Gervase were accustomed to the saddle, produced a sluggish palfrey. Checking Beata's protest with a smile, Gervase said the palfrey would no doubt be excellent if he intended to amble along, writing letters on horseback, but as he wished to encompass two manors that day . . . ?

A frenzied barking interrupted them, and Flash tumbled into the yard, tail oscillating. He flung himself on Gervase, who pulled his ears and disentangled the frayed end of rope which had been tied round the dog's collar.

"Oh, no!" groaned Beata. "Has he got free again?"

The head groom hid a smile. Jaclin stared. Gervase looked at the head groom, who kicked thoughtfully at a pebble. "Well?" said Gervase. "Are you going to give us away?"

"I will take him back to the Glebe with me," said Beata.

"I doubt he will go willingly," said Gervase, fondling the dog, who expressed his appreciation by rolling over on his back, with his legs in the air, wriggling and growling with mock ferocity.

"Fetch the roan," said the head groom to one of his lads.

"And as to dogs . . . dogs come and go, and we don't take no notice of 'em . . . right?"

"The roan?" queried the stable lad.

"Yes," said the head groom, smiling at Gervase. "The sooner Master William is out of my yard, the better . . . with all his party . . . . "

The roan was a good horse, and after a small difference of opinion with Gervase as to who was going to be master, suffered him to do as he wished. They rode west to the Glebe, where they left Beata, and then went on to the first of the outlying manors administered by Rocca. Jaclin became loquacious, pointing out this and that, condemning a neglected coppice here, and a tumbledown cot there. The eyes of the peasants were sullen as Gervase and Jaclin rode among them. They worked listlessly, and the ribs of their beasts of burden showed as sharp ridges through their hides.

"They all look half-starved to me," said Gervase to Jaclin.

"They're a feckless lot," replied Jaclin, shrugging. "Doubtless they've been drinking. Father Anthony says they're a den of sinners down here. Rocca's always complaining he can't get them to do a proper day's work."

"An empty belly does tend to slow you down," said Gervase. He slid off his horse to visit the mill, to which the peasants must take their corn to be ground. He came out looking thoughtful."Not enough corn going through the mill to feed the sparrows! I thought this was supposed to be the most prosperous of the manors hereabouts . . . that is, according to the taxes levied last Michaelmas by Rocca. I see no signs of prosperity here, except . . . ." He pointed to a large house which was even now being extended by an extra wing. "Is that Rocca's house, by any chance?" It was. Gervase looked at the bailiff's house, and then looked at the lathe and plaster hovels that made up the rest of the hamlet.

"Come on!" urged Jaclin. "We're wasting time. There's a convenient glade in which to practise half a mile on."

Stripped to the waist, Gervase tried to teach Jaclin how to throw the sword from hand to hand, and how to wield it with equal skill in either hand . . . and failed. Jaclin began to curse, and to become angry with Gervase who could manage it so easily.

"I am left-handed," said Gervase, trying to explain.

"A sign of the devil in you," snarled Jaclin.

"Then why seek to master the trick of it?"

"Because I want to be the best! I must triumph at the tourney at Christmas. My uncle shall give me the prize, and then I shall go to the wars, and earn fame and fortune . . . . "

Gervase put his head between his hands, fatigue immobilising him. He was too soon out of a sick-bed, too ill-equipped to teach a healthy young animal like Jaclin . . . and above all, he was out of sympathy with what Jaclin wanted to do.

"Surely your uncle needs you here, checking such creatures as Rocca . . . ?"

"Such work is for peasants! Come, we will at it again!"

"I can do no more today," said Gervase. "But tomorrow at dawn I will meet you in the tiltyard – or where you wish – before I commence the day's duties. And whenever I ride out, if you wish to come with me, we can take the opportunity of practising in secret. It may be some time before you are able to take on a fully-armed knight in combat."

It was soon after dawn in the tiltyard. Jaclin, on horseback, had been trying to hurl his lance through a ring which dangled from a chain above his head. Three times had he driven his horse past the ring, and three times failed to score. Now he beat at his horse until it reared, protesting at this ill-treatment.

"It is not the horse's fault," said Gervase, growing angry. He threw off his cap and gown, and as Jaclin slid down from the horse, Gervase gentled the nervous animal with hand and voice. "You must ride parallel with the wall, and not at it," said Gervase. "You are pulling the horse to the left at the last minute, and thus spoiling your aim. Also, I think you changed your grip at the moment you thrust forward . . . . "

"You think you could do better?" Jaclin's temper was mounting.

Without a word Gervase picked up the lance, mounted the horse, steadied him, and set off down the yard . . . steadying the lance, lifting it with elbow crooked, thrusting it at the ring, which did not even twitch as the weapon passed through, and then catching the lance again as he cantered forward.

"Bravo!" Captain Varons came out of the shadows, yawning, pulling his sword belt straight. "That was a neat trick."

Gervase slid to the ground, biting his lip. He had not intended to show off like that . . . would not have done so if Jaclin had not nettled him, if he had thought there would be onlookers.

"A fluke, merely," he said.

"I can do better than that!" Jaclin swaggered, drawing the long sword from its sheath, and making a sweep with it in the direction of Gervase. Jaclin laughed as Gervase jumped back, and swept in again with the sword, relishing the opportunity to make Gervase give ground . . . to wipe out the humiliating memory of his failure and the older man's success.

"Steady!" said Gervase, as the blade whistled past his head. He looked into Jaclin's eyes and saw there only the consciousness of power . . . the lad was going to hurt him, to pay him out . . . .

There was a shout from Varons, but little Jaclin cared. His lips were drawn back over his teeth, and he swung the sword with both hands. Again and again. And then there was the sharp smack of a stick connecting with a hand outstretched for it. Varons had thrown a pike to Gervase, who had caught it, and was now using it as a longstick, parrying Jaclin's blows at first, and then staying his advance, setting his own weight against that of the younger man, twisting and twirling the unwieldy-looking weapon between capable hands, thrusting at Jaclin's body now and then with the blunt – and never the spiked – end. Now Gervase was raining blows on Jaclin's ribs as if there were no weapon interposed between him and

Jaclin, and Jaclin cried out and dropped his sword – Gervase's long sword – to the ground.

Varons looked at Gervase, and Gervase watched Jaclin, ready to resume the conflict if there were the slightest sign of more trouble. Then Jaclin said, breathlessly, that he thought Master William had learned his lesson, and went away with uncertain, heavy steps.

Gervase looked down at the pike in his hands, as if uncertain how it had got there. He was interested to see that he was not even breathing hard. His muscles had benefited from those daily bouts with Jaclin. He leaned the pike against the wall, and turned to thank Varons.

But Varons was staring at him, ruffling his thatch of grey hair. Gervase resumed his cap and gown, making conversation. He had an uneasy feeling that Varons had discovered the secret of "Master William's" identity.

"Do you mind – that is, do you remember the gate?" asked Varons.

Gervase gave him a blank, enquiring look. Yet he remembered the gate in the foreign town well – and the fight before it when the men under his command had been inextricably mixed with those who fought under another emblem – and the man with the thatch of thick black hair who had wielded a double-headed axe at his side.

"Gate?" he queried.

"Escot!" said Varons, snapping his fingers. "I thought I knew you. You remember how my sword broke, and you used a pike to cover me when I was down? I have often wondered what became of you. I would have sought you out to thank you, but we were moved on at dawn next day."

Men were beginning to move about the castle. A groom took Jaclin's horse away. Flash arrived and sat on Gervase's feet, to attract his attention. Gervase bent to fondle the dog, thinking hard. Did Varons mean to give him away? Probably not. Men like Varons did not forget favours done them, although he, Gervase, had long forgotten the incident.

"Well?" said Gervase. "You may have heard that a man called Escot left Ware in the middle of the night, with the sheriffs after him. He had been falsely accused of robbing his uncle . . . and convicted. He could not prove his innocence, and while in prison, men came to kill him in the night, intent on making it look as if he had committed suicide – and so he fled."

"Walk apart with me," said Varons. He ruffled his hair, to help him think. "I believe you were innocent. You would not have stolen from your uncle. When the story was brought here, I said as much to Hamo. I will not give you away . . . but what happens when Sir Bertrand de Bors comes to Malling?"

"That is a question which is rarely out of my mind."

"You are needed here." Varson touched Gervase on the arm, and indicated they should take the stairs to the battlements. "Jaclin is greatly improved, though not as much as he believes. You have checked Rocca simply by being on your guard, by watching him . . . the affairs of the castle run smoothly. Telfer is heard to defer to your judgment, and my Lord Crispin has grown to depend on you. Then there are all the preparations for the tourney, and the masque. These things are not within Telfer's sphere . . . without you they would fail."

"No-one is indispensable."

"I am in two minds about that. If I were gone, I know very well what would happen to my idle, good-for-nothing men-at-arms . . . a sloppy, ill-mannered crowd of louts at the best of times, and without me at their back . . . ." He spread his hands.

"And without me?" Gervase smiled his twisted smile. "Not much would be altered, I think. There is a clerk under me who, with a little more training, would do very well."

"And Jaclin? You have kept him usefully employed for two months or more; without you he would have no chance at all in the lists at Christmas. As it is, he does you credit."

"No, he does not do me credit. You have a lad or two in your garrison who has an instinctive idea of what he is about, but young Jaclin lacks innate skill. I can teach him a trick here and there, but I cannot give him the gift of timing his actions, of adapting. He throws a lance, and his aim is true, but his arm is stiff. He hits the target four times out of five now, but to succeed in the tourney he must hit it five times out of five, for in the hour of trial there will be so many distractions as must dishearten him. Above all, he has no sense of discipline. He practises hard for an hour, and then despairs. He will try and try again, but lacking that one vital ingredient of perseverance, will not try the twentieth time and the thirtieth. And then perhaps he will not practise at all for three or four days. No, I do not look for him to do very well."

"He talks of entering the lists in Crispin's little army of knights, to tilt against those headed by Sir Bertrand."

"He will keep his seat in a mêlee, unless he is very unlucky. It is in the single combats that I fear for him. He cannot imagine being defeated, yet I cannot envisage him standing up to a man of experience."

"He has the family hot temper."

"As witness our recent bout." They grinned at each other, and paced on together, talking of arrangements for the tourney. Gervase felt sure that Varons would not betray him . . . or not betray him wittingly. Too many people knew his secret. And what would happen when Sir Bertrand arrived? Would he recognise Gervase?

"I wonder if I should go before Lord Henry arrives."

Gervase and Telfer were sitting together after supper one evening. Outside a storm raged. It had been pounding at the castle all day, stopping work on the stands which were being erected along the length of the tiltyard, and even preventing workmen from adding the finishing touches to the new kitchen which had been built in the outermost courtyard, to feed the horde of invited guests and their retainers. On the table between the two men lay a flagon of wine, goblets, and a dish of nuts. Under these lay a medley of papers and reports on which they had been working.

Gervase took off his coif, and smoothed back his hair. Soon he would have to have his hair cut, or it would peep out from under the back of his cap.

"Does that gown chafe you?" said Telfer. "Is that why you wish to leave?"

"No, I am grown accustomed to the gown. But the cap and coif irritate me. I was always wont to go bareheaded."

"A tall-tale," said Telfer, his eyes on Gervase's hair, so many shades darker than his beard.

"Too many men to tell tales," said Gervase, speaking lightly. "Varons knows, and you know, and I would take my oath on it that Master Thomas the clerk knows . . . ."

"And who is to tell the tale on you? Not I, or Varons . . . nor Master Thomas, either, unless I miss my guess. We all wish you well. Who does not? Do not affairs run as smoothly now, as when Hamo was in his prime?"

"On the surface, maybe."

"You find it humiliating to take Lord Crispin's orders?"

"Some of his commands are unwelcome, and yet I am accustomed to taking orders which do not please me. I appreciate his dilemma. I think I am even a little sorry for him."

They were silent awhile. The wind redoubled its efforts to break into the castle, and somewhere not far away a shutter banged against a wall. In the round tower Crispin's only son and heir, the deaf and dumb child, lay in the throes of a fever. Lady Joan wept and ate, drank and wept, while the child was nursed by Beata. Crispin went in and out, uncertain whether to hope that his son would live, or to wish he might die.

"If the child dies, and surely only the strength of the Lady Beata holds him here still," said Telfer, "then we must look for further changes. My lord will undoubtedly wish to repudiate the Lady Joan, who has proved a bad bargain as a wife . . . ."

"Apart from the manors she brought him by way of dowry," murmured Gervase.

"I believe the church would support him in a divorce," Telfer nodded. "Father Anthony seems to think so, anyway."

"With the Lady Beata about to be received into their arms," said Gervase, "bearing her enormous dowry with her . . . why should the church not agree?"

"If only the Lady Joan will go quietly! I fear she may tell her woes to her kinsman, Sir Bertrand. Suppose he take her part?"

"What, when he is so soon to be allied to this house by marriage himself? Surely he would not be so foolish."

"Hamo never thought Sir Bertrand wished for the match, until Lord Henry pressed it. Of course it is a good marriage for Sir Bertrand, but Hamo said there was talk at Ware about Sir Bertrand and another lady . . . ?"

Gervase sighed. "Telfer, I wish I knew the truth of that matter. Yes, there was talk. It seemed to me then, and to others about the place, that my very new and very experienced aunt, Lady Escot, had a habit of familiarity with her cousin, Sir Bertrand, that was . . . suggestive. There was no proof that they had had carnal intercourse. She was already a widow when my uncle courted her. There was no good reason why she should not have married Sir Bertrand instead . . . save that they were cousins. Yet it is not unusual for cousins to obtain a dispensation, in order to marry. Perhaps . . . I thought she might be a couple of years older than he . . . and he would know that, and wish for a younger wife, who would bear him children. My aunt's first marriage had proved barren . . . perhaps it was that which kept them apart . . . ."

Telfer nursed his goblet, resting one ankle over the knee of his other leg. He was a wise old bird, thought Gervase, rather like an owl. If Telfer had been at Ware when Gervase had been accused of theft . . . . How absurd that charge was . . . had not Gervase handled all the money for the estate every year, without any of it sticking to his fingers?

"Looking back," said Gervase, "I see that I should have cut my losses and departed when my uncle married. I resented the marriage, and though I would not let the servants speak against my aunt in front of me, I probably did show my feelings. And yet what right did I have to resent it, even though my uncle had promised I would be his heir? Did he not have every right to marry and get himself an heir of his own loins? I only wish that I had not parted from him under such circumstances as must lead him to think of me with anger . . . or regret. Possibly he may regret my going . . . he was fond of me, in his way. His anger never lasted long . . . ."

"I do not think I could forgive a charge against my honesty."

"He is a foolish old man. . . . If it had not been for Sir Bertrand, I am sure I could have made him see sense . . . questioned the servants . . . found out how the ring got in my pouch. Then I could have gone from him, without feeling that I had to carry a shameful secret around with me."

Telfer sat up with unusual energy. "You are not thinking of going back . . . of challenging Sir Bertrand for the truth? That would be worse than folly. The man is so well entrenched there, has taken over all your duties . . . your uncle ailing, your aunt the only one who sees him. No, no. You must not think of it. You have made a new life for yourself. You are valued here, as you were never valued at Ware. This is where you belong."

"Do I really do any good here? Have I succeeded in lifting the yoke of Rocca from the peasants? Have I gained Crispin's confidence? No and no. Master Thomas could do what I do."

"No, he could not. There is some quality in you, Gervase Escot, which makes men hold themselves straighter when you speak to them. You expect them to show you their best side, and so they do. They see that you yourself would never behave boorishly, and so in your presence they shade their own behaviour – not by much, but a little. Enough. Consider Jaclin!"

Gervase smiled his crooked smile. "You think he behaves better when I am by? Swears less? Bullies less?"

"Hamo said you would make a jest of anything. You must be more careful. You make people laugh, and they go away with a smile on their lips, and the world seems a brighter place for a while."

"That is dangerous?"

"It is dangerous for you, because those who do not laugh feel shut out, and the devil works in them, causing them to envy you, and the good terms you are on with the family here."

"Rocca . . .!"

"My Lord Crispin smiles when he speaks of you. He would, I think, be rid of Rocca if he knew how. Crispin is not a wicked man, and he is uneasy when he does wrong. The trouble is that he thought he was doing a clever thing by accepting the Michaelmas dues direct from Rocca, instead of keeping them for his father; but in doing so he has not only earned his father's wrath, but also put himself – to some extent – in Rocca's power. He begins to suspect, perhaps, that Rocca is a far greater villain than he had thought. He dislikes the idea of being tied to Rocca and yet how can he be rid of the man who has done so much for him? Rocca was appointed bailiff against Lord Henry's wishes, remember . . . and against Hamo's advice. How can Crispin now acknowledge that he made a mistake?"

Chapter Eight

Gervase rose and opened the shutter over the window. By leaning out he could catch sight of the windows in the round tower nearby. There was a light still burning in the chamber where the deaf and dumb boy fought for his life . . . with Beata holding him, bathing his forehead, caressing him all the time . . . how many days since she had walked in the sunlight, ridden out into the country?

Gervase leaned his forehead against the edge of the shutter for a moment before closing it once more. He felt dull and heavy. For some reason he had been thinking much of his uncle of late, remembering the bluff manner which concealed kindness, Lord Escot's hearty sneezes, and his loud laughter . . ..

"I am poor company tonight, I fear," he said to Telfer. Telfer continued to massage his right ankle, and look into space. There was a feeling of tension in the air. Gervase believed it came from him, and did not blame Telfer for it. Beata: her courage, her wildness in grief, and rebellion – her love for Hamo and for her father, a father who had disposed of her life as casually as Crispin had thought to dispose of the dog, Flash.

Flash lay snoring in a corner now, but Beata . . . . Gervase felt an unfamiliar black hole open up around him. He despised those who wallowed in self-pity. He told himself that it would help no-one – and certainly not himself – to be seen to grieve. And yet he grieved. At last Telfer departed to his own room.

Gervase resumed his coif and cap, drew a cloak around him, and went to walk up on the battlements. The men were accustomed to seeing him there, either with Varons, or alone. Now and then heads turned as he passed, and he would exchange a word with the sentries.

He leaned on the wall, overlooking the sleeping countryside, and thought about Telfer. That quiet man knew of Gervase's love for the Lady Beata. Nothing had been said of it – nothing could be said of it – and yet Gervase had been aware for some time that Telfer knew. A lifted eyebrow, a hesitation, and all was clear; for men that work closely together hour after hour, day after day, develop forms of communication other than speech.

Yes, Telfer knew. It eased Gervase's troubled mind a little, to know that Telfer knew, and to a certain extent understood. It was some solace to him that Telfer wished Gervase to stay on at the castle, felt that he had found a place for himself where he might be of some use in the world.

It was Beata who was lost, without a place. A word here, an outburst of angry grief there, and to one who watched and listened as closely as Gervase watched and listened, the truth was easy to come at. He even divined the reason why she spent all her energies on saving the life of a child whom no-one else – not even his mother – thought worth preserving. Beata was daring all, risking all, spending herself because only thus could she keep at bay the thought of what was to be . . . the thought that she could not face, the future she could not contemplate. And yet she would have to bring herself to do so, sometime.

And yet . . . although he felt his own life was without purpose if she went . . . why did he suddenly think of his uncle, bending to give a small boy an apple? Beata . . . his uncle . . . Hamo . . . . Life was a dark affair, indeed.

"It is very pleasant to be admired," said Elaine, trying the effect of a ruby ring on her forefinger.

"Yes," said Beata. She was sitting on their bed, with her knees to her chin, and her arms clasped round her ankles. She looked ill, and though she was pale it seemed that the fever had passed from the dying child to her eyes, for they burned and sparkled as surely they had never done before.

"Oh, I didn't mean you," said Elaine, laughing, and throwing a kiss at her sister. "I ought not to boast, to you!"

She did not mean to be unkind. Whatever else she was – shallow, selfish and ignorant – Elaine was a kind-hearted girl, and not nearly as spoiled by her elevation to the role of Queen of Beauty as many another girl might have been. Only she was so accustomed to thinking of herself as beautiful and sought after, that she never thought her dark, busy little sister might also be admired. Lord Henry had often congratulated himself on his decision to dedicate the smaller and darker of his twin babes to the church, for who could have justified for existence as a marriageable daughter better than Elaine?

"No," said Beata, in the same indifferent tone. "I knew you did not mean that I was admired."

Something in her manner perhaps, more than in her tone, stirred Elaine's sympathy, and she pushed aside her jewel-box, and signed to the waiting-woman to leave them alone. Elaine put her arm round Beata, and drew the dark head close.

"I am sorry the boy died. You tried so hard."

"He could never have been happy, or useful," said Beata. "Let us talk of something else. I envy you, Elaine, for you always seem to be happy."

"I?" Elaine considered the matter, pretty head on one

side. "I suppose I have been fortunate . . . ." She sighed. "Except about Gerald, poor fool. He swears he will throw himself under Sir Bertrand's horse and be killed in the tourney . . . or take on all comers single-handed. He is not sure which!" Elaine laughed, and Beata managed a smile. "He has asked me to give him a token of my favour to wear in the tourney. I said no, of course, because Crispin was listening, and frowning at me not to encourage Gerald. But I might do so, perhaps. Gerald had the impertinence to ask for a lock of my hair!" And again she laughed. Beata pulled at one of her curls, twining it around her fingers.

Elaine took up a comb, and pushing her sister's hand aside, began to reduce her curly locks to order. "You have lovely hair, Beata. A pity it should have to be cut every year."

"Well, I shall be properly shaven and shorn at Christmas. A pity I am not fair-haired, too, or you could have had my tresses to add to yours." Her tone was bitter.

Elaine frowned, trying to think of a topic of conversation to lighten her sister's mood. "The alms-giving!" she cried, her brow clearing. "Did I tell you that I did as you asked, and went to the gates every night when you were nursing the little boy? Three nights now I have gone, and the poor people are so grateful, and they call out to me to bless them, and say how lovely I am . . . the silly creatures!"

Beata kissed her sister. "Thank you. I am sure it did them good to see you."

"You must thank the others, too, for I could not have done it all by myself. There are the two pages – the smallest ones – who say that they have to come because Master William needs help in such matters, being a stranger hereabouts."

"Master William?" Beata got off the bed, and busied herself folding and putting away some of her sister's clothing.

"Leave that . . . the women will do it. Yes, the children think he's ancient. I suppose at their age, he must seem quite elderly . . . ." She yawned. "But he is not, of course. As I said before, it is pleasant to be admired."

"By him?" Beata's activity became feverish. "The

secretary? I should have thought you could have left him alone, Elaine. Is he not beneath your notice?"

"I daresay he is," said Elaine, beginning to comb her own locks. "But then, he is surely of noble birth, and there is something about him, when he smiles at you and gives you his hand . . . ugly, of course . . . but with a certain something . . . ."

"You have studied him, indeed!" Beata turned her back on Elaine. "And did he tell you his history?"

"Has the man a history?"

"You . . . are . . .so . . . stupid!" Beata uttered the words in such a low tone that Elaine was not sure she had heard aright, but sat with the comb in her hand, staring at her sister. Beata threw down the clothes in her arms, and ran out. Elaine called after her, but Beata did not hear her – or if she heard, she did not heed the cry.

Down the stairs she went and across the courtyard. He was not in the great hall, although there were a number of men there waiting to see Crispin with petitions . . . . nor in the green solar, where Joan sat drinking and crying. He was not in the tiltyard, where Crispin was doffing his armour. Crispin called out to her in merry fashion that he seemed to have lost none of his skill . . . .

She paused with her hand on the chapel door. He would not be in there, and perhaps Father Anthony would be. She beckoned one of the pages to her, and asked where the secretary might be. She dreaded to hear that he was gone out to one of the outlying manors . . . but no, the lad said Master William was in the newly-finished apartments off the small courtyard, in the rooms which were being made ready against the arrival of their guests.

She found him there, checking over a list of furnishings, with Master Thomas. Though she had sought him for some time, she did not know what to say to him. He, though, seemed to know what to do. He gave his list to the clerk, and invited Beata to inspect the bedding which had been sent over . . . was the quality of the linen good enough? He feared not, but would abide by her opinion.

They were in a small room, by themselves, with the door

open . . . no-one could see them. He lifted a sheet from a pile, and held it out to her. She did not take it, or look at it. She did not hear his words of censure. He talked on, saying that this was really Telfer's business, and none of his . . . or hers, either, come to think of it.

She walked about the room, seeing nothing of what was there. The clerk left the apartments . . . she could hear him going down the stairs . . . and there was silence. When had he stopped talking? She discovered that she was leaning against the wall, with her cheek against the cool plaster. In a moment she would cry. He had that effect on her sometimes. But she would not show him that he had any power over her, any influence . . . .

She said, "I wish I had died with the boy."

"I know." How had he known? And yet she had felt instinctively he would understand. He was a dangerous man. He knew too much. She must keep him at a distance, for her own sake.

She thought: that was all I wanted to say to him . . . what matter if he does admire Elaine? Or even, if he loves her . . . . No, he does not love her. I can feel his care for me, his anxiety, even though I have turned my face from him. It is as if he were reaching out to enfold me in his arms, though he has never touched me . . . never will touch me . . . .

"Hamo's property," she said, in a high, an unnaturally high voice. "The money, as well as the land. Father Anthony declares that I must take it into the church when I go, in addition to the dowry my father will give. Crispin approves, naturally, for he, too, wishes to stand well with the church."

"Are you to pay everyone's debts?"

"Yes, I am the scapegoat for them all. But I will not go bleating to my death . . . nor will I beg for mercy any more . . . did I tell you I had begged my father to release me, and he would not? Nor will I permit myself to speak of this again. I wanted you to have Hamo's money, and his lands, but it appears that I am not to be allowed to dispose of them as I wish."

"You want me to leave?"

"Yes."

Now she could feel his moment of rebellion. He did not want to go. He would fight against it. In a moment he would have marshalled his arguments, and she knew he could out-think, out-talk her, so . . . .

"Yes, Gervase," she said. And felt his shock that she knew. Then she felt anger that he should not have guessed that she knew. Did he think her such a fool as not to have put two and two together . . . the red-headed man with the long sword, and the tale of the theft brought to her by travellers arriving on his heels, and she looking for his return every day thereafter though she had known that if he were wise he would never come back . . . every day, scanning the face of everyone who came to the gate . . . and that alone ought to have warned her how dangerous he might become to her peace of mind . . . .

He said nothing at all. Well, she had silenced him, and she was glad. His voice was so deep, so melodious, so pleasant to the ear that he might perhaps have persuaded her . . . . No. She jerked herself upright.

She said, "I am going to cut my hair off today. Now. I do not want to see you again."

Those last words had been a mistake. They had hinted at a weakness in her. Yet she would show no weakness. She clenched her hands at her sides, and turned round, looking at him and through him, aware of him only as a shadow against the deeper shadows in the room, not daring to let her eyes rest on him. She could see the door before her. She walked towards it, and knew that he had stepped back, his head bent . . . and yet she had not looked directly at him. She could have described every detail of his long pale hands that were gripping at his belt, as they had been since the beginning of their interview, and of the harsh lines that had appeared on his face when she had said . . . what she had said.

And she had meant it. She would do it, now, that instant. A pair of scissors, a few minutes by herself, and no more would she need to look in a mirror, no more twist her curls in her fingers, no more watch his eyes go to her hair, and that beloved crooked smile alter the grim line of his mouth.

And his mouth was so hard-set, so thin . . . . It hurt. She acknowledged that she had hurt him, was hurting him, and was going to hurt him even more in the future. So. He must go. Now. Before Sir Bertrand came and denounced him. She would find him some money, somehow, somewhere . . . even if it meant taking some of that intended for alms-giving . . . a suit of clothes, a horse . . . surely Telfer would help her to equip him to set out on the road again. It would be easier for her to go into the convent, when he had left Malling.

She was in the bedroom she shared with her sister, and all around her were the outward trappings of beauty: gold and green, silk on satin, the jewel casket open, and the comb left on the coverlet of the bed where Elaine had dropped it. Well, she would not need a comb again.

She swallowed. She would not cry. She must find scissors at once, quickly, while her resolution lasted. If she were not careful she would begin to cry, and to tremble, and then . . . .

She could not find her own shears, which should have been attached to a ring on her belt, next her purse. The waiting-woman had been using some scissors, working on a gown for Elaine . . . she dashed silks to the ground and the shears fell, glistening, at her feet.

She picked them up, took a deep breath, and closed her eyes. Seizing a lock of hair in one hand, she opened the shears and, made clumsy by haste, tried to cut too low. The shears would not cut so much at once. She lowered her arm. She was shaking. The shears dropped from her hand onto the coverlet. She stood there, shaking and trying not to cry, until she heard someone mounting the stairs outside. Swiftly, as if ashamed of what she had intended to do, she put the shears in her hanging purse, and drew the strings tight. A waiting-woman came in with yet another pretty veil for Elaine.

Beata fled. She ran down the stairs, and halted, leaning against the wall. She was panting, terrified of herself, of she knew not what . . . . She told herself to be calm. She went to the chapel, where Father Anthony was counting over his store of candles.

She stood before him with her hand on her purse, on the handles of the shears.

"Father, will you cut off my hair for me?"

He looked at her without really seeing her, candles in either hand. "Fifteen, sixteen . . . did you say – cut your hair? No, no. You know perfectly well the bishop is to oversee your robing at Christmas. Your hair will be cut then."

"I want it done now!"

"Sixteen, seventeen . . . . Child! Can you not see that I am in the middle of . . . ?"

She turned and fled out of the chapel. It had begun to drizzle. She closed her eyes, leaning against the chapel door, letting the rain tingle against her skin. She must have it done now, or else . . . she dreaded to think . . . his own hair was of a wondrous hue, and she had grieved when Anselm had cut it short, when he had been ill . . . .

Something moved in her throat, and she heard herself groan, as if she were in pain. Well, there was only one way to end this temptation. Once she had shorn her hair, she would have put such a barrier between herself and men that they would never more look at her with that look of . . . of love.

There. She had acknowledged it at last. Gervase loved her, and she loved him, and she could not bear it.

Her old nurse was passing through the courtyard. Beata ran to her, and taking the basket from the nurse's arm, said, "Will you do something for me, Nursey? I want you to cut off my hair now!"

"I never heard the like!" said Nurse, taking the basket back with a wrench. "What do you want to cut off your lovely hair for now, before you have to? Is it not enough that you have to dress in those plain gowns, and go without all the pretty little things that someone-I-could-mention has? Go along with you, do . . . ."

"My lady . . . ?" He was there, at her elbow, and although his head was bent in courteous fashion, yet his hand was reaching for her upper arm, and he was turning her away, and walking her . . . she knew not where . . . tears . . . . She was shaking, and his arm was shifting to support her while he spoke on and on about some emergency in the infirmary . . . and there were the cloisters safely about them, and she could at last let the tears flow without anyone noticing.

Her legs gave way, and he caught her up in his arm, and held her high, close against him. She closed her eyes, savouring the moment through weakness, knowing he had anticipated her collapse, and not caring who saw them . . . his arms, so safe . . . .

Then she was being set down on a bed in the end cell – Hamo's cell – and he was taking off his gown and folding it close about her. The tears ran down her cheeks and she made no sound.

He was rubbing her hands, and Anselm was setting a light to the kindling in the fireplace. He was asking when she had eaten last, and she was trying to tell him, though for some reason it seemed she could only whisper, that she was supposed to fast in Advent . . . and he was cursing all priests, and Anselm – dear Anselm – was nodding his head, and tottering away to fetch her mulled wine, and chicken breasts and soup, and the two of them were pressing food on her, and encouraging her to eat, smiling at her . . . and she began to feel warm for the first time for days, although the tears still came, without sound, without effort.

He laid her down to sleep on the bed, with the firelight all about his form, and sat beside her, comfortably close. She tried to sit up, to protest that she had duties to perform . . . and he pushed her back, saying he would attend to everything, that she was, simply, to sleep.

And she slept. He was not there when she woke, but she looked out of the half-open door and saw that it was twilight, and she knew that he would be at the gate, distributing alms for her. And she was content to wait for him. She decided she would stay awake until he returned.

He was there . . . he had come while she was asleep. They smiled at each other and for the first time he touched her cheek; only with the back of his hand, but it was enough to make her tears flow again . . . but peacefully, now. She said, "I must have been missed . . ."

"Of course. But I sent Anselm to explain to your brother that you had a touch of the child's fever, and needed to spend a few days away from your sister and your family, lest the infection spread. Your nurse has been sitting here with you. She says you will do nicely if you'll only mind your own business, and not try to do everything for everyone else, as well."

This echo of her nurse's concern made her smile, but she asked, "I don't really have his fever . . . do I?"

He shook his head. "You are worn out. You need a rest. The fiction will serve to keep them away for a few days."

A few days by herself . . . with him . . . .

Only now did she realise that she had been lying with clenched fists and jaw. She gave a long sigh, and sighing, felt some of her tension leave her. She said, "Will you not take off your cap and coif awhile?" She wanted to watch the firelight on his hair, for just a few minutes . . . a few minutes of stolen pleasure, to set against what was to come.

He obeyed her, and then took her hand in both of his, holding it firmly. He said, "I am glad you did not cut your hair. If it has to be done, it must not be done like that, in anger or despair. That robs the sacrifice of its value."

She was quite calm, now. "You mean that I am robbing my father of his due, by not going gladly into the convent."

Yes, he had meant that, but he would not say it.

She sighed again. "It is strange. This afternoon I could not do it. I thought I would never be able to do it. And now, if the scissors were in my hand, I could."

After some time, he lifted his eyes from contemplating her hand, and looked her in the eye. "Do you really want me to go, straight away?"

She shook her head, but did not speak.

He said, "Would it help . . . . I am not sure if it is the right thing for me to do or no . . . I could return to France and enter the community of brethren there . . . ."

She was silent. She could not judge what might be best for him. She had had this shining picture of him from the beginning, of a knight without a sword, of a capable, kindly man who would have given her a goodly brood of children and loved her well. If that was not to be, then she was without purpose, for herself or for him. Her father's vow would dispose of her future, but for him . . . She sighed, and was silent.

Then he was gone, and her nurse was there, nodding, and the fire was low. She lay looking out into the shadows of the night, and it was as if he had left his gown about her, comforting her. For she knew now that the parting at Christmas would not end his love. He loved her deep and he loved her true . . . to the end, and beyond.

Chapter Nine

For three days Beata stayed in the infirmary, seeing only her nurse and Anselm. Most of the time she slept, and when she woke she ate whatever they put before her. Father Anthony came to the door several times when, feeling too weary to argue with him, she would close her eyes and pretend to be asleep, that he might go away again. Which he did. On the fourth day Crispin sent his physician to see her.

"They are afraid I will die before Christmas, and cheat them of their sacrifice," thought Beata.

The physician found her weak and listless, but on the mend. He prescribed various noxious draughts for her – which she told Anselm to throw away – and talked much of low fevers and of putting your faith in God. He said it was her duty to recover quickly, and went hastily away, fearful lest he catch her "fever".

On the fifth day the nurse sent for Gervase. Beata had known he would have to be summoned . . . perhaps she had not wanted to recover too quickly, knowing that if she seemed worse, he would come to her.

He smiled at her from the doorway. He did not come in at

once, but stood there, hesitating. She knew why he hesitated. Nurse had gone about some business of her own, and they would be alone. She smiled back at him, and put out her hand to draw him into the room. She was dressed only in her shift, but wrapped in a cloak, sitting on a stool before the fire.

She said, "Did you think I was a ghost? I feel as if I were one. I feel as if I died that day you brought me here, and am only lingering till Christmas, that they can bury my body at the right time."

He seated himself on a stool on the other side of the fire, and without being reminded, took off his cap and coif with a sigh. He ran his hands back through his hair, and shook his head. It seemed to her that his attention was not wholly with her; once this would have enraged but now it merely saddened her. She thought he looked weary, though it was not much past noon.

Then he was looking at her, and smiling again. She did not know what anxiety had preoccupied him, but it was gone, and she was content.

"That you should have to be sent for . . . !" she said, in mock reproach.

"It is an open secret in the castle that I am devoted to you, and that is no great matter, I think. But it must not be said that I am of any importance to you."

"Oh, prudent man! Oh, wise steward! To think you might have been married to my sister by this time . . . ."

He laughed, low and soft, and shook his head at her.

"Do you not admire her?" She could not resist probing the wound.

His eyebrows zigzagged. "She is delightful, in her own way. She does everything with such an art–and she is fond of you, Beata." He used her name deliberately, for the first time, bringing light to her lacklustre eyes. "She has asked every day if she may be permitted to visit you, and when my Lord Crispin and the physician have denied her, she has wept. She weeps beautifully."

"I am glad," replied Beata, leaving it unclear whether she rejoiced because Elaine had asked for her, or because her lover did not really admire her sister. "Do you enjoy working as a secretary?"

Again he ran his hands through his hair, and this time grimaced. "Telfer asked me if my gown chafed, and I said no; only the cap and coif. Perhaps that is about right. I like to bring order out of chaos, prosperity from neglect. I was trained to be a soldier, but the years of combat brought only a feeling of emptiness . . . the waste of it all! I like to build, and not to destroy. The years in which I was allowed to administer my uncle's estates were busy years, and I never stopped then to ask myself if I were content with such work. Now I know that I was. Hamo was right about my having a talent for it. If I were allowed a free hand here, I could do such things . . . ! I ought to be riding to the Midlands now, for there is a dispute about pavage in the town. Your father writes that we must refuse the townsmen's claim, but when I studied their charter . . . !" He stopped short, laughing at himself for having become so enthusiastic. The light died from his eyes. "It is true that my place is here at the moment. Your brother says that after Christmas . . . ." He shrugged. "Well, I must obey him, of course, and help Telfer as best I can. Yet this delay will not soothe the tempers of the men in the Midlands who are disputing the tax. Yes, the cap and coif do chafe me."

"Oh, if you could only have talked face to face with my father about it, he would have bid you go! What is a steward for, if he cannot act for his lord in such cases?"

"But I am not steward here. I am only acting–temporarily – for Crispin as his secretary. I see what should be done, and cannot do it because I have to wait on his moods. If I could fawn on him, and flatter him, it would be easier to get my own way, but I cannot. And yet . . . a dozen times I have been on the point of throwing up the post, and then he has turned round and given me everything and more than that which I have been working for. And why does he give in? Because I have convinced him that this or that is the right course to follow? No. It is all caprice. No, not all. I must be fair. He seems a warm-hearted man at bottom, but . . . perhaps it is because he is entangled with Rocca that he tries to play the tyrant. Yet he has quite accepted that I keep the dog Flash beside me. That takes a forgiving spirit, does it not?"

"My father is not capricious. You will like to serve him."

"I think not. I think I will go at Christmas. Perhaps I should go before Sir Bertrand de Bors arrives, for fear that he recognise me . . . ." He looked at her steadily.

She smiled faintly. "I know about it. Did he put the ring in your wallet? Did he arrange the whole thing to please his cousin? Tell me . . . ."

He looked into the fire. "It all seems so long ago, now . . . as if it happened to another man, in another age. I was falsely accused, convicted, and would have been branded as a thief. Awaiting punishment, two men came to kill me in the night. But I had been forewarned, and my sword had been thrust through the bars of my prison, so that I could defend myself, which I did. And escaped. And came here. I do not know how the ring got into my wallet. I cannot clear myself. When my uncle turned his back on me, I knew all was lost." He shook himself out of his reverie. "Well, Telfer tells me no-one would recognise me, dressed like this, and with a beard. So, I will serve Malling as best I may till you go, and then I also will be on my way."

"You must appeal to my father to reopen the case."

"Against his son-in-law?" He smiled, and shook his head. Then he extended his hand to her. "Come, will you dine with us in the hall tonight? You are needed."

"I think not. I am always tired by evening, and everyone says they can manage well enough without me."

"Who says so?" He spoke sharply. "Ah, I know who told you that! Your nurse? Is that not the usual way to talk to invalids, to keep them happy in their beds? Did she tell you of the floggings that Crispin orders every day? Or that there are now two pairs of stocks in the courtyard, and both filled from dawn to sunset? Did she tell you of Jaclin's drinking bouts, and of his thrashing Crispin's squire, who can ill be spared at this time? Did she not tell you that Telfer has lost his voice? That my clerk Thomas has developed a nervous twitch? That Joan denounced Crispin at Mass . . .?"

"What?" She half-rose from her stool. Her colour de-epened to something approaching normal.

"She had been drinking, I suppose. She interrupted Sunday Mass, despite everything her women could do, to denounce him. She said a great many foolish things, about Crispin's desiring the child's death, and wanting to put her away. I think he would indeed like to divorce her, poor creature, but dares not say so as yet, for she comes of a powerful family . . . is not Sir Bertrand her cousin? As she reminds Crispin daily. Yesterday he sent his physician to her chamber, and the rumour is that the physician so dosed and purged her that she is now abed, and likely to stay there, weeping . . . ."

"Why, this is not to be borne!"

". . . and leaving the castle without a chatelaine just when the first of your father's guests are arriving – they come from so far, they started early, and are expected on the morrow – you cannot ask your sister to act as chatelaine, can you? She confuses people's names and status, and gives offence without intending to do so. Also, she is very prone to tears since young Gerald was found by Jaclin with his arm about her, and that caused some stir, I can tell you! Your brother couldn't order Gerald to be whipped, but he screamed and shouted that he would like to do so, in front of everyone. Then Gerald, who does not lack for courage, tried to challenge your brother to meet him in the tourney, and Crispin was going to accept!" He put his hand over his eyes, overcome at the memory. "Well, Telfer and Varons and I got them apart, and talked some sense into them, but by that time your sister was in another pickle. The silly girl fled from the scene between Gerald and Crispin and after coming here and being turned away by your nurse, she went weeping to the armoury, looking for I know not whom. There she discovered a good-looking young ostler, who was old enough to know better than to try to touch her. However, she threw herself on him in tears, he put his arm round her to comfort her, and is in consequence under threat of losing his eyes."

"I must dress! Where is . . .?"

"Of course he has been flogged already," said Gervase. "Your brother, foiled of his vengeance where Gerald was concerned, fell on the ostler like a gift from heaven. Once more Telfer, Varons and I tried to intervene, but though we have gained a stay of execution for the moment, the lad is still in danger of losing his eyes. Your sister ought to have been married at sixteen – though, come to think of it, she has been so taught to display her charms that she is as likely to cause trouble as a young married woman as she is without a ring on her finger. Then . . . ."

Beata ran to the door, and called for her nurse. She clapped her hands, looking around her for her clothes. Gervase picked some stockings from the chest nearby, and handed them to her while he went on with his report.

"There is also the question of the masque to be perfomed on the night before your joint nuptials. I was told to compose some trifle, to be performed by the pages, the waiting-women, yourself and your sister. Unfortunately my effort did not meet with approval. I lack talent for fulsome praise, you see, and my drafts were greeted with scorn. Only this morning Father Anthony informed me that he was taking over the direction of the masque, which would have as its climax the ascent of a staircase by you and your sister, to be greeted at the top by Sir Bertrand in all his glory as the God of War . . . and our own Father Anthony in full canonicals, who will join with you in a song in praise of some minor saint or other – I forget which."

"Never!" cried Beata, laughing yet angry. "What a ridiculous . . . hand me my shoes . . .!"

He went on one knee to fit them on, as she sat on the bed. "It is a sight better, I can assure you, than the ode in praise of Chastity which I had been trying to compose for you to speak."

"Chastity?" His hands were warm about her ankles. They both fell silent. He sat back on his heels, and stroked his beard. She stood up, pulled her dress over her head, and fastened it at the neck.

"Has Crispin gone mad?"

"With anxiety, I believe. He receives directives from your

father daily, and these are filled with such contradictory instructions that he knows not how to manage. The work on the stands in the tiltyard overlooking the lists has been held up by bad weather, and if they are not finished, then how can we stage a tourney? The bishop writes one week that he will certainly be here, and the next that he will assuredly not be here. Some abbot or other has now been invited, as stop-gap, and the abbess of the convent to which you are bound. The numbers of guests fluctuate from day to day, but usually in an upwards direction. All this would be as nothing to Cripsin, of course, if he were not so anxious about his wife. I believe he has come to hate the very sight of her; yet his is a kindly nature at bottom, and therefore he takes refuge from his misery in striking out at any who cross his will."

"At you?"

"Not as yet, but that will come, no doubt. Rocca is ever at your brother's elbow. Crispin has grown to hate Rocca, and yet cannot be rid of the man. Like Joan, in a way. He has a talent for tying himself to people he does not really like. Rocca opposes me in everything, on principle, which is very wearing. I would keep out of the internal affairs of the castle if I could, but Telfer has begged me to help him, and I cannot refuse."

"Besides, it is a challenge to your sense of order, is it not?"

"You are right." He smiled. "Yes . . . . I think I would quite enjoy it, if it were not for having to watch Rocca at every turn. You see, if I have a finger in this pie, and it pleases Lord Henry, then Rocca will be at a disadvantage when it comes to a confrontation between us over the Michaelmas dues. He knows very well that if he does not destroy me first, I will destroy him in time."

Lacking a comb, she ran her fingers through her curls. "What do you want me to do?"

He lifted his hands and let them fall. "Help us, all of us. We are all overtired, trying to get everything ready in time. Some trifling incident may spark Crispin off again – set yourself close to him, listen to him, and when he is in a receptive mood, reason with him. You are needed everywhere . . . ."

"My lady!" The nurse came in, anxious-eyed. "you are never up and dressed! You cannot mean to go out!"

"Not before time, it appears," said Beata. "Could you not have told me that all was not well in the castle?"

"If I had thought you could mend matters . . . . "

"I do not know whether I can or no," said Beata. "But of a certainty, I must try."

Gervase went straight from the infirmary to the armoury, where Crispin was inspecting the armour he planned to wear in the tourney. This would not be the heavy armour of the battlefield, but was lighter, specially made for such purposes. Lances and swords would be prepared with blunt tips, and no heavy maces allowed.

Crispin was absorbed in his choice, so Gervase leaned against the wall and allowed his thoughts to wander. He was tired. He had been up all night, trying to devise a solution to the seemingly impossible problem of how to hold the tourney if the weather continued inclement. Thomas the clerk came up, with a bundle of newly-arrived letters which ought to have been attended to that morning, but which Crispin had brushed aside as being of no importance. A self-important little man had been sent down from London by Lord Henry to act as Clerk of the Lists, and Crispin was more anxious to confer with him than to deal with business matters.

Thomas nudged Gervase. Crispin was asking for him. Perhaps they could get some work done now . . . but no, Crispin was merely seeking confirmation that his armour would be the best, the most ornate, the most highly gilded to appear in the tourney. Three helmets had been laid out for his inspection. Crispin ran his fingers over the chasing on the helm before him. A scarlet ostrich-feather plume floated from the crest, which was wrought in the semblance of a man's hand. Gervase nodded and smiled, but his own eyes went to an unadorned helm which Crispin had pushed aside. Now there was a helm made for fighting, instead of display; that helm had lines that would deflect a sword-blade, instead of catching it in their intricacies . . . It was a thing of beauty, to Gervase, that plain helm, because it was so well designed for its purpose.

Crispin had talked himself into a sunny mood. Perhaps now would be a good time to speak with him about the ostler condemned to lose his sight . . . the poor lad's father and mother had been waiting to plead his case since dawn yesterday, and . . . but no! A page had come with a request for an audience from the Lady Joan, and at once Crispin's good humour was gone. He cuffed the page from his path, bidding them not to trouble him with that woman any more. So. Now Crispin decided to go to the stables, to inspect the horse he planned to ride in the tourney, and the clerks would not be required. Gervase bade Thomas snatch an hour's sleep, and went to take another look at the tiltyard.

"Master William!" The tone of Gerald's voice was nicely poised between condescension and entreaty. "Master William, one moment of your time. I believe you taught young Jaclin a trick or two . . . ?" Gervase bowed. For the last week he had gone daily to the tiltyard or the armoury at the time appointed by Jaclin, only to be kept waiting for an hour and then dismissed, or told to watch while Jaclin beat a number of stable-lads, untrained in such work, at the quarter-staff. It had not been an edifying experience.

"I wish . . . ." Gerald reddened. "That is, Captain Varons suggested . . . I have difficulty in holding my lance steady, and this will be my first tourney."

Gervase stifled a yawn. What next would be required of him? As Crispin's secretary, he could refuse. Yet he was sorry for the lad.

"I have watched you tilt," Gervase told him. "You take your lance out of its rest just before impact. Therefore you lose control."

"It is so hard . . . will you not practise with me? Jaclin says he has no further need of you . . . tomorrow at dawn?"

Gervase sighed. Then he thought, perhaps if I get a good night's sleep tonight, I might be able to do it. He said, "If my duties permit, and time allows, I will certainly be there. It is certainly difficult to keep up that arm-breaking posture up to and beyond the moment of impact. There is one way. You must want to kill your opponent. If you think only of that, you will hold the lance steady enough."

Gerald started. How had Gervase known that Gerald hated Crispin? Gerald was out of his depth in such a situation. He turned on his heel and walked away, stiff-legged. Gervase shook his tired head to clear it, and went out into the rain.

"I did not mean it!" wept Elaine, her head buried in Beata's lap. "I am fond of Gerald, and when Crispin said . . . what he said . . . oh, Beata! I am not a . . . what he called me! And I went to the infirmary to see if you were well enough to talk to me, and Nurse said you were asleep, so I went along to the armoury, because I thought Jaclin might be there, or Master William, maybe; but they weren't and I was leaning against the table to cry in peace and one of the ostlers asked me what was the matter, and I suppose I did hold onto his arm, because he was so big and comforting . . . and then Crispin came in with everyone, and he said the man must be flogged . . . and I went on my knees and said I supposed it was my fault, and that I'd only let him comfort me because he had such nice eyes, and then Crispin said . . . .

"Hush, dear!" Beata smoothed her sister's hair. "We will try to save the man's eyes . . . ."

"Father Anthony says it is all my fault because I am so vain, and display myself like the Whore of Babylon! But I'm not a Jezebel, truly I am not!"

"No, you are not." Yet Beata sighed.

Elaine sat up, eyes still brimming with tears. "Don't you believe me?"

"I don't think you are aware of the damage you do, that's all."

"Crispin said I ought to be whipped, but instead he sent me to Father Anthony to be scolded . . . I wasn't very sympathetic when Father Anthony scolded you, was I? The things he said – he made me feel so sinful!"

"Not sinful, dearest. Thoughtless, perhaps."

"He said I led men into sin, by the way I behaved. That isn't true, is it?"

Beata gave a sad little laugh. "I don't think I know enough about it to judge. Perhaps it would have been better if you had been married at sixteen."

"Y-yes. Though I wouldn't have been Queen of Beauty then, would I? I would have been bearing children, one a year . . . ugh! Or dying in childbirth . . . I wish . . . I wish I need never get married. . . ."

"You are not still afraid of your bold Sir Bertrand, are you? Why, he is sure to be Champion of the tourney at Christmas, and at your feet . . . ."

"Father Anthony says that the masque must be completely rewritten. He says Master William is no poet."

"Would you have expected him to be?" And Beata smiled.

Elaine sighed, pushing back her hair, and drying her eyes. "We are lucky to have him, aren't we?"

"Father Anthony?"

"I meant Master William. He is so kind. Do you know, he always makes me stand at the back when we distribute alms so that my dress does not get spattered with mud . . . oh, this rain . . . will it never stop? Crispin says Father is to send me some gold tissue to make up into a gown for my wedding, but the roads are going to be impassable if the weather does not improve soon. You are to have one exactly the same, of course. If the material doesn't come in time, I have ordered them to make up another blue gown for you, like the one I wore at the last tourney . . . with the silver cloth undergown. It is here, half-made, somewhere . . . also I have been thinking how much the nun's wimple and veil will suit you . . . so helpful to disguise a sagging neck as you grow older." She stopped and put her hand to her head. "You think I'm heartless, don't you? Well, I'm not. Only I must think about something else quickly, or go mad!"

"I hate wearing things on my head," said Beata, following Elaine's lead. "Yet I dare say I shall grow accustomed to the cap and coif in time."

"It's not a cap, dearest . . . why are you smiling like that? And where are you going?"

"I'm going to see Joan."

"You won't please Crispin by paying attention to her. No-one goes near her, now. He swears he doesn't wish to see her, ever again, only of course he will have to. For one thing, who else would receive the guests at Christmas? Crispin said I should do it, but I really couldn't." She stood, finger tapping cheek, looking around her. "I know I saw that gown last night . . . ."

"I hope to persuade her to divorce Crispin. If he returns her dowry, she may yet attract another husband. . . ."

"I doubt he'll wish to return her dowry. Rocca says Crispin needs her dowry, in order to pay ours. The cost of the tourney and all the entertainments at Christmas! Rocca says . . . ."

"Are you so friendly with the man that you repeat everything he says?"

"Why . . . no. Not exactly. He took the trouble to talk to me when everyone else was so busy, and you were sick. He asked me to help persuade Crispin to let Rocca raise a loan from the Jews. Only Crispin refused. I can't think why!"

"I can! I see one thing, and that is that Rocca will die a rich man!"

"I know you do not like him, but . . . ."

"Who says so?"

"He did. He told me it was a great sorrow to him, and that he wished he knew how he had come to offend you. I admit I don't care for his manner, but he is a useful man. He knows everything. I asked him to find out Master William's history for me . . . ."

Beata stifled a shriek, with both hands over her mouth. Elaine's lips began to tremble, and her eyes to brim. "Now what have I said?"

"Do you not know that Rocca is Master William's enemy, and would give anything to bring him down? Do you not know that Master William is the king-pin round whom this castle revolves, and that without him – do you really think the tourney would be ready in time, or anything done that ought to be done?"

"Well, I don't suppose he has anything to hide."

"Everyone has something to hide," said Beata, with a wry smile.

"It was you who hinted he had a mysterious past, in the first place!"

"I had done better to cut out my tongue."

It was late in the afternoon, and Crispin had been led to his chair in the green solar by a mixture of persuasion and gentle bullying which had left Gervase weary even before they started on the letters.

With mechanical movements Gervase broke the seal on the latest letter from Lord Henry, who was still in London. He began to read it aloud. Crispin could read when he had to, but he was a poor scholar, and preferred to have his correspondence read aloud to him. Before Gervase could proceed beyond the greetings, Crispin interrupted him, with a request to go over the order of events at the tourney once more, so that the Clerk of the Lists could familiarise himself with them. And there came the Clerk, bowing to left and right as if he were visiting royalty.

Holding back a sigh, Gervase took the roll of parchment from the ever-helpful Thomas, spread it out on the table, and checked off the various items. This was the third programme he had prepared, and he was not anxious to alter the order again. The celebrations were to last over the two days before Christmas and Christmas Day itself. On the morning of the first two days there would be archery contests for the yeomanry, followed by bouts of singlestick, and certain local games of skill such as climbing greased poles and foot races. If necessary these could be held in the Great Hall. On the afternoon of the first day – weather permitting – there would be a procession of all the knights and squires in full armour, on horseback, past the Queen of Beauty and her sister, at which time the Queen of Beauty would give a knot of ribbons or some other favour from her dress to Sir Bertrand, to be worn on his helm. The Lady Beata would likewise award her brother Crispin a favour. The two knights would then pick sides, and there would be a mock battle, which it was tacitly assumed that Sir Bertrand's side would win. And then a feast, with dancing.

On the second afternoon, after the usual festivities for the peasants in the forenoon, six knights would challenge six others to single combat in the lists. Again, Crispin would be matched with Sir Bertrand, and so on, down to Jaclin, Gerald, and the rest. In the evening there would be another feast, at which would be performed the masque over which Father Anthony was now labouring.

On Christmas Day the marriage of Sir Bertrand and the Lady Elaine would be celebrated, followed by a nuptial mass for all. Later that day the Lady Beata would be received into the arms of the church, and Lord Henry would be given quittance of the vow he had made at the birth of his daughters.

"It is well enough, I suppose," said Crispin. "Let the bishop be given the best seat at all times. It is important he be well disposed towards us. If only it would stop raining! Whatever possessed my father to stage a tourney in the depths of winter!"

"It occurred to me," said Gervase, rubbing his forehead in an effort to concentrate, "that . . . ."

"Very well, then. I will hear my father's letter now."

Gervase did not actually shrug, but he certainly gave the impression of having done so. Crispin scowled, and taking out his dagger, began to clean his nails with it. His restless eye met Rocca's smirk, and Crispin's scowl deepened.

Gervase stopped reading in mid-sentence. Crispin looked up with an oath, but Gervase, without asking permission, had handed the letter to his clerk Thomas, and was walking away to the window, with his head averted.

"Is the fool taken ill?"

Gervase could be seen to shake his head, and spread his hands. Thomas hesitated, with one eye on Gervase, and then resumed the reading of the letter, which was concerned with the exact date Lord Henry intended to arrive at the castle, and with the number and style of those he was to bring in his train.

"Shall I send for your physician to attend Master William?" asked Rocca, fawning at Crispin's elbow.

"One moment," said Gervase. He seemed to be fighting pain. "One moment," he repeated.

"My lord will not find the physician in any of the places where he ought to be. Shall I send for him, my lord? I know where the man has gone – against your orders – you recall you said no-one was to go near the ostler who behaved so shockingly to your sister? But there it is, some people find it difficult to obey your orders – your very clear orders – Master William never seems to learn, does he?"

The dagger flashed through the air, hooking itself in Rocca's gown. "Speak clearly, man! Or it will be the worse for you!"

Rocca went grey, and sweat stood out on his brow. "That treacherous secretary of yours . . . the man you choose to honour, he flouts your orders and speaks slightingly of you behind your back . . . . He ordered your physician to go to the cell of the villain who would have dishonoured your sister . . . to succour him in secret . . . ."

Crispin threw Rocca from him, and turned on Gervase. "Did you do that? You knew I had ordered no-one to go near him!"

Gervase threw out his hands. He was very pale. He said, "My lord, they said he had a fever, because of the flogging . . . ."

"Silence! What, am I to be mocked to my face? And behind my back, too! Why, you disobedient . . . Rocca is right, and you will need a taste of the whip yourself before you understand who is master here!" He swung on Varons. "Take him to the West Tower and set him in fetters, neck and ankles . . . and be sure I will send to see my orders have been faithfully carried out!"

There was a moment when the confused echoes of Crispin's voice seemed to hold everyone still. Varons did not move first. Gervase did. He walked across the room without haste, without showing any sign of fear, looking straight ahead. Varons lifted his arms in despair, and followed Gervase out.

Beata was mounting the stairs to visit the Lady Joan, her

nurse at her heels. She stopped short, as if she had mistaken the step on the stair.

"What is it, my dearie?" said the nurse.

"Nothing . . . at least, I'm not sure." Her rapid heart-beat gave the lie to her words. "I was disturbed by a thought . . . something is wrong."

"You have risen too early from sick-bed. I told you . . . ."

Beata ran on up the steps till she came to a window overlooking the courtyard. From above the two figures were foreshortened, yet both men were easy to identify. Gervase was being escorted to the West Tower by Captain Varons.

"I should certainly have cut out my tongue," said Beata.

Chapter Ten

The head gaoler sorted through his keys. "Leave your outer clothes and your shoes over there, if you please, Master William."

"That will not be necessary," said Varons, rubbing the back of his neck. "And we will have a nice, airy chamber for the secretary, if you please; with a window."

"Like that, is it?" The gaoler's eyebrows rose. "Think he'll not be with us long?"

"I hope not," said Varons. He looked at Gervase, and bit his lip. Gervase hardly seemed aware of what was happening to him. "And you'll not give him one of those collars studded with bolts inside," said Varons. "A plain affair, if you please, and the fetters on his ankles are not to be so close as to give him gangrene . . . ."

The gaoler shrugged, and led them up, instead of down the stairs to a slip of a room with a high barred window. The aperture was unglazed, and small, but did admit adequate light. A stool, a pitcher for water, and some straw comprised the furnishings, apart from the chains which dangled from staples set into the walls. Gervase allowed the gaoler to fasten the heavy collar about his neck, and set his ankles in fetters, with the same air of inattention that he had worn all along.

"You are ill, my friend," said Varons, shaking Gervase's arm. "Shall I send the physician to you?"

Gervase shook his head. For the first time he seemed aware of his surroundings. Colour stained his cheeks. He clenched his fists, and moved his feet so that the irons about his legs clattered along the floor. "A better lodging than I might have expected," he said, with his habitual courtesy.

A man panted up the stairs calling for Varons. "Lord Crispin – you are to come at once – that ostler is to lose the sight of his eyes within the hour, and we all ordered to look on . . . ."

Varons cursed. The gaoler said he must lock up sharpish then, if he might make so bold as to ask the captain to move.

Gervase looked up at that. He rubbed his eyes, and yawned. He said, "Will you tell Thomas . . . the tithe barn, the one that's disused . . . they must make that ready against the tourney. He'll understand."

Varons halted at the door, unwilling to go, and yet aware that he was awaited elsewhere. "Do not listen, if your window overlooks the courtyard . . . ."

"Thank you," said Gervase. "I shall do well enough."

Thomas the Clerk sought for the Lady Beata, and found her crossing one of the antechambers. She drew her mantle closer, against the draughts, as she listened to his tale.

"And he sent me a most strange message, about using the old tithe barn, which is nigh on a ruin, as you may know . . . and we cannot make head nor tail of it, none of us, and wondered if perhaps you might . . . knowing him so well?"

She noted the hint, and yet seemed not to notice it. "I? No. If it is so important, and I can see that he must have held it so, can you not ask my brother for permission to visit him? Or better still, to have him released?"

Thomas shrugged, and spread his hands. Rocca was openly triumphant, swaggering about the castle as if it were his personal property. Crispin was drinking so heavily it were folly to interrupt him.

"If Master William is ill . . ." suggested Beata, and if you had not been watching her closely, you would not have noticed that she found the idea alarming. But Thomas was watching her.

"He is worn out, merely. Or perhaps a touch of that fever which took the little heir, and laid you low? That is the excuse, and in time no doubt Lord Crispin will accept it, and release Master William. It is for that end we work." Then, with apparent irrelevance, he added, "I have put the letter from Lord Henry in with a pile of other such papers, in case it fall into . . . certain hands."

She stood so still . . . only her eyes showed she still lived.

Thomas went on. "I was curious, of course, as to why he had faltered at that point. It was so very unlike him. His self-control has always been something to admire. Lord Henry wrote that he was bringing Lady Escot with Sir Bertrand at Christmas . . . the newly-widowed Lady Escot . . . ."

She could say nothing . . . pretend she knew nothing. Yet the fact that she had listened and found nothing to say, would have told Thomas that he had guessed aright. How had he known? Ah, but he was another of the spiders of Castle Malling, in the tradition of his master, Hamo. Naturally he would have guessed, as she had guessed, and Hamo and Telfer and Varons . . . too many people knew this secret. So Lord Escot was dead. What would this mean to Gervase? Her mind darted among various possibilities, only to be brought back to the present by a cough from Thomas.

"Humble suggestion . . . might Father Anthony intervene on Master William's behalf? He's not afraid of my Lord Crispin, even in his cups. Suggestion to the effect that the bishop is not going to be pleased, if the tourney is put off . . . the weather being so bad . . . most unfortunate, of course, that the one who might have been able to solve the problem has offended my lord, no doubt due to the fever . . . and so forth?"

"You are as bad as Hamo," said Beata. "Yes, of course I

will go to Father Anthony – and at once. You really think the old tithe barn could be made into a tiltyard?"

"I don't." Thomas stressed the pronoun. "Did I say the old tithe barn? No doubt you misheard me. And no doubt I misheard the message I was given by Captain Varons. All I know is that Master William said he thought he knew the answer to the problem of holding a tourney in bad weather."

"It will do very well . . . although . . . I fear my brother will have to be allowed to sleep off his present indulgence, which means an overnight stay in prison for our friend."

"Captain Varons assures me he is well housed in a dry cell, and that he is provided with a light. Master Telfer has commanded an excellent supper to be sent over, and a pallet with some bedding. The physician has visited him –after he attended to the . . . ." Master Thomas swallowed and Beata shuddered, remembering the screams of the ostler as his eyes were burned out. "Afterwards. The physician reported that Master William was asleep. I think sleep might be a better physic than the purges the good doctor left for our friend."

The knowledge that the blinded ostler was not like to live the night through hung between them. They both knew they were running a risk in seeking to soften the rigour of Gervase's imprisonment.

"Thank you, Master Thomas," said Beata.

The man smiled, an open and most unexpectedly wide smile. Then he was his anxious-eyed self again. He bowed and left her. Beata went in search of Father Anthony.

It was still raining next morning, when Gervase was brought from the West Tower direct to the tiltyard. Crispin awaited him, surrounded by a worried-looking group of people. Rocca was not there.

"Well?" demanded Crispin, as Gervase approached.

Gervase gestured to the high blank wall above them. Around them rain fell, gently, persistently, and the hammers of the men working on the stands opposite – even though they were protected by covers – struck with sad irregularity.

"It occurred to me," said Gervase, "that a wall has two sides. This side is open to the elements, and the ground beneath our feet suffers accordingly. Even if the rain ceases before noon, we would need a strong drying wind for days before the ground would be fit for horses. It occurred to me that we might investigate what lay on the other side of the wall, which must of necessity run in length for as many paces as are required in a tiltyard."

The Clerk of the Lists came bustling up. "What's this about staging the tourney under cover? A preposterous idea, if I may say so . . . ."

Gervase gave him a cold look. "It is true that we could not hold a mock battle inside, but the individual encounters with lance and sword, and perhaps also the entertainment provided by and for the peasants, could easily . . . ."

"Without the mock battle, you have nothing," argued the Clerk.

"Peace!" said Crispin. His eyes were deep-set today, and a muscle twitched at the side of his mouth. His scar had darkened, till it seemed almost black. "Let us hear Master William out. If I had not been so hasty yesterday . . . come inside out of the rain, Master William! I don't want you falling sick again."

They went round the corner into a secluded courtyard, formed in an angle of the curtain wall of the castle, and clustered with ramshackle sheds, broken farm wagons, and the like. The litter of the castle had drifted here over many years, yet behind it, now that they looked closely, they could see the shape of an immense and very ancient, half-timbered barn.

They stepped into the gloom of the barn. It had no windows, and the only light came in through two great doorways, whose wooden leaves lay in shattered pieces at an angle against the walls inside.

"The light . . . impossible . . . ." said the Clerk, yet his nose twitched, and he began to pace out distances.

The barn was partially filled with sacks of grain, and although a stack of discarded barrels and farm implements impeded their view, nothing could disguise the fact that the building was nobly proportioned and in a reasonable state of repair. The roof was tiled, sloping to within some fifteen feet of the ground on either side, but rising in the centre to double that height. Along the whole length of the side opposite the doors, a platform had been raised to facilitate the storage of grain.

"Our stands are ready-made for us, you see," said Gervase, gesturing to the platform. "If we put up handrails, and drape them suitably . . . staircases at either end. We have been making stairs for the stands outside, and they can easily be adapted for this place instead. The common folk can come and go beneath the platform, once we have fenced them off from the body of the barn. There are two doors already made for entrances and exits of opposing knights, and there is no reason why we should not cut more – we can effect a barrier down the centre of the barn, with the poles we had intended to use outside."

"The light!" bawled the Clerk of the Lists, from the far end. "How could we possibly light the place?"

"Our smiths must work overnight to produce some large iron rings, on which we can spike candles. We will suspend the rings from the roof at intervals. The lack of light is, I agree, the greatest problem we face."

"No mock battle?" said Crispin, frowning and pulling at the ring on his finger.

"It requires an area of ground greater than we can provide. Yet we can still have the procession, here in the barn. The knights can still pick their sides and challenge an opponent. Or we could go back to the Round Table method, and match a challenger against all comers to fight not only with lance but also with swords, the knight who acquits himself best to receive the crown of honour."

"Single combat only? Yes, I like the idea . . . ." Crispin put his arm round Gervase's shoulder. "Master William, I do not know what we should do without you! I shall certainly recommend that you be the next Steward, when my father comes."

The Lady Beata was descending the ramp into the courtyard when Gervase met her, going up.

She said, "What is it? You do not really have the fever, have you?"

"I am well enough." And yet he did not look it. There was a pallor about his cheek-bones that spoke of ill-health, or strain, or . . . .

"You are angry," she said. "Yes, I can see that you are. Once in the stocks, and then . . . yes, I can see how being imprisoned would anger you. But my brother has made amends, has he not? He has promised to make you Steward?"

"Lady," he said, and there was an infinite distancing effect in the way he gave her her title. "Lady, I served a fool for many years because I loved him. Your brother is no fool; he is something worse. He is not to be trusted. Do you really think I would serve him, after this? I go at Christmas."

She held her head high, and he passed on with a slight bow.

Crispin lay in his great chair by the fire after supper, drinking, and staring into the fire. He called Gervase to him.

"My father will be here next Friday or possibly on Thursday . . . . I will speak to him on your behalf, about the Steward's position. You have my word on it."

Gervase bowed, but made no reply.

Crispin pulled the ring off his finger, looked at it, and then put it back again. "Advise me," he said. "What I should do about my wife."

"The bishop is surely better qualified than I to . . . ."

"He is one who bends with every wind that blows. You do not bend. I like that in you. You might have supposed that I did not like it, and for a while I did not. And yet, when all is finished, I find I have come to trust you. You say you wish to leave us at Christmas . . . ." Again Gervase bowed, and said nothing. "You will not go," said Crispin, looking dark. His hand began to beat on the arm of his chair.

"Until Christmas you may count on my loyal service. After that, I think you will find Master Thomas satisfactory."

"Christmas . . . it may never come. I wish my father had never conceived the idea of a tourney. It will bring all the riffraff in the county to our gates. What the devil am I to do about my wife?"

"I think you have already decided, my lord."

"Yes, but the manner of it . . . this damned tourney, and she the rightful chatelaine of Malling, with her cousin about to marry into the family . . . tell me how to get out of that, and I'll fill your purse with gold."

"My lord, divorces are not uncommon. There are precedents. If these affairs are conducted with dignity and resolution . . . ."

"Dignity! I can make myself feared, I know. Or can I? You don't fear me, do you? Do you?"

"No, my lord." Gervase spoke wearily, as to a fractious, tiresome child.

Crispin laughed aloud, and smote the arm of his chair. "I like that in you. Here!" He took off his ring, and held it out to Gervase "Take it. Put it on your hand and wear it always. I know myself well enough to suspect there will be times in the future when I shall forget that you are a good man, and I shall wish to hurt you . . . if that should ever happen again, you must hold up that ring, or remind me of it . . . Understand?"

Gervase contemplated the sapphire, and perhaps his mind went back to another ring, found in his wallet at Ware. He shook his head. "My lord, it is too valuable. What would men say if they saw me wearing that?"

"They would say that I valued you as I ought to value you. Come, I can be a good friend, when I choose. You cannot refuse me."

Gervase put the ring on his forefinger, with reluctance. "I will wear it till Christmas, if you so wish. After that . . . ."

Crispin gave him a tigerish smile. "You will not leave, Master Steward. I know how to hold on to my own, and you are my man now. I have shown you my bad side hitherto, have I not? Yet I have a better nature . . . when I am not overwhelmed with problems."

"The lady Joan is your legal wife," said Gervase, somewhat hesitantly. "And surely she is also the chatelaine of Malling. Yet she is much worn down by the tragic death of her son. Doubtless she would be glad to share the duties of chatelaine with your sisters. . . ."

"Elaine! A beautiful, destructive fool! If I had not punished that ostler, we would have had half the servants in the castle putting their arms round her!"

"The Lady Beata, on the other hand, is accustomed to acting as unofficial chatelaine in the frequent absences of the Lady Joan . . . and I believe she does not lack for sense. If the three ladies were to receive your guests together, especially since the celebrations are in honour of your sisters' marriages . . .?"

Beata stood in the chamber she shared with Elaine and looked about her. Clothes and jewels were everywhere, but none of them belonged to her.

Ten days, she thought; and her fingers curled within her palms. Only ten days, and she would have to part with everything that she loved. At that moment she hated her father. He had rejected her plea that she be spared her fate . . . well, and good. That was his right. Yet could he not at least have written to her himself? Need he have belittled her so? To send a message through Crispin that she take her maidenly scruples to the priest was hardly helpful. . . .

Father Anthony had said that she must pray for faith, and resume her fast. 'I don't believe in prayer," she said. "What is more, I'm not sure that I believe in a God who can let such things happen . . . though when it comes to Rocca, I can manage to believe in the devil."

Prayer, she thought, was useless. Only deeds were of use in this messy, workaday, heart-aching world.

She took out the knife with which she cut up her food, and setting it within the neck of her gown, ripped it to the waist, and then to the hem. She kicked it aside, and advanced on her sister's clothing. If there were only ten days of womanhood left to her, then for those last few days she would at least dress becomingly.

Eight days. Beata danced in the hall, twined flowers in her

hair, and laughed . . . and just when her laughter verged on the hysterical, she felt Gervase's eye on her, and checked herself. And then rebelled that he had dared to check her. What if she did laugh too loudly? What if she were to curse and make lewd jokes as other noblewomen did? If he could have danced with her, she would not have cared . . . but he could only watch, in his cap and coif . . . .

She lay in the great bed she shared with Elaine, but she did not sleep. She lay on her back and stared up at the ceiling, and her eyes glowed in the light of the lamp which had been left burning nearby.

Elaine could not sleep, either. She propped herself up on one elbow, and considered her sister's tense body, and shining eyes. "What are you thinking of?"

"Of men," said Beata, and closed her eyes with a shiver. "I think of how it would be to lie with a man. . . ."

"Beata!"

"Why so shocked? Did not God give us these desires that we might procreate? Am I not a woman first, and only destined for the convent by a man-made whim? May I not think as other women think, feel as other women feel, for the few days of life left to me?"

"You talk as if you were going to die!"

"It feels rather like it." She turned her head to look at her sister. "There's no one to overhear you, little sister, if you wish to speak openly. Listen – the women are snoring in the next room. Do not tell me you have never dreamed of a man taking you in his arms, and laying you down, with his strength leaping to meet and mingle with yours . . . and his leanness . . . his long back . . . his strong arms around you, and his strong thighs . . .!"

"Don't!" said Elaine, in a frightened whisper. "Of course I don't think of men like that. I didn't know that you could . . . ."

"Have you lived all your life in a blindfold? Have you no ears, that you have not heard the women talk of life and birth? Or seen them coupling in the hay at harvest, or behind the buttery, which is the usual place of rendezvous in this castle?"

"I have thought, now and then . . . ." She fiddled with her hair. "But of course it could never be!"

"Of whom? You intrigue me. Not Gerald, I dare swear! Nor that wretched ostler! Of Jaclin?"

Elaine buried her hot face in her pillow. "Don't be absurd!"

"Of whom, then? Not Sir Bertrand, I must suppose. Who can have caught your fancy about this place? Tell me, my sweet. You know I will keep your secret."

"Well, if you promise not to tell – and of course I know it would never be possible, but there is a man in the castle who, if he is not of noble birth, yet was surely gently born . . . ."

Beata's mind leaped to the truth. She said nothing, but something in her attitude caused Elaine to shrink away from her.

"Beata, you frighten me. You said you would not tell. Indeed, he has said nothing, and I have been discreet. No-one would ever guess! Just because he is not a knight, you look down on him, but I assure you that I do not. He is so kind, so gentle, and yet so clever. If I could only have married someone like him, I think I would have been happy."

"Why not ask Father if you may marry him, instead of Sir Bertrand?" Beata burst into wild laughter.

Elaine said, with a forlorn attempt at dignity, "I know I am a fool, but I am not so foolish as to wish to harm him. I would not want him to suffer, as others have suffered for my foolishness."

Beata gave a great sigh, and turned from her sister. Presently Elaine slept, but Beata lay awake for a long time, pondering what Elaine had said.

The corpse of the blinded ostler was taken out of the infirmary and buried. Beata did not attend his death-bed nor did she have a mass said for him. Father Anthony enquired of Elaine – who had substituted for her sister that morning at Mass – why the Lady Beata neglected her duties. Elaine bit her lip, and wished herself elsewhere.

"I think . . . that is, I believe . . . some cousins arrive at noon, and Beata wished . . . that is, I did remind her about Mass, Father . . . "

Father Anthony sent a page with a request that the Lady Beata attend him in chapel. She returned a negligent answer, and did not go. He went in search of her, and found her in the Great Hall, consulting with Telfer on domestic matters. She wore a gown of dark blue, into which a pattern of light green leaves had been woven. One of Elaine's tire-women had been at work on Beata's hair, and it shone as it waved and curled about her head and shoulders. She had confined her locks with a fillet of gold, but discarded her nets and veils.

When Telfer had departed, she turned on the priest with a fierce gesture.

"Can you not see I must be about my father's business?"

"Lady Beata! That is nigh on blasphemy!" The priest was much perturbed. "I must recall you to a sense of your duty. . . ."

"Am I not my father's daughter? I am not yours, Father, until Christmas. So leave me be."

The priest could hardly believe his ears. Was this the quiet girl whose spiritual life he had overseen for so many years? "This is not like you!" he exclaimed. "That wretched creature we buried this morning . . . if Master William had not sent for me to be with the man, he would have died alone and unshriven. Moreover, I hear you are eating meat, which is strictly forbidden you in Advent . . . and you have not been to Mass this five days, nor to confession. . . ."

"And shall not. What, am I to be a nun before my time? I warn you, Father, leave me alone. My father constrains me to enter the church; well, he has the right, and I know my duty. I will come to you on Christmas Day, and you will hear no word of complaint then. But not even the bishop will get me into that church, or force me to bend the knee to your futile God, before that time.

"My child!" He was not accustomed to defiance, but he was no coward, and was merely collecting his thoughts for a return to the attack when she walked away. He could not believe it; the girl had simply turned her back on him, and left him in mid-sentence. He opened his mouth to recall her but it was too late, for she was even now greeting a group of guests who had just arrived at the castle.

"I will write to Lord Henry about this," said Father Anthony.

Seven days, and still Lord Henry dallied in London.

For the first time in weeks, Beata went to the gate at sunset to distribute alms. Elaine was there, as she usually was nowadays, and Gervase, accompanied by one small page and one large dog.

"This will not do," said Beata, as they gathered up their baskets at the end. "Who can we ask to take on this duty for us? The alms-giving must not cease at Christmas, when we go."

Gervase seemed in a reflective mood. "It is true that one tend to think everything ends at Christmas . . . that one has no responsibility for what happens here after that . . . ."

"But you are not going, too?" said Elaine to Gervase. Her colour rose, and her eyes widened.

"Why, of course he is going!" said Beata. "He finds the uncertain temper of our family distasteful, and the rewards. . . ." She snapped her fingers. "A prison cell."

"And a ring," said Gervase, turning the sapphire round on his finger, "which I must remember to return before I go."

"I don't understand," said Elaine, and now tears began to fill her eyes – those fatally beautiful, blue eyes. "Why do you have to go? And where will you go?"

"He will go to the devil!" snapped Beata. She swung one basket into the other, and lifted both to her hip. As she turned, she stumbled over the dog . . . with her arms full, she could not save herself.

But Gervase was there, reaching for her arm, breaking her fall, and then setting her back on her feet. She stood, trembling, not looking at him or Elaine. He also was speechless. The baskets lay tumbled on the floor, but neither Beata nor Gervase moved to pick them up. Elaine had given a little cry of alarm, but it seemed that neither Beata nor Gervase had had heard her.

Without looking at them, Beata walked rapidly back into

the castle, brushing down her arm, where Gervase had held her.

Elaine might not be very clever, but even she could pick up and interpret the complexity of emotions which had been involved in the incident. She saw that Gervase's eyes were following Beata, and she remembered the look on his face when he had leaped forward to save her sister from falling . . . and now Elaine, too, began to tremble. For she understood that Beata and Gervase loved each other, and that Gervase would never . . . could never . . . love her.

Chapter Eleven

Six days, and the atmosphere in the castle was charged with excitement. The population of the village below had trebled, for a number of landless knights had been drawn to the neighbourhood by the tourney. Two heralds had appeared and were even now consulting about titles and escutcheons, muttering to each other of saltires, chevrons and the like. Many of the invited guests had arrived, but still the lord of the castle tarried in London, although letters had been received from him saying that he was to be expected shortly. The retainers of the guests swelled the ranks of the servants, and by night as by day a subdued murmur hung over the castle, as from a hive of bees about to swarm.

The guests were received by the two sisters who led them to the Lady Joan, where she sat in her black veils in the solar, being tearfully consoled by their sympathy. Beata seemed to be everywhere at once, flashing out a witty retort to an ancient, lecherous cousin; commiserating with a young damsel whose neck had come out in a rash, chivvying Crispin into taking care of a restless young knight. The tiltyard and its environs rang with the clangour of practice throughout the hours of daylight; at night relays of jugglers, minstrels and jesters entertained the company.

Elaine seemed to have lost all her arts of pleasing. She was silent, unless directly addressed, and she disregarded the smiles of invitation addressed to her by the young gallants. Her tiring-women sewed knots of ribbon on her sleeves at the shoulders, that she might bestow them on those young knights she favoured for the tourney . . . reserving the biggest knot, of course, for Sir Bertrand. But now it was Beata who was asked for a favour. She swung into the bedchamber, laughing at Gerald's folly.

" . . . . So of course I told him not to be so absurd. He only asked me for a ribbon in order to make you jealous!"

"I don't think so," said Elaine. "It is you who are the Queen of Beauty now."

"Idiot!" Beata tore off her gown, dropped it on the floor, and pulled on a dark green damask dress, threaded with gold in a trellis pattern. She tugged a comb through her hair, bent her head just long enough for her nurse to settle a wreath of fresh flowers on her curls, and was ready to go. Elaine stood among three women, all twitching and pulling at her brocade to make it fit more closely. She had been standing like that for some time, but it seemed she took little interest now in how she looked. The woman who was combing her hair, braiding this tress here, and looping that one over a fillet of gold there, was creating a work of art, but Elaine told her to desist.

"Yes," said Elaine to Beata. "You have become beautiful, and I have lost my looks."

Beata burst out laughing. "What! I, beautiful?" The tire-women and her nurse all turned to look at Beata. She met their gaze, and expecting to find merriment there, found only agreement with that Elaine had said. "I?" said Beata. She bit her lip, repressing laughter, while the doubt set in her mind grew, little by little. She picked up a hand-mirror, and gazed into it. Her hand went to her hair, tweaking a curl, settling the wreath more securely on her head.

"Joan said that there was a radiance about you nowadays . . . . " Elaine signed to her women to go, and they did so. Nurse lingered in the door, but finally departed too.

"A radiance?" said Beata, still looking into the mirror. "I see nothing new, save that my cheeks are red, and that this wreath is becoming. Fine feathers."

"No, it is not that." With a patient air, Elaine began to adorn her fingers with costly rings. "You take no trouble with your appearance, and yet you have such a shining look that no man can see you without acknowledging that you are beautiful. You need no jewels to attract men's eyes. You should have given Gerald his ribbon."

Beata laid down the mirror and looked at her sister. The light fell across Elaine's face.

"You are ill?" said Beata.

Elaine shook her head. She wound a jewelled belt twice round her waist, and buckled it in front. There was an exhausted look about her, which contrasted with the vitality of Beata. Elaine's features were as perfect as ever, her hair as long and plentiful, and of as fair a colour; yet there was a suggestion about her now as of one who had passed her best, like a leaf touched with the fingers of tomorrow's decay.

"What is it, little sister?" And now it seemed apt that Beata should call Elaine her "little sister". Blue eyes met eyes of brown, and held. Presently Elaine half-closed her eyes, and Beata put her arm round her sister's shoulders.

"Dearest, if I could only see you happy. . . . I would go with a light heart. But you know it cannot be. Put him out of your mind . . . . "

"Have you put him out of yours?" The query was made gently, without edge, and yet Beata shivered.

"Why," she said. "I have tried. I did try. But from the first moment . . . when our eyes first met . . . it seems so long ago, now. It was too late . . . though I did not know for a long time what ailed me. I thought I was immune, you see. He is too much a part of me, now. And yet there has been nothing done, nothing said . . . and nothing will be done, and nothing will be said. And there is an end of it."

Elaine touched Beata's cheek, and smiled, more to herself than to her sister. There was suffering in that smile, and yet there was much love, also.

"I wish," said Beata, "that this waiting were done . . . and yet when it is done, I think I shall die. When I think of it, even now, I die a little. Will you come to visit me in the convent? Will you? Say you will! Swear it!"

"I will, I swear it."

The girls embraced, and parted. And each was thinking it was unlikely Sir Bertrand would permit his wife to travel to the convent very often, and that they would be parted for ever in six days' time.

Five days. Early in the morning Jaclin summoned Gervase to the tiltyard. The sky was overcast, the ground muddy, but it was not raining at that particular moment. Lord Henry was expected the following night before supper, and everyone was on edge. Jaclin was walking up and down, slashing at imaginary opponents with his sword – with Gervase's sword – when Gervase arrived.

"So . . . you've deigned to come!" Jaclin sheathed his sword, eyeing Gervase sideways. "I wanted to tell you . . . ." He scowled, and turned his back on Gervase. "Did you know that my uncle is going to knight me the day after tomorrow?"

"Yes, indeed. I am glad for you."

"He said I couldn't take part in the tourney until I was knighted. It's the first time he's taken any notice of me for years. It's due to my having this sword, you see, and what armour I like to choose from the store . . . and having practised a lot."

"I believe you may do well. I shall be watching."

"I want you to go over those passes again with me. I want to challenge Gerald, d'ye see. Crispin says I may." He hunched his shoulders, and, still without looking at Gervase said, "Varons said you wouldn't want anything to do with me, after the way I . . . ." His voice tailed away.

Gervase held back a sigh. He was sorry for Jaclin – a little. He could remember how it was to be young and graceless and neglected. Yet the lad had behaved badly, and Gervase was busy. He was worried about Rocca, who had disappeared without saying where he was going. Now what was he up to? Gervase felt a pricking at the back of his neck when he thought of Rocca's being out of sight at this time . . . .

Jaclin held out both his arms to Gervase, and Gervase saw that there were tears in Jaclin's eyes. For a moment the young man held the gesture and then, as Gervase made no move towards him, Jaclin turned away, reddening, and muttering a curse.

"Your pardon," said Gervase quickly. "Of course I will help, if I can." The younger man turned such a wide grin on Gervase that for a moment there was more than a passing look of Beata about him. Gervase was shaken, not only by the resemblance, but by the depth of emotion which the lad was showing. Graceless Jaclin might be, unfeeling he was not.

"When and where?" demanded Jaclin. "Tonight? Now? There are always people practising here . . . and I wanted to tell you . . . I told Varons that I wanted to do it, but he said I could not . . . but if I fall in the lists, if I am killed, then I want you to have your sword back."

The blood leaped in Gervase's cheek, but he checked himself. "Now that is a generous thought, and appreciated. However, it is most unlikely that you will be so badly beaten you will have to retire from the lists for good. And if you are beaten, you must remember that your victor takes both your horse and armour. As for being killed . . . what! In light armour, with blunted swords and lances?"

"There are accidental deaths sometimes, aren't there? And some not so accidental, they say. I do not know why, but I have this recurring dream . . . ." He looked beseechingly at Gervase. "Tell me it will not happen!"

"It will not happen," said Gervase. "And now, show me your problem."

It was the evening of the fifth day. Gervase, Telfer and Varons had gathered in Gervase's room for a final conference. They were all very tired, but reasonably pleased with what they achieved. Their content was muted, however, for this might be the last time the three friends would sit together.

"How you manage to look so fresh, Gervase, I do not

know . . . ." Varons gave an enormous yawn. "If any of us has had more than four hours' sleep these last few days . . . . By the by, we got that fellow who's been cutting purses – clapped him in fetters in a cell below the waterline."

Telfer groaned, easing his aching back. "That consignment of Gascony wine is still held up twenty miles away. I doubt we'll have enough good wine to last us through . . . ."

Gervase tossed cap and coif into a corner, and ran his hands through his hair. Then he rubbed his eyes, and like Varons, yawned. "What do you say to our lighting the windows and ramparts overlooking the courtyard with torches tomorrow night to greet Lord Henry and his party? I saw it done once, in France. The effect was remarkable . . . ."

Varons said, "God in heaven! That's a marvellous idea. Gervase, what would we do without you? One thing is certain; Lord Henry will never let you go when he sees how well you've done."

Telfer added his voice to Varons's argument. "Reconsider, Gervase! We need you here, and what will you do when you leave us? You cannot go back to Ware. Crispin is ready to eat out of your hand, now. A word with Lord Henry and you will be able to expose Rocca . . . then nothing stands in the way of your being appointed Steward."

"He must not go!" declared Varons. "Did he not save my life once, and has not fate brought him here, that I may repay him?"

"I don't think life's like that," said Gervase. "I think it's more like a circle . . . or a chain . . . a man receives a favour, and passes it on to someone else."

Five days, he thought. Like Telfer and Varons, he had expended so much energy on planning for those five days that he had given little thought to what might happen to him thereafter. When thought of the future had intruded, he had found it intolerable. It seemed to him impossible he should stay in Malling, where every room, every face, would remind him of she who was gone.

Besides . . . .

"You may have thought me ungrateful in wishing to leave you," he said. He looked at Telfer – Telfer, who had been so wary of him at first, but who had clasped him in his arms when he had been released from the West Tower – and then at Varons, whose straightforward, honest personality had come to mean so much to him . . . .

"I am not ungrateful," said Gervase. "But . . . ." He sighed. "I have been thinking, of late, that we have overlooked something. You say Lord Henry is a very different man from his son, that he is a man who prides himself on his reputation for justice, that he appreciates the good qualities of those who serve him, that he is not capricious. You say he even invites you to sit down with him, to discuss the affairs of Malling as if you were all equals. This may all be true, but he could never offer me a place in his household if he knew my history, and I will not serve a man and deceive him in that matter. It was chance that brought me here, and for a while Malling succoured me, and I have served it all these months, in order to discharge my debt. But if Lord Henry had been here all this time, you must surely have told him my story . . . or he would have guessed it. And knowing that, he could not have offered me sanctuary, because he is so soon to take Sir Bertrand into his family. In some sense I have abused Lord Henry's hospitality."

"Why, "said Telfer, "we did not look at it like that. Surely there was nothing wrong in . . . . "

"Then why did you not tell Crispin the truth? Or why did I not tell him? Perhaps we did not wish to think clearly on the subject, but the truth is that we have all betrayed our trust by not being frank."

The two men were silent, their eyes on the table, and not on Gervase.

"And so I will go, as I said I would, at Christmas. I will not go before then; you need me, and I have promised . . . . But I will not ask you to introduce me to Lord Henry. I will keep well in the background. Thomas will take over my duties, and I will run errands for Telfer, or for you, Varons . . . whatever is required. Then I will go, as I came, with nothing but the clothes on my back for wages."

Varons swore, and shook his head, but voiced no other objection.

Telfer said, "You may be right," in heavy voice. "And yet . . . I feel it is all wrong. Crispin does not wish you to go. No-one wishes you to go. He was asking me today why you were determined to go, and I could give him no good reason. He was vexed. I said you intended to return his ring before you left, and he gave the table such a buffet I thought it would crack . . . then he vowed you should keep the ring, and that you must have the roan horse for your own, as well."

"The roan?" Gervase looked pleased, and then he frowned. "I doubt Rocca will like that . . . where has the man got to? Did Crispin say?"

"He is worried about the bailiff being absent at such a time, too. One thing, Rocca has gone without Crispin's permission."

"Rocca is surely up to no good," said Gervase, turning the ring on his forefinger. "And I think Crispin suspects . . . I doubt he actually knows, for he is not a devious man . . . he does not take easily to plots and stratagems, any more than I do. But Crispin suspects that what Rocca is doing is intended to harm me. Therefore he says I must keep the ring, and gives me the roan horse. It's his guilty conscience . . . ."

"Hold hard," said Varons. "There may be nothing in it but gratitude. Crispin is like that. You know he gave the ostler's parents a purse of gold, swearing them to secrecy?"

"Like Jaclin," said Gervase, thinking how the lad had offered him his sword.

"Well, they are half-brothers, after all," said Telfer. "Did you not know? The lad's mother was a washer-woman here, and a rare beauty. Jaclin knows, of course. So does everyone else. But Lord Henry has never recognised the boy as his son, and so no one else does. Of course, if Jaclin distinguishes himself in the tourney, and is allowed funds to go abroad to the war, and does well there – who knows? Lord Henry will probably find him an heiress to marry."

Lord Henry and his party were in sight of the castle.

Gervase, Telfer and Varons came out onto the head of the

ramp that led down into the courtyard, and looked about them with identical expressions of critical approval. Everything was as they had planned. Men holding flaming torches lined the ramp and more torches were suspended from windows overlooking the court. A small page – Flash's special friend – knelt at Gervase's feet to buckle a jewelled collar onto the dog, and put the leash in Gervase's hand. Grooms were waiting to take the horses away as the company rode into the court, and a crowd of retainers – all those who could easily be spared from the kitchens at this hour of the night – had been positioned to give a rousing cheer of welcome to the lord of the castle on his return.

Telfer settled his chain of office more comfortably over his shoulders, and smoothed back what remained of his hair. Varons tightened his sword-belt one notch, and then put it back where it had been before. Gervase watched the door of the keep.

She came out and stood looking out over the courtyard and then up at the windows, with her head on one side. She seemed nervous, and her hand played with her curls. She did not look at Gervase. Elaine followed, leading the Lady Joan by the hand, bending to hear the bereaved mother's whispered words of complaint. Elaine's jewels shone more brightly than her eyes. The light of the torches set Beata's flashing beauty aglow, but drained all colour from Elaine.

Crispin strode out, humming, brushing a speck from the rich damask of his furred tunic. The air was chill. A few flakes of snow flickered down into the light of the torches, and sizzled there. All was quiet. Then the leading horsemen clattered into the court, Telfer lifted his hand, and the courtyard erupted with cheers.

Lord Henry smiled to left and right. A groom led his horse to the mounting-block, and he dismounted, stiff from his journey. Gervase saw, with a sense of shock, that the man was below average height . . . almost a dwarf. One side of his neck was thicker than the other, setting his head slightly awry on a powerful pair of shoulders. Lord Henry's eyes passed over the group of upper servants waiting to greet him at the head of the ramp, passed on to where his daughters, his son, and his son's wife were coming down to greet him . . . and Gervase forgot that the man was ungainly of body, and short of stature, for this was a person of considerable presence. Lord Henry's iron-gray hair was carefully curled under his wide-brimmed travelling hat, and the heavy face beneath was dominated by thick-lidded black eyes . . . eyes that saw and judged and condemned . . . .

Beata, running ahead of her brother and sister, came down the slope like a great bird, with her green and gold skirt flowing behind like her wings, to sink to her knees at Lord Henry's feet. She was lifted up with a smile that was fixed and meaningless, to be scrutinised by eyes that sharpened as they took in every detail of the change in her. Lord Henry had left her a brown girl, whose insignificance of person he had been able to overlook with ease. Now . . . he drew in his breath. Was this truly his daughter Beata?

Then Crispin was leading Elaine to his father, with Joan treading on his heels. Courteously, but without Beata's spontaneity, Crispin bent his knee before his father. Lord Henry's smile thinned, so that all men, watching him, understood that their lord was displeased with his son and heir . . . and possibly also displeased with his daughter Elaine, who moved like a shadow at her brother's side.

There was a great jingling and neighing of tired horses as the rest of the company dismounted. The horses were led away, servants darted here and there with bundles and packages as the first of the train of carts came into the courtyard, laden with the effects of the travellers. Each new servant was taken into the charge of one of Telfer's men or women, to be directed to the quarters in which their master or mistress was to lie. Some eight extra noblemen and women had now to be assimilated into the castle, and perhaps three times as many more servants. The abbot and his train, nuns and all, were still on the road, later than they ought to have been, delayed by the bad roads.

Varons frowned as he looked over the newcomers. So many haughty nobles, so many even haughtier servants, strange to the ways of the castle . . . so many possible causes of friction . . . . He was glad the stocks had been left standing: the sight of them might cause the guests to hesitate before reaching for their knives in trivial disputes.

Lord Henry turned to a big man in scarlet and black, who was throwing a fur-lined cloak back over his shoulders. At his elbow stood a beautiful woman, and the woman looked not at Lord Henry, her host, but at Elaine's tired face . . . and smiled. Then the big man said something to her which caused her to turn from him with a shrug and a scowl . . . and now it could be seen that she was no longer beautiful, or even very young . . . .

"My lady aunt . . . " said Gervase, low in Telfer's ear. "Is she still trying to hang on Sir Bertrand's sleeve, do you think?"

"And what will the Lady Elaine have to say about that?" replied Telfer, equally low.

Lord Henry had taken Sir Bertrand's hand, and was laying it in Elaine's. Elaine had dutifully gone down on one knee before Sir Bertrand . . . but his gaze was riveted on Beata's parted lips and brilliant eyes. And Sir Bertrand said, loud enough for all to hear, "I salute the Queen of Beauty!" And all who heard him, and who saw his look, knew that the compliment was not for Elaine, but for Beata.

Crispin bit his lip, and the scar on his cheek grew dark. He lifted his sister from the ground with a hand under her elbow, so that she stood between the man she was to marry, and the sister whom Sir Bertrand had so obviously admired. Sir Bertrand was forced to lower his gaze, and to acknowledge Elaine's existence.

"Trouble . . . nothing but trouble," said Varons. "If it's not the servants, it's their so-called betters."

Lord Henry lifted one of his short, awkwardly-hung arms, and waved his hand, collecting his noble guests into one group. "Welcome!"

At that point Beata turned her head and looked up, and it was a marvel how she knew where Gervase was, for she had not seemed to look at him before. He let slip the leash that he had been holding, and gave Flash a nudge. That sagacious animal, who had been sniffing and yapping from the moment he saw his old master below, slipped down the ramp, his tail oscillating so fast it could barely be seen, and jumped up at Lord Henry, uttering sharp barks of pleasure.

Now Gervase watched Lord Henry even more closely. Would the man show any sign of emotion? They said he cared for nothing and nobody since his wife had died . . . except perhaps for his dog, and one of his horses . . . if the man showed no emotion even now, then he was as good as dead inside.

But Lord Henry, though a cold, was not a hollow man. He grasped the dog's collar, and shook his head from side to side, in a game that, plainly, both were accustomed to. His smile became, for a few moments, something to hearten those who watched.

Beata spoke a few words, explaining that the dog had been nursed back to health by their new secretary, Master William, and at that Lord Henry's smile vanished. He nodded to Beata, and led the way up the stairs without comment. Gervase slipped back into the crowd, but Telfer and Varons stepped forward to greet their master. Telfer was greeted by name, and with a smile, and so was Varons. But Gervase, in the shadows, was aware that Lord Henry was paying scant attention to his trusted lieutenants. His eyes ranged over the crowd of waiting servants, searching for the one face with which he was not familiar, and when he had found it, the gaze hardened for as long as it took a man to breathe in and out. Then Lord Henry passed within, and his family and guests went with him.

"That went off very well, I thought," said Varons. He clapped Gervase on the shoulder, and passed into the keep also.

"He knew you," said Telfer. "He knew who you were. He looked for you."

"Yes," said Gervase.

Telfer took a deep breath. "You had best go, now. They will lower the portcullis and shut the gates as soon as the abbot and his train are here . . . ."

"Too late!" said Gervase, pointing to where a train of cowled and hooded figures came clattering into the courtyard. In the distance could be heard the clangour of gates shutting, and villagers shouting their farewells as they passed out into the countryside . . . free . . . .

Telfer said, "I must go down to greet the abbot. What will you do?"

"Nothing," said Gervase. "The game is out of my hands now."

As Telfer went down the slope into the courtyard, a man in a murrey gown came out from where he had been riding with the baggage wagons, and looked up at Gervase. Rocca . . . laying a trail of poison with the father, as he had once laid a trail with the son. How much did Rocca know, and what had he told Lord Henry?

Gervase turned into the keep as the men with torches dowsed their lights, withdrawing them from windows and ramparts. The courtyard was silent now. All the noise was within, in the Great Hall.

A prick of fear assailed Gervase. He could smell danger. He had the faculty many soldiers acquire of knowing when he was being watched. Yet Rocca had stayed outside. Gervase did not move, but his eyes probed the shadows around him, and still the sense that he was in danger grew, and reason would not disperse it. One of Varons's men-at-arms came out of the hall, and beckoned to him.

"The captain asked me to take you to him."

Gervase nodded, and the sense of danger increased until he could almost smell it. Fear was in the air, and yet he could not see how or where the attack would be made, if Rocca was outside.

Gervase followed the man with his chin on his shoulder. And yet no-one came after them. A servant crossing an anteroom muttered an apology as they nearly collided. Then they were within stairs and going down again. The undercroft was normally used as a store, and was but poorly lit. They went across it, and into another passage leading to a small room in the bowels of the earth. The door was opened by another man-at-arms, and Gervase paused, his mouth dry. Now he knew where the danger would come from . . . had come from. A lighted torch had been thrust into a sconce set high in the wall, and below it stood Varons, with a crumpled sheet of paper in his hand. Varons did not look directly at Gervase, but thrust the paper into his hand, and turned away. The door closed.

Gervase smoothed out the paper, and held it up to the light.

The handwriting was that of Rocca, but the signature under the warrant for the arrest and detention of the fugitive Gervase Escot, also known by the name of Master William of Leys . . . the signature was that of Lord Henry. The terms of Gervase's imprisonment were spelled out in detail. All his clothing and effects were to be given into the keeping of Master Rocca, bailiff of Malling.

"Rocca has had two days in Lord Henry's company," said Varons, in a strangled voice. "He made the excuse that he must take part of the Michaelmas rents to Lord Henry, who needed extra money for travelling expenses. But when Rocca joined Lord Henry's party, he made it his business to tell Sir Bertrand de Bors about you . . . and Sir Bertrand demanded that you be arrested and held against his coming. Lord Henry called me to him just now, together with my sergeant. Orders have gone out to the gates, to watch for you . . . otherwise I would have said you should knock me down, take my dagger . . . tie me up and escape."

"With two men at the door?" Gervase studied the warrant. The conditions under which he was to be detained were dreadful, so dreadful that he could not contemplate them without shivering. He must be calm. There must be some way.

"My keys!" said Gervase. "That is what he's after . . . access to the manorial rolls which would prove that he's been cheating his master. He knows very well that those keys never leave me, by night or day. Once in possession, he can alter the entries on the rolls to cover up the loss of those monies which he has extorted from peasants who appear so poor, and yet should be so prosperous . . . to explain the loss of those sums of money which he has given to Crispin, over and above monies which . . . yes, there will be a grand altering of totals, if we do not stop him."

"Tell me what to do?"

"Take my keys and give them to Telfer." Gervase slipped them from the leather belt he wore, and handed them over. "Have the chest containing the rolls taken from my room and placed where Rocca cannot reach them, until you have a chance to explain to Lord Henry what we suspect has been happening. Thomas will help you." Gervase took off the sapphire ring. "And take this, also. I would not have it fall into Rocca's hands. Take it back to Crispin and tell him . . . tell him nothing. He cannot interfere without denouncing himself for having cheated his father. He is caught in Rocca's trap, just as I am. Well, it is one way out of our difficulties, I suppose."

Varons embraced him. There were tears in his eyes. "I will speak to my lord, at the earliest possible . . . confound this tourney, and all those guests . . . . Telfer and I, we'll have you out of it in no time at all."

Gervase smiled and nodded, but he did not believe Varons. This was, this must be the end.

They went out, and down the stairs yet again.

"What! Him again?" said the gaoler. Varons showed the gaoler the warrant, and he sighed, and shook his head. Gervase was told to discard his outer clothing and his shoes, which he did. As he shook out his hair he thought numbly that Beata's hair had never looked so beautiful as tonight, in the light of the torches, with the wreath of flowers so delicate, so hardy . . . like herself. Well, it was unlikely he would ever see her again . . . perhaps it was better so.

This time there was no favoured treatment. This time there was no window, no light, no fresh air. They went past barred doors and men roused from slumber, past hands clutching at bars, and voices calling out to them for mercy.

"We like to have the cells full for when Lord Henry comes," said the gaoler. He thrust his torch into a low passageway, indicating that Gervase should precede him. The passage was narrow and low, but debouched eventually into a chamber whose stench caused Gervase to recoil . . . only to be pushed forward, over and into the foulness on the floor. There was a phosphorescent slime on the walls. Gervase swallowed, trying to think of some plea that he might make, some protest . . . and knew it would be in vain.

An iron cage rested some foot or so above the floor, suspended by a chain from a ring in the ceiling, and the ceiling of this chamber was high indeed. The chain went through the ring, and then wound itself around a spindle, controlled by a wheel.

"Only the worst – murderers and the like – get put in here," said the gaoler. "They commonly scream when I leaves them here . . . good echo . . . I can hear them nigh to the top staircase."

Gervase stared in fascinated horror at the cage. He had heard of such things, but never seen one before. He remembered someone in France telling of how his sister had been suspended in one such cage over the battlements of a castle till she died . . . for what offence he could not remember.

The cage was large enough to accommodate a small man standing, but Gervase was above average height. A man might lie down on the barred floor, if he bent himself into a foetal position. There was a door, and it was open, a staple and padlock dangling from the central bar.

The gaoler pushed Gervase to the cage. He thought of trying to make a fight for it . . . but that would be useless, and only incriminate Varons if his friend tried to help.

He got into the cage, aand it swung. Before he had turned round, his hands clutching at the bars, the door was being padlocked on him. Then the gaoler was turning the wheel, and Gervase was rising into the air, rising, with the foetid smell all around him, rising above the piles of filth left behind by previous occupants of the cage . . . to which he prayed he would not add while Varons and the gaoler were there, watching him rise . . . and jerk to a halt.

Then they turned and left him, taking the torch with them. And he was alone in the dark . . . in a cage . . . half-naked, in a cage.

He bowed his head on his hands, and began to pray.

Chapter Twelve

The Lady Beata was queen of the feast; unofficially, that is. Officially the honours were shared between the Lady Joan as Crispin's wife, and the Lady Elaine, who had so often borne the title of Queen of Beauty in the past. But poor sad Joan – all black veils and hysteria – was accorded lip service only, as chatelaine of Malling. She had made it clear she would not exert herself to help Crispin with the guests, since Crispin had made it clear that he wished her to the devil.

Once in the hall, Lord Henry took Joan by one hand and Crispin by the other, and he joined the hands of man and wife together before the whole company, smiling at them and at Sir Bertrand in meaning fashion. More, he bade Sir Bertrand welcome not only as an old friend, but also as a cousin of the Lady Joan. Crispin, loosing his wife's hand, scowled and turned his head from her, so that the Lady Joan, who had smiled when Lord Henry took her hand, now put her kerchief to her eyes and wept. Beata, impatient because Joan ought to have been greeting their guests by name and directing them to their seats, stepped forward, in front of the weeping Joan, and performed the office of chatelaine herself.

Lord Henry's eye rested on Beata, and he marvelled at her poise.

Elaine, standing silent and awkward beside Sir Bertrand, was nudged by her sister, with a hissing reminder of duties to be performed. So Elaine pushed back her long hair with a lax hand, and looked around, only to find that Beata had already summoned Telfer to her aid, and that the guests were already seated according to their rank. And then Elaine shivered, for Lady Escot was staring at her with a wicked, sly, knowing look . . . .

Beata sat very straight in her chair, and smiled and laughed, and ate and drank, and was conscious of herself as queen of the feast . . . and mocked herself because she was extracting pleasure from something so transient. And then she was sitting still, not breathing, her eyes fixed on the floor of the hall, and seeing it not . . . seeing nothing, scenting filth, while a voice filled her brain, praying for courage. And then the voice and the smell faded, and she was looking at the jugglers in the hall, and accepting a cutlet from a spit handed to her by a page, and her goblet was being refilled, and her father was looking at her with shrewd black eyes, eyes that saw everything and noted everything.

Gervase! She wanted to scream to everyone to be silent, to cease that terrible hubbub, the echo in the hall, that she might think. But Crispin on her left, and Sir Bertrand on her right were both talking, and the one was laughing, and inviting her to laugh with him, while the other was scowling and muttering that their father was an unfeeling tyrant.

Quiet! She said to the hollow space inside herself. Quiet, Gervase! I heard you . . . .

She laughed with Sir Bertrand, and when he put his hand over hers, removed it without showing any sign of offence. She said to Crispin, "Do you know what has happened to Master William? He is not sitting with Varons and the others, and I am afraid . . . . Father snubbed him; looked at him, but would not speak to him . . . .

"How the devil should I know?" said Crispin, downing another goblet of wine. "What am I to do about Joan, if Father won't allow a divorce?"

"I will think . . . ." said Beata, and beckoned a page to send for Telfer, who was hovering nearby, directing servants, his eyes everywhere. And Lord Henry looked at Beata, and she looked back at him, and once she would have dropped her eyes from his and bent her head . . . and now she did not, but stared back at him . . . eye to eye, strong will bent against strong will, and neither willing to yield. Then Lord Henry smiled and lifted his goblet in a toast to her, and she flushed, and smiled back. Each knew the other's mind. He knew she would not refuse to do her duty, and she knew he would not break his vow to send her to the convent. Yet there was now a consciousness between them that they were, in a sense, equals.

Telfer bent his head beside her and she said, in a voice barely stronger than a whisper. "Gervase . . . in trouble. Will you investigate?" Telfer bowed and passed on, his face impassive – yet she knew he was to be trusted. She clapped and laughed as a juggler finished his act and dancers came on, turning somersaults.

And the pain stabbed her. She could feel the burn of bars across her back, yet nothing had touched her. Quiet! she said to herself again. Quiet, Gervase . . . Telfer is sending to look for you.

They were feasting well . . . pray heaven the provisions would last out till after Christmas, with so many more guests than they had anticipated. Thank heaven the Bishop had not come after all, though how many nuns had the abbot brought with him? Five . . . six . . . seven? And no doubt an equal number of servants to look after them.

And here was young Jaclin and another youth – a distant cousin brought down by Lord Henry from London – and they were approaching the high table, bending their knees to Lord Henry, with Father Anthony smiling in attendance. And at least the preparations for the knighting ceremony would keep the priest out of Beata's way for tonight.

Lord Henry was bending forward and speaking in kindly fashion to Jaclin – far more kindly than was usual with him. Jaclin had fired up and was boasting of the work he would do in the tourney, and how he had learned so many good tricks from a man who had been a soldier.

"Who is this man?" enquired Lord Henry, pleased to be graciously amused by Jaclin's chatter.

"The new secretary, recommended by Hamo for the position of Steward," said Beata, in a clear, metallic voice that hardly seemed to be her own. "He has been good to Jaclin, as he was good to Flash, your dog, that he healed."

Lord Henry's brows drew together, and seeing this Jaclin made haste to remove himself, with his comrade and the priest. They would spend the night fasting and praying in the chapel, in preparation for the ceremony of knighting early on the morrow.

Crispin, who had been sitting slumped forward in his

chair, now roused himself. He had become aware that for some reason Lord Henry had taken a dislike to Master William, and his better nature urged him to defend the secretary. "Master William is a good man, and without him I daresay we would never have been ready in time for the tourney. If my word is worth anything, he should have the post of Steward tonight."

"Your word promoted Rocca," said Lord Henry. "I am not certain that your word is worth anything." So saying, he turned to the abbot, who was on his other side, and began to talk to him.

Telfer was coming back up the hall, catching Beata's eye, shrugging. He had not been able to find Gervase – now he had stopped to have a word with Varons, and the two men were turning to look up at the dais, and then drawing apart from the others, frowning. Bad news, thought Beata.

Something heavy dropped onto her feet. Something warm, and living. She put down her hand, and dragged Flash out. He jumped up at her, wagging his tail.

"He has a new trick, Father," she said. "He sits on your feet when he wants attention. Did he not sit on yours just now? He always sat on Master William's feet. It's his way of begging for scraps at mealtimes."

Lord Henry smiled at the dog, flicked his fingers to draw him near, and gave him a bone.

"We are wearying our guests with this talk of a fugitive clerk," said Lord Henry. "Now, my dear Joan . . . ."

Telfer was bending over Beata's shoulder again. "He has been arrested as a fugitive on a warrant signed by your father. Varons says Rocca is at the bottom of it. Rocca made mischief with Sir Bertrand, who demanded Gervase's arrest. Varons has the ring your brother gave Gervase . . . ." Beata and Telfer both looked at Crispin, who was drinking steadily, head on hand, leaning on the table. Beata shook her head at Telfer, indicating that it would not be wise to ask her brother to intervene on Gervase's behalf at the moment. Telfer bowed, and passed on.

Beata turned in her chair to consider Sir Bertrand. He was only too ready to talk to her, for Elaine paid him no attention at all. He talked about tourneys he had attended, and accidents that had occurred to other people – though never to him. And she smiled and nodded, and laughed at the right points and felt herself divide into two. There was her body, sitting at the high table, eyes everywhere, ears bent for the significant word, watching, waiting . . . brilliantly the queen of the feast, gathering power from the admiration of all those who dined in the hall and watched the nobility.

And there was her inner self, calculating, planning, vigilant . . . holding Gervase wrapped in her arms as she had held him twice when he had been on the verge of death – though he had never known – trying to tell him that she was doing what she could . . . trying to give him hope and patience and courage. . . .

Bars . . . and the tumblers in the hall formed themselves into a pyramid, and for a moment inspiration came through a trick of the light: faces glimpsed through spreadeagled arms and legs, and she knew where Gervase was. In a cage. Rather, in the cage. She had never been in the dungeons, of course, but she had seen prisoners brought out of the West Tower, and compared the ways they had endured the punishment and whether or not they could walk afterwards. The cage – she drew in her breath, and held it – the cage was the most feared, the most terrible . . . .

She would not cry. She smiled at Sir Bertrand, and threw back her head and laughed. He laid his hand on her arm, and leaned over the space between her chair and his, and said in her ear, with his breath hot on her cheek, "If I had only known . . . .

She felt a sense of shock. This man was to marry Elaine . . . Elaine, who sat so still and silent on the far side of Bertrand, playing with her food, while her father watched his two daughters and Bertrand: three pawns on his chess board.

Beata felt desperate. She wanted to run away and hide, to burst into tears, to scream. She gritted her teeth, and clasped her hands round the arms of her chair. She said, inside herself, "Help me, Gervase . . . ."

Suddenly there was warmth around her. She closed her eyes for a moment, and let out her breath, the tension leaving her . . . and letting him in . . . relaxing, feeling his strength around her, his self-control, his clear, uncluttered mind.

She opened her eyes and looked about her, seeing everything now as if through his eyes, making calculations as if with his mind, noting that the clerk Thomas was talking with Varons, and that they were both turning to look at a man in a murrey gown: the serpent Rocca. Now how much did Rocca know? Enough to point the finger at Gervase as a fugitive. He was a clever man, but not quite clever enough. If he had been really clever, he would have confessed his peculations to Lord Henry, throwing the blame on Crispin to ingratiate himself with his father. A hundred to one Lord Henry knew nothing of Crispin's little deal with Rocca. It was a card she could play, if she could only see how.

Beata's eyes moved on. Lady Escot, pouting, talking across young Gerald to Joan, comparing notes on fashions, gossiping . . . Lady Escot was well past thirty, if Beata were any judge, and she remembered what Gervase had said about her; and then Beata's eyes narrowed, as she had often seen Gervase's eyes narrow, when a thought struck him. She leaned forward to ask Joan a question, and Joan, like the obedient pawn that she was, seeing no ulterior motive in the query, repeated it to Lady Escot, who threw up her hands in what was meant to be a pretty, spontaneous gesture, and replied honestly, raising laughter around her. Beata leant back against her chair, well-satisfied. And there was card number two, if only the game could be twisted her way.

And she saw Lord Henry frown at his daughter Elaine, who was being told to get up and lead the dancing with Sir Bertrand, and Sir Bertrand was not looking at Elaine, but at Beata. There was a hand pressing on Beata's thigh, but she did not start or push it away; instead she looked Sir Bertrand full in the eye, so that his colour rose, and he turned away.

Then Beata turned her head and saw that her father had seen the movement of the hand, his daughter's rejection of it, and Sir Bertrand's discomfiture. Once more the eyes of father and daughter met and clashed, and this time it was Beata who looked away first.

There is another card, she thought. I could tell him I will

make a public declaration of my unwillingness to go into the convent. I could shame him before everyone and he knows now that I am capable of doing it if I set my mind to it. I would still have to go, of course, but the humiliation of its being known that I did not wish to . . . that he had had to force me . . . no, he would not like that.

And Crispin. Or rather, Crispin vis-à-vis Joan. There is something there that I could use, if only I could think how.

Elaine was half out of her seat, her eyes downcast, making no attempt to summon Telfer to instruct the musicians about changing to a dance tune . . . making no effort to pair off the rest of the guests. Joan? No, Joan would not dance!

Beata leaped to her feet and clapped her hands, catching Telfer's eye, smiling, holding out her hands to Gerald and Crispin, urging everyone to their feet, to dance and make merry. She swung on Crispin's arm into the dance, while her mind still wrestled with the problems around her.

Lord Henry's determination. He would be justice itself if Gervase were to ask for the trial to be reheard at Malling. No, Lord Henry was in a cleft stick and could not move in the matter. He could not offend his son-in-law . . . .

The cage! How to get Gervase out? Perhaps Varons could . . . no, Varons always obeyed orders, however much he disliked them. Varons could not help, however willing he might be. Telfer had influence with her father. . . . No, no. Her father could not help, she saw that quite clearly. He had been appealed to, as a fellow justice of the peace, to detain an escaped criminal. How could he do otherwise than comply? Yet, if a way could be found to re-open the case?

Lady Escot was dancing with an ancient fool of a knight who would probably fall off his horse at the first pass of a lance in his direction, though he boasted loudly enough of years of experience. Lady Escot was glancing over her shoulder at Sir Bertrand, smiling at him . . . pleased to see that Elaine was not pleased with her cousin?

Sir Bertrand de Bors. Consider him well, Beata. Six foot tall and well-built; broader in the shoulder than Gervase, with thighs like tree-trunks. Clumsy-footed, heavy with power. Red-necked, hirsute, blue-chinned, with dark eyes that were of unusual size and beauty. Such eyes, combined with a soft voice – unexpectedly soft and small for a man of his bulk – speaking of his love of women, of his pleasure in their company, of his triumph. The accepted son-in-law of a wealthy nobleman, the victor in the contest with Gervase – he must know that Gervase was even now in a dungeon, at his behest – and still he smiled at Beata rather than at Elaine. He wore a powerful scent, too, to disguise his own strong odour. He was a man who would hold a woman's wishes in contempt . . . a man used to having his own way in all things. A man without scruples.

He smiled at her with teeth that were a little too large and confident.

Beata clapped her hands, and laughed, and swung into the dance again. Her mind cleared, and she knew what she must do.

The feast was over, the dancers gone to their beds. Lord Henry had bidden his children good night and retired to his chamber, taking Telfer with him, to receive his report. Beata took a cloak from the hands of her nurse, had a quick word with Varons, and made her way to her brother's chamber. He slept alone nowadays . . . or rather tonight he did not sleep, but sat drinking by the fire, attended only by his valet. She signed to him to dismiss the servant, and he did so, staring at her in half-drunken curiosity.

"What do you here, Beata?"

"You asked me to help you get rid of Joan. I have thought of a way. Suppose Father could be persuaded to break off the match between Sir Bertrand and Elaine . . . ."

"You want him for yourself?"

Beata's face flamed. "Crispin!"

"Oh, very well. But you hide your dislike better than Elaine."

"Believe me, I detest the man! Now suppose I could so arrange it that he were discredited with Father . . . perhaps even disgraced. I know of someone who could do this for you. Someone who has suffered at Sir Bertrand's hands . . . . and if that someone were brought into court before Father, and allowed to tell his story, then I think Sir Bertrand's hopes of wedding Elaine would be nil."

Crispin put down his goblet with an unsteady hand, and squinted at Beata. "Master William? Rocca tried to tell me something . . . ." He shook his head. "His word against Sir Bertrand's?"

"My dear, mud sticks! Let us so arrange it that mud be thrown at the right target this time, and there will be no more talk of marriage with Elaine. Think of her dread of the man! Think how grateful she will be to you!"

He shook his finger at her. "Rocca said you and Master William . . . . Told him not to be a fool! Beginning to think there might be some truth in it . . . eh?"

"I saved his life once, and I would not have it thrown away. Yes, I like the man . . . and so does Elaine . . . . No, not in that way! Oh, Crispin, have some sense! Has she not dropped all her old airs and graces? Is her behaviour not discreet nowadays? And is the man himself not worth helping? Have you not found him helpful? Consider this; Father once thought to marry him to Elaine. Suppose that that match were once more to be revived . . . would not Elaine's new husband be grateful to you, instead of trying to work against you?"

"Well . . . yes; I suppose so. But it would be quicker to end it in the lists tomorrow. A pity we are to fight with blunt lances, or . . . ." He laughed unpleasantly.

"My way is more sure. You must send Varons down to the dungeons to get Master William out. You must hear his story, of course, before you move any further in the matter. Then we will confer together how best to approach Father." She went to the door, opened it, and beckoned Varons to come inside. Then she went to a nearby table, and began to write.

"My lord," said Varons, going down on his knee. "Master William sends you this." He held out his hand, and the sapphire ring winked in the light of the candle, and the fire.

Crispin shook his head to clear it. "I cannot possibly interfere . . . in the dungeons, you say?"

If you will sign this warrant to release him from the dungeon into Varons's custody," said Beata, scratching away, "then you can hear his story here, without anyone being the wiser. If you are not satisfied, once you have heard his story, then he can go back to the cage, can he not?"

"The cage?" said Crispin. "Why did they put him in the cage? That is absurd!"

"Indeed it is," said Beata, handing him the paper to sign.

Crispin snorted. "As if he would ever have stolen that ring . . . he's too damned keen on the letter of the law, as I know to my cost. And I'll tell you another thing, Beata; you think I haven't got much in the way of brains, and maybe you're right, but if he had wanted to revenge himself on his uncle, he could have milked the estate's rent-roll, and no-one would ever have noticed."

Rocca! thought Beata. Crispin does suspect that that's what Rocca's been doing, and it's preying on his mind. "Of course he could," she said, in a soothing voice. "That is, if he'd been that sort of man. You are clever, Crispin!" She set the quill in his hand. Then she remembered the advice Gervase had once given her, to flatter Crispin if you wanted him to do something – advice which Gervase himself had never been able to follow – and she smiled as Crispin scratched his name on the document which would free her lover.

"I'm not all that clever," said Crispin, holding the pass out to Varons. "But when I set my mind to a matter, I can usually puzzle it out. He's an honest man, and my friend. He'll get me out of this marriage, if anyone can."

"Oh, be quick!" said Beata to Varons.

He nodded, and was gone. Beata paced the floor, wrapped in her cloak. Crispin stared into the fire, and though he had picked up his goblet once more, he did not refill it.

Presently there was a stir at the door, and Varons came in, followed by a tall bareheaded figure.

Beata said, "Greetings, Lord Escot."

Chapter Thirteen

Crispin stared, first at Beata, and then at Gervase. "Lord Escot? Why, so he is! I never thought of that!"

Gervase put out a hand to steady himself against the wall . . . but the wall was too far away, and his hand grasped only at the air. A small sound escaped Beata's throat; a sob, perhaps . . . perhaps a laugh. She took off her cloak, and gave it to Gervase. Then she extracted the goblet from Crispin's hand, refilled it with wine, and handed that also to Gervase. He looked steadily into her eyes as he took the goblet; then bowed his thanks, and drank.

Gervase said to himself, "This is not happening to me. I am not really here, standing barefoot in Crispin's bedchamber. I was never in the cage. Perhaps I am dead already. Perhaps it is all a dream."

But the goblet was a reality, the wine in it catching the light as he lifted it to his lips and drank, and it burned down inside him, reminding him that he had not eaten that day . . . was it still the same day, the day of Lord Henry's return? There was no time in the cage, only timeless agony . . . .

"Did you not guess, Crispin?" Beata was talking to give Gervase time to recover. He tried to follow what she was saying, because she had mentioned his uncle's name. She was saying something about his aunt's pregnancy.

"But she is not pregnant!" Crispin said.

"That is the point," replied Beata. "I could see she was not . . . and I counted on my fingers, and thought it just possible she might have borne a child already, so I made Joan ask her whether she had been brought to bed of a boy or a girl."

"She had a girl? That is why the title passes to Master William . . . Sir Gervase Escot, I should say?"

"She was never pregnant," said Beata, smiling. "She admitted it quite freely. She said it had been a 'mistake'. She said that men would do anything for you – especially elderly husbands – if you told them they were about to become a father. And everyone laughed, as she had intended they should. It gives me pleasure to think that a widow can only retain one third of her husband's property, and that the rest must pass to his heir . . . to Sir Gervase Escot . . . with the title."

"But how does that help me?" asked Crispin. "Master William – Lord Escot, I should say – the devil with this tangle! Listen, man! I got you out of gaol because Beata said you could help rid us of Sir Bertrand. If you will do this for me, I will . . ." he gestured widely. "Whatever you wish! Can you do it?"

Gervase looked at Beata. He was tired, so tired that he could barely stand upright. The cage had set its mark on him in more ways than one. There was dirt on his cheek, and the palms of his hands were scored where he had clutched at the bars . . . his feet were grazed and bleeding. His eyelids dropped. She was asking too much of him . . . and yet had she not a right to ask? Would he not still be in that infernal cage, if it were not for her? He knew how highly to evaluate Crispin's aid.

He said, "I cannot prove that Sir Bertrand gave false evidence against me, but I think I can prove that he was behind the attempt to kill me, afterwards. If you challenge him with this, and have witnesses by you at the time, he will very likely betray himself. He is not a man who thinks quickly, and he will not be expecting a challenge."

"I might be able to draw the truth out of him," said Beata. "The man is a lecher. One look at him told me that. If I can get him alone – or what he thinks is alone – with witnesses hidden nearby. If I could get him to make love to me, and then Crispin could jump out, and charge him with being false in more ways than one . . . ."

"I'll ram my dagger down his throat!" exclaimed Crispin, and meant it.

"It would be better simply to tell your father the truth," said Gervase, passing his hand over his eyes. "I do not say that a trap such as you describe would not work, but so much would have to be left to chance, and . . . ."

"No, I like the idea," declared Crispin. "We will do it in the evening, after the jousting, and before the masque. Master William – Lord Escot, I mean – you must be hidden close by, to advise me when to jump out on him, and what to say."

"He is not to go back to the cage, then?" asked Beata.

"Of course not," said Crispin. Then bit his lip. "Only . . . his being out of the dungeons must not be known before we spring our trap."

"I will go to the infirmary," said Gervase. "And shave off my beard. I shall find some old clothes to wear there, no doubt."

"Better still," suggested Varons, "I will send you over such clothing as might be worn by retainers attached to some nobleman visiting the castle; Telfer will know which one. Then if you wish to leave the infirmary walls and are challenged – which is unlikely since so many strange faces are about the castle now – you will say you serve such-and-such a man."

"And keep your ring," said Crispin, handing it back to Gervase. "Yes, I insist. It has acted as your messenger once, and you may have need of it again. Till tomorrow . . . ."

Gervase bowed his thanks, and withdrew.

A circle of tiring-women surrounded Elaine. The Queen of Beauty was seated, having a wreath of gold leaves set upon her fair head when Beata hurried in, her nurse at her heels. While the tiring-women laced Elaine's dress even more closely to her slender figure, Beata pulled on a matching gown, and rammed another wreath of gold leaves on her head. As her nurse pulled Beata's lacing tight, Elaine said with a sigh that she had been nigh on two hours getting dressed.

Beata had been going to say something about how well her sister was looking, but desisted. She frowned. Then she saw that the tiring-women were also frowning.

Beata said, "Perhaps it is the gold of the silk that makes you a little pale. It is too near the colour of your hair, or . . . ."

Elaine said, smiling as if at a secret, "Yet it becomes you well, Beata."

"Oh, what does that matter!" Beata brushed her nurse aside. She was wearing a dress identical in cut and material to that of Elaine and yet, as was plain to them all, the Queen of Beauty appeared drab beside her darker sister's flashing vitality.

"A different wreath?" suggested Beata. "Something with colour in it?"

"No," said Elaine. "We have to wear identical wreaths of gold leaves, that they may be given to the victor in the tourney. You will enjoy being Queen of Beauty jointly with me, will you not, Beata?"

"Oh, that! I suppose it depends who wins." She made a gesture of dismissal, and the tiring-women and her nurse faded away. Beata seated herself by her sister, and began to stroke first her hand, and then her cheek. "Elaine, dearest. You look so pale. I was not going to tell you, but now . . . ."

"He's been arrested, hasn't he? I noticed he was not at the feast, and one of the women said . . . ."

"He is all right. Crispin had him released last night. But that is a secret, and you must not breathe a word of it . . . promise?" Elaine nodded. There was a slight smile on her face now, which pleased Beata, but her cheeks remained pale. "What would you say," began Beata, "if I told you there might be a way of preventing your marriage with Sir Bertrand?"

"I would like it," said Elaine. "You know that."

"Yes, I do. I had not been in company with him above a minute before I understood the sort of man he was. I wonder what woman he took to his bed last night, to keep himself warm?" The two sisters smiled at each other.

Elaine said, with a sigh, "It is useless to dream of such things. Father would never allow me to refuse him."

"Perhaps the man can be induced to withdraw. Perhaps I am trying to arrange it. Perhaps the man who can force Sir Bertrand to withdraw was once one of your suitors, someone it would not make you miserable to marry."

"Gerald?" There was a touch of hauteur mingled with incredulity in Elaine's tone, which made Beata stare.

"No, not Gerald. Of course not Gerald. What would you say to . . . ." Beata set her sister's hand aside, and stood up. It had been one thing to talk of reviving the marriage between Gervase and Elaine to her brother, as if it were a remote possibility, but when it came to speaking of it directly to her sister, Beata's nerve failed her. "It is asking too much!" she said, and put her hand over her eyes.

"You have a headache?" Elaine asked softly. She put her arm round her sister. "There, now. It is all in the hands of God. I have prayed that this marriage will not take place, but if it is to be, then . . ." she sighed. "I would rather not wed him, I must confess, but I will not have you making yourself ill with worry about it. You know what you are, Beata; always busy with other people's affairs, just as Nurse says! And yet I thank you for it." She kissed her sister. "There! Now, you must look your best today . . . as indeed, you do! I wish the beggars at the gate could see you in this dress, with the gold leaves in your hair; they would never think of calling for me, then. I have been such a vain, silly creature in the past, have I not? Well, I am trying to mend my ways. I know now that when the people at the gate called down blessings on me, they were pleased to see someone looking pretty, but they would have been even more pleased if you had gone among them in an old gown, attending to their wants with your own hands. Beauty is nothing. It has brought me nothing but trouble. I am glad to be done with it."

"I don't understand you. You are still beautiful, Elaine!"

"You are more beautiful now than I ever was, and you will grow more lovely with age."

Beata threw off her sister's hand, and thrust her fingers through her hair, forgetting the splendid wreath set there. She said, "Do you want him, or don't you?" Then, seeing that Elaine did not understand her, she stamped her foot, and frowned. "Gervase Escot that was . . . Master William that is . . . Lord Escot, by the grace of God . . . ."

But Elaine only stared at her sister, until Beata ran out of the room, and slammed the door behind her.

Crispin woke late, and in a foul temper. He was only just in time to slip into his place in chapel before Jaclin and his comrade were knighted by Lord Henry. Jaclin, freshly bathed and shaved, wearing new clothes, made his vows in a ringing tone, earning the grudging approval of all those who knew his history. Perhaps he might turn out all right after all, they said, trooping back to the Great Hall after the ceremony. There a light repast was set out before a roaring fire, and there the women awaited them, clad in their most gorgeous gowns, ready to tease the men on their hopes for the tourney.

Crispin, trying to catch his father's eye, was disappointed. Instead, wherever he turned he seemed to find Sir Bertrand in his way, laughing too loudly, swearing too much, his roving eye confidently assessing the women in the hall; serving-women, washerwomen, noble-women . . . it was all one to him–or so Sir Bertrand's eye seemed to say.

Crispin ground his teeth and looked black. When Sir Bertrand made some jest about their letting the ladies pick the two sides for the mock battle, Crispin retorted that whatever side he led would beat Sir Bertrand's. At which Sir Bertrand whistled, and one or two of the older men looked uneasy. It was not wise to take ill feelings onto the tourney field, said one. Blunt weapons or no, rules or no, you could not foresee what might happen if enemies met on the field.

"Laws," said Crispin, looking at Sir Bertrand, "are broken now and then . . . or bent to the advantage of the judges . . . but rest assured that those who break the law will themselves be broken by the law."

"Whatever that might mean," said Sir Bertrand, setting his jaw at Crispin. Whatever else he was, Sir Bertrand was no coward.

But Crispin only showed his teeth in a mirthless grin, and tried to catch his father's eye again. If only Lord Henry would see reason . . . .

Beata, meanwhile, had succeeded in doing what Crispin had merely attempted to do. She took her father's free arm while he walked with Lady Escot, and drew him to one side. Lord Henry looked at her with sharp black eyes and said, in a tone whose mildness belied its content, "I hear ill news of an undutiful daughter."

She gave him a brilliant smile and said mockingly, "Pray allow your undutiful daughter to remind you it is time we began the morning's sport. And while we lead the company to their places, let your undutiful daughter tell you that though she has given serious consideration to such desperate remedies as running away, or throwing herself off the ramparts, yet she considers that since you were the instrument of bringing her into this world, and have fed and clothed her for nigh on nineteen years, so her body belongs to you . . . though her soul is still her own."

"Her soul – I devoutly trust – is with God!" Lord Henry bowed his head no more than two inches as he fronted the company, with his daughter on his arm. Smiling, he indicated to the Clerk of the Lists that he was ready to proceed.

"My soul?" said Beata, seating herself beside him. "Why, my soul remains my own – if I have such a thing, which I sometimes doubt. But that is no business of yours, Father. My body is yours, and you may dispose of it as you wish, but do not ask for intangibles as well. . . ."

"My vow to the church binds you body and soul, Beata . . . ."

And they smiled and bowed as they indicated that the abbot and the other noble guests should be seated. The Clerk of the Lists marshalled his helpers, directing the peasants to this side and that, re-aligning targets and benches on which the onlookers might be seated.

"Your vow, dear Father, promised something you could not wholly fulfil. You, being at a loss for something with which to bribe God, promised him something which was of no great value to you: to wit, a girl child. I submit to you that though her body is yours to sell as you wish – as much or as little as any bond-woman on your estates – yet her soul is her own, and remains her own property, and does not fall within the scope of your vow."

"Well, well. We will let the Mother Abbess deal with your scruples."

"If I ever get there . . . ."

His hand tightened on her arm. She turned a smiling face on him, and said, "I reserve the right to hope, even until the eleventh hour."

"You were content enough before. You will be content again."

"Now of that you cannot be sure, any more than you can be sure that Crispin will ever sire you another grandchild, if he is forced to remain shackled to a woman he finds repugnant."

"Do you try to bargain with me? Your willingness to go quietly into the convent, against Crispin's divorce? Folly! You will both do your duty. You have no choice in the matter, either of you."

"Why, the letter of the law may be observed, truly. But the spirit? Can you force me to fulfil your vow by going with a willing heart? Can you force Crispin to enter Joan's bed with eagerness? I think not. Any more than you can force Elaine to smile when she marries a man charged with attempted murder."

A great throng of country folk began to cheer as the first of the contestants were singled out by the Clerk of the Lists, and bowed before Lord Henry, prior to starting the first game.

Men such as Lord Henry can smile and smile, and think of other things. So now he smiled, and his eyes flicked from Elaine's pallor to where Joan sat beyond, munching on some nuts, with her eyelids puffy and her fat white fingers covered with rings . . . and beyond them to where the young maidens sat, fingering their locks, and whispering to each other, laughing and glancing at the young men out of the corners of their eyes.

"That is a grave charge," said Lord Henry, low in Beata's ear. "Attempted murder? You can prove what you say, I trust?"

"Lady Escot knows . . . ." Beata avoided answering directly. She bent forward, applauding the winner of a wrestling bout. Her voice was a murmur, easily lost . . . yet Lord Henry did not lose it.

"You know nothing of the matter," said Lord Henry to Beata, under cover of the applause. "You know nothing of life. My plans are well-conceived . . . ."

"And include a faulty knight . . . ."

Lord Henry set his teeth. The winner, a sweating, brawny smith, came up to receive a prize from Elaine; and then it was the turn of the archers.

"Your suit prospered in the London courts?" asked Beata.

"Thanks entirely to Sir Bertrand."

"Ah, the faulty knight. I wonder how impartial a judge he will find you, when he is brought up in court on a charge of attempted murder?"

Lord Henry's eyes narrowed, and for a moment his look of good humour vanished. Beata turned to look full in his face, and for a moment the two stared at each other. It was a contest as deadly as any they would see on the floor that day. Lord Henry had the advantage of years, and experience, but Beata's superb beauty and will-power were founded in love, and would not be denied. Yet neither could say that they had won, when the plaudits of the crowd below dragged their eyes thither.

"You have proof?" said Lord Henry, for the second time.

"If you will come secretly to the green solar this evening, an hour before the masque is to begin, I believe you will be satisfied. . . ."

"Beata!" But his daughter, smiling at him, had risen, and gone to bend over Joan, asking to change places with her.

Lord Henry's eyes glittered, for he was not accustomed to receiving a challenge on his home ground. In spite of years of self-discipline his first reaction was a violent one. But he could not order his daughter to be taken out and whipped in the middle of the games, and so he turned to Joan and was courteous, and smiled down at the contestants, who looked up so eagerly to catch his eye, waiting for a word of praise. And beneath his smile his brain began to work on the problems propounded by Beata.

But Beata took Joan's seat a little way along, where she could look across the contestants below to where a man in a hood, with whitened eyebrows and moustache, stood a head taller than the retainers around him, and watched her, and the contestants, and her . . . and her . . . .

It was as if something had burst into flame inside her. She thought she could not bear the pain of seeing him and knowing there were only two more days . . . and on the second of those she would be turned into a thing of black and ugly poverty . . . and yet, although she knew it was folly that he should have come, she was glad and glowing with beauty and consciousness of his love, she leaned over to hand the prize to the winner of the single-stick contest. And the winner, poor fool, thinking the smile and the radiance for him, was so struck out of his wits that he could not even mumble his thanks, but had to be dragged away with his chin on his shoulder, still looking back at her.

Presently Lord Henry beckoned Crispin to take his place and withdrew to a recess in a window nearby, where he might still oversee the company, but also talk in some degree of privacy with whomsoever it pleased him to summon to his side. As he settled himself Telfer and Varons came discreetly up, and behind them, though in more hesitant fashion, came young Master Thomas.

"I am displeased with you, Telfer . . . and you too, Varons," said Lord Henry, still smiling, but allowing his eyes to grow chill. "What an impossible position you have placed me in, allowing a rogue like Rocca to force my hand! The man came whining to me before church this morning, complaining that you have withheld Master William's effects from him, against my orders."

Now Telfer and Varons had met that morning with the Lady Beata, while the better part of the company were in chapel, and they were well informed on the matter.

Telfer lifted his arm, to show that he had an extra bunch of keys on his belt. "It was not Master William's effects Rocca wanted, but the keys to the chest in which the accounts are kept. Master William thought they would be less misused in my hands than in Rocca's."

"Ha! Rocca has cheated me? With my son's approval?"

"Your son now realises how hasty he was in putting Rocca

forward for the position of bailiff. If you were to dismiss Rocca and set in hand an investigation into his accounts, I believe Crispin would be extremely relieved. As to Rocca's villainy, Master William believed that if a search were to be made of Rocca's house, papers might be discovered which would make all clear. More, if Rocca were to be detained here for questioning, the peasants would lose their fear of him, and talk freely. At the moment he has power of life and death over them, and they will not speak."

"Powers of life and death? Rocca? Who says so?"

"Master William made a memorandum on the subject, which he entrusted to Thomas the Clerk. If you will cast your eye over it?"

"You believe it?" Telfer nodded. Lord Henry expelled his breath with some force. His smile had vanished, and his fingertips drummed, lightly, on the arm of his chair. He said, "I am indeed in an impossible position! Everything that you told me last night, everything that I see around me, bears out your statement that I owe much to Gervase Escot, and yet . . . my hands are tied!"

Telfer exchanged glances with Varons. Telfer said, "The man was wrongfully convicted."

"How can we be sure of that?"

Telfer paused. "You looked into his face last night, my lord. You had already given the order for his arrest to Rocca. Once you have made a decision, you rarely have doubts, and yet it seems you have doubts this time . . . ."

"Why should I have doubts?"

"Because of what you saw in Gervase Escot's face. You saw integrity, my lord. As we did. As Hamo did. You know now that Gervase Escot was not guilty of stealing his uncle's ring. You cannot send him back to Ware in chains, to be branded, imprisoned and perhaps murdered by his enemy."

"The man should have left Malling before I returned. I could not ignore the presence of a fugitive from justice, once I had been officially informed of it."

"Let him go now, then . . . quietly. Let him be given means to escape. Varons will see to it. You need know nothing of it, and can make a great show of anger when it is eventually discovered that the man has gone."

Lord Henry sank back into his chair. "When we were both young, Telfer, you and I . . . everything seemed so clear-cut . . . right and wrong . . . good and evil. We thought it strange that a man should find it difficult to choose, when morality and self-interest conflicted. Now I am older and they say I am a wise man . . . yet I find it very difficult to choose. Let the matter rest as it is for the moment. The man cannot run away now. Perhaps I will question him sometime in the New Year, when Sir Bertrand is safely wed to Elaine. In the meantime, I forbid all mention of the subject. No, not another word!"

"My lord! Uncle!" It was young Jaclin, bowing before them, awkward and nervous. "Uncle, a boon! You have been pleased to dub me a knight, and indeed I am grateful, but I heard that Master William was arrested last night and sent to the dungeons . . . my lord, he is no rogue, and has been of much service to me. I wanted him to watch me in the lists. I thought, even, that he might act as my squire."

"That is enough!" said Lord Henry. "My mind is made up! Forget him, as I intend to do. . . . "

Chapter Fourteen

"My lord! Father!" Crispin hastened up even as Lord Henry still frowned at Jaclin. "A word with you, Father . . . in private . . . ."

"What, sirrah?" said Lord Henry, his smile a thing of the past. "Is this my disobedient son, who has foisted a rogue and a scoundrel on me? Peace, sirrah! To your duty, sirrah! I will have none of your selfish whining! Go sit beside your lady wife, and show that you love her well."

"Father, it is not possible!"

"Silence!"

And there was silence. Lord Henry had not even raised his voice, but his guests, applauding the last of the contestants, were aware that something was amiss, and began to look round, and to mutter amongst themselves.

Lord Henry beckoned to the Clerk of the Lists, who was hovering nearby. "Is the ground fit for us to hold the mock battle?"

"My gracious lord, I fear not. However, plans have been made against this contingency, and if my gracious lord would care to lead guests out to the impromptu tiltyard, we could hold the procession of noble knights shortly, and then . . . ."

"I will challenge all comers to tilt against me!" cried Sir Bertrand, coming up behind them. He was yawning, stretching, loosening his muscles at the prospect of action. "I'll declare my Lady Elaine the fairest Queen of Beauty that ever was, and so on and so forth. Then you may come at me one at a time, or all together . . . what you will!" And he laughed, showing all his teeth.

Crispin cast him a look of dislike. "I challenge you here and now, on behalf of my sister Beata. And I will strip you of your armour and your horse by nightfall. Aye, and belabour your carcase till you cry for mercy!"

"Crispin!" said Lord Henry in warning tone. His son started, changed colour, and bit his lip.

"Aye, well . . . !" said Sir Bertrand, laughing. "And if the Lady Beata had been offered me, in place of her sister Elaiine, I doubt not I would fight alongside you. There's a maid meet for mating. . . ." He chuckled, with meaning. "She wears the look of a woman who knows her lover's eyes are upon her. Which of our company, think you, does she favour?"

Crispin's hand was on the hilt of his sword, and the scar on his cheek burned. "You son of a . . . !"

"Enough!" said Lord Henry, and once again Crispin was checked. "More than enough, Sir Bertrand. My daughter Beata is destined for the church, and the only lover she has ever had, or ever will have, is our Lord Jesus Christ."

"Then my jest was ill-timed indeed," said Sir Bertrand. But his eyes, those bold, large eyes of his, slid round Crispin to where Beata was standing with one hand up to her curls, laughing and causing a group of young men to join in her laughter. And Sir Bertrand's tongue came out, and touched his upper lip, and Crispin made a sound deep in his throat . . . and Varons moved to stand directly behind Crispin.

Lord Henry leaned back in his chair, watching them all beneath heavy lids, until Crispin took his hand from his sword and, tapping Jaclin on the shoulder, strode away to arm himself.

"Varons, Telfer!" The two men drew near Lord Henry. "Sir Bertrand, though uncouth, is no fool where women are concerned. Does my daughter Beata have a lover?" There was no reply. Lord Henry's hand came down lightly, caressingly, on the arm of his chair, and began to stroke it. The threat of violence hung in the air, all the more telling for being so understated.

"One who loves her; yes," said Telfer. "A lover? Not in the sense that Sir Bertrand intended."

The solid white hand stilled on the arm of the chair; only the forefinger twitched, twice. "There is a name on the tip of my tongue," said Lord Henry. "Is it he, indeed? Or some other . . . ?"

"My lord," said Varons, "he is a man of honour, and she understands her duty. You have not been betrayed, my oath on it."

The white hand closed convulsively around the arm of the chair. The black eyes watched Beata. "So . . . she does not know he has been arrested? She cannot, or she would not behave like that. It cannot go deep with her . . . I must say, I am relieved." He permitted himself a chuckle. "She is grown so much, she might have given me trouble, if she but knew . . . ."

Varons met Telfer's eyes over Lord Henry's head. Telfer shook his head. This was no time to disillusion Lord Henry.

The Clerk of the Lists came hurrying up, followed by the two heralds. The musicians had now formed themselves into a group by the door, and had struck up a martial tune.

"My lord," said the Clerk, bowing low and walking backwards as Lord Henry proceeded to lead his guests out of the hall. "The challenges . . . so many! My Lord Crispin and Sir Bertrand so very eager to fight each other! Might I suggest that we revert to the Arthurian method of matching knight against knight in single combat? The least experienced being given their moment of glory first, and then building up to a bout between the finest, the most illustrious . . . oh, my lord! The vigour of your son, the prowess of Sir Bertrand . . . !" The little man kissed his fingertips, and nearly fell over a hovering page in his enthusiasm. "Entirely at your discretion, of course, my lord . . . but perhaps four pairs of knights this afternoon, and the same again tomorrow? First they must break three lances against each other, and then . . . light permitting . . . and if they so wish . . . a second bout on foot, with swords? Only the best of the knights will wish to descend to fighting on foot, but . . . the vote among the ladies to say which knight deserves the golden wreaths . . . though perhaps, tactfully, one each to Lord Crispin and Sir Bertrand?"

Thus talking, the Clerk led the procession out through the courtyard, and along to where the tithe barn had been made ready for them, with braziers placed at intervals along the sides to take the chill off the air, and scarlet cloths hanging over the rail of the balcony. There were bench seats for the ladies in front, and standing room behind for those of the gentry who did not care to risk themselves in the arena. And below the balcony crowded a couple of hundred poor folk, and many not so poor, who had come from far and wide to see the gentry disport themselves. The light was not as good as on a summer's day, but the great iron rings swung high above the Lists, shedding the glow of a myriad candles upon the ground below. Lord Henry looked round him, long and hard, and Telfer knew that his master would not have missed any of the alterations that had been made and that, though he barely smiled, he was pleased with all that had been done.

"Keep my son and Sir Bertrand apart as long as you can," he said to the Clerk of the Lists. "Match Sir Jaclin with the other new-made knight, and the rest as the heralds suggest."

Lord Henry beckoned his daughters to sit one on either

side of him, and saw that all his other guests were appropriately settled. "Elaine, my dear; you are not smiling. Yet this is a joyful occasion, is it not?"

"Yes, Father," said Elaine. She turned her head to where the head of the knights' procession was coming into the barn, and smiled.

"Beata, my dear," said her father. "You smile too much. Remember your destiny lies in the arms of no earthly man. . . ."

"And if any man question my smiling," she replied, "you must say it is with joy at what is to befall me. What else?" And she laughed in her father's face.

Lord Henry's eyelids drooped, and he thought: assuredly she has no idea her lover is in the dungeons . . . or perhaps she did not care for him deeply? No, this change in her is too great to be accounted for in any other way. Sir Bertrand spoke truly; she looks as a woman does who is aware of being admired . . . as her mother used to do when I first went courting her. So who is the man? Suppose it is not Escot; then who?

His eye passed over the procession of mounted men as they made their way before him, displaying their horses, with plumes and gilding on their harnesses, and rich cloths covering their flanks. The knights rode in the light armour intended for the tourney, covered with silken surcoats in brilliant colours, with pennants fixed to their lances, and shields displaying heraldic devices. Sir Bertrand and Crispin rode side by side at the head of the procession, but it seemed they found such proximity annoying, for first Crispin edged in front of Sir Bertrand, and then Sir Bertrand made a spurt to catch up and overtake Crispin. Thus they came to the centre of the balcony, immediately under the place where Beata and her sister sat. Sir Bertrand raised his lance high in the air, and in a resonant voice cried out that the Lady Elaine was the Queen of Beauty, and begged that she give him some favour to wear on her behalf. Elaine rose and, taking a knot of ribbons from the shoulder of her gown, dropped it into his waiting hands. She smiled and smiled, but her fingers were unsteady, so that she fumbled with the ribbons, and dropped them so clumsily that Sir Bertrand had to lunge forward to catch them. Not so Beata. She jumped up, laughing, as Crispin cried her name aloud. The knot of ribbons was off, and thrown into his hand with a flamboyant gesture.

Lord Henry thought: Varons was wrong. Her lover is here. . . somewhere!

He looked along the line of esquires, for each knight was accompanied by a young man versed in arms, but not yet ready for knighthood. But there was no-one there, he thought, who would hold Beata's attention.

Jaclin also besought a favour from Beata, and so did Gerald. But Beata turned so naturally to include Elaine in the little ceremony, that Gerald's favour came from Elaine, instead.

"That was well done," said Lord Henry to Beata, as the last of the younger knights passed before them. It was, perhaps, the first word of praise he had ever given her.

She said, "Father, I love you for that!"

And he, master of plot and stratagem, knowing himself generally more feared than loved, understood that this expression of her love for him was but an overflowing of her love for another man. At first he was angry that it should be so, and then he remembered how Beata had nursed him the previous winter when he had been ill so long . . . and he thought of her as she had been then, going silently about the castle with her hair cropped short and a plain gown concealing instead of ornamenting her figure . . . and he marvelled again at the change in her. And with that marvelling came a pang that she was to be lost to him so soon, just as she had become of value to him.

He followed the direction of her eye, and saw only Jaclin entering the lists, followed by a squire who carried his lances and his shield.

Jaclin? thought Lord Henry. Could Beata love Jaclin, and not Gervase Escot? This idea troubled him so greatly that he had to be reminded to give the signal for the bout to start.

The knights rode one from each end of the barn, to meet at the centre, under the place where Lord Henry sat. The lists were divided lengthways by a flimsy barrier, and the knights on their horses kept one on either side of this barrier as they levelled their lances at each other. Jaclin held his horse straight, his powerful shoulders bent forward, his shield well up, and his lance steady, remembering all that he had been taught. The point of Jaclin's lance took his opponent full in the centre of his shield, and the power of Jaclin's body, locked onto his horse by rigid thighs, kept him steady, so that his opponent tumbled off his horse with a cry.

"Bravo!" cried Beata, jumping to her feet. "Oh, bravo Jaclin!"

"Bravo Jaclin, indeed!" said Lord Henry, as the fallen knight was helped from the lists. "You favour Jaclin, Beata? He has gained his opponent's horse and armour with that thrust." Jaclin cantered past them, and out of the tithe barn, holding lance and shield high in acknowledgment of the cheers that greeted his victory.

"Oh yes!" said Beata. "He has worked so hard, and been so much less troublesome of late."

So it was not Jaclin she loved. The next pair of knights came into the lists; an elderly knight and a distant cousin. Three lances, and neither of them giving the other an opening . . . fairly matched, the company growing restive, for neither man seemed anxious to take risks. Lord Henry shook his head when the Clerk of the Lists enquired whether the bout should be prolonged on foot.

Then Gerald, and a knight who had come in Sir Bertrand's train. And the first lance nearly unseated Gerald, causing Beata once more to jump up from her seat . . . but he made a good recovery, and managed to shatter his opponent's shield on the third lance, so that Lord Henry was graciously pleased that the two men should continue their fight on foot. But now it could be seen that the stranger knight was far heavier in weight than Gerald, and more experienced, so that Gerald was soon forced to submit, but on such terms that he did not consider himself badly treated. It was in the rules that the victor could take not only his opponent's horse and armour, but—at the discretion of the Clerk of the Lists—might also in some cases exact a ransom. On this occasion

Gerald did not lose his horse or have to pay a ransom, but surrendered his armour and sword.

Jaclin now came on again, tilting against an older knight. Such was the younger man's ferocity that on the third charge he managed to make his opponent sway dangerously in the saddle, casting shield and lance from him in an endeavour to remain upright. Lord Henry pronounced Jaclin the winner and in mercy to the older knight, who seemed dazed, forebore to order that they continue to fight on foot. Jaclin would gain both armour and horse, for the second time that day.

"Sir Jaclin is eager to try again," said the Clerk of the Lists, consulting Lord Henry. "But although he is courageous enough, his horse is blown . . . ."

"I doubt he is capable of fighting any more experienced knight," said Varons, low in Lord Henry's ear. "He has done better than Master William anticipated, as it is."

So Lord Henry gave the signal for the last bout of the day There was a sudden hush as Crispin came on at one end, and Sir Bertrand at the other.

"I thought they were to be kept apart," said Beata to her father. "Why, what sport shall we have tomorrow, if we let them wear themselves out today?"

"Perhaps the weather will improve, so that we may still have our mock battle outside tomorrow," said Lord Henry, but he raised an enquiring eyebow at the Clerk of the Lists nevertheless.

"My lord, it was not so I arranged the matter. But my Lord Crispin overruled me, and there were some hard things said out in the courtyard . . . neither man will listen to reason."

"Trouble!" said Varons, in Telfer's ear. Telfer nodded, anxious-eyed. Varons slid back through the company, and made his way along the balcony to the stairs.

Crispin adjusted his ornate, gilded helm. From its crest floated a long red plume, around which he had tied the knot of ribbon from Beata's dress. Sir Bertrand was smiling as he bent to take his own helmet from his squire, and fit it over his chain-mail hood. Now the two men faced each other down the length of the lists, with the slender rail of the barrier between them, like a string joining them together.

The first of the lances was handed up to the two knights, adjusted to their satisfaction . . . the signal given . . . and away they went, cantering, galloping faster and more heavily then any of those who had gone before them.

There was a crash and a splintering, and both horses checked as their riders rocked back in their saddles.

Beata said, "Father . . . ."

"They are well-matched, truly," said Lord Henry, but his brows flattened.

The two knights cantered back to their own ends, and took a second lance each. Again they set off towards each other, power against power, heavily bearing down as they met . . . and the lance of one caught the shield of the other off-centre, and slid away harmlessly . . . but Crispin's lance shattered, and he laughed, the laugh echoing within his helmet.

Beata put her hand over her father's. "Father," she said, a second time. But it was not in Lord Henry's power to stop the bout, even if he had wished to do so.

For the third and last time the horses turned and checked at the end of the lists, and each knight took a fresh lance.

"Father," said Beata, "you will not let them continue the fight on foot!"

"No," said Lord Henry. "After all, we must save some excitement for the morrow."

"There is the masque," she said, and smiled awry. "We can dance, instead of fighting."

"It is expected that knights do both," said Lord Henry.

The two knights were off again, crouching low, their dented shields covering their bodies, the plumes floating from their helms . . . they would meet exactly in the centre. There was nothing in it as regards distance; and yet perhaps Crispin was the faster, the more accurate, and his lance aimed at the exact centre of Sir Bertrand's shield, and would surely shatter against it once again . . . and so he be declared the winner. But Sir Bertrand lifted the point of his lance at the last moment, and even as they crashed together, the tip of that lance caught in the vizor of the ornate helm that Crispin wore, and as he was borne forward by the momentum of his horse, Crispin drove himself forward onto the lance . . . jolting in his saddle, his own lance shattered on his opponent's shield . . . fighting with his horse for control, dropping his weapons.

Sir Bertrand cantered on, holding one half of the lance, the shaft . . . for the other had broken away, embedded in Crispin's helmet.

Crispin swayed in his saddle, both hands to his helmet.

Beata's hand was a claw on her father's, her face as white as his.

She said, "My God! What have I done!"

Lord Henry half-rose in his seat. His lips moved. No sound came. Suddenly, he was an old man. At the third attempt he said, "Crispin loses this bout, evidently. He forfeits horse and armour to Sir Bertrand."

Telfer moved forward and said, his voice shaking, "See, he is not hurt . . . he is still in the saddle."

"Yes," said Lord Henry, yet he moved stiffly as he resumed his seat. "Sir Bertrand is the victor, undoubtedly."

Beata fell back in her chair, breathing through her mouth.

"Not much hurt, you think?" asked Lord Henry.

Crispin was struggling with the tip of the lance, trying to break it away from his helm. His squire was running down the length of the lists . . . and how long it was taking him to get there! A great hubbub and outcry rose from the people. Sir Bertrand brought his horse to a halt, and waited to see what might happen.

"But he is not badly hurt . . . is he?" said Lord Henry.

Someone screamed. It was Joan. Lord Henry looked at her as if he had never seen her before.

Beata rose, with an effort. She said, "I must go to him."

Crispin brought his horse to a standstill. Sir Bertrand walked his horse round the barrier, and dismounted, taking off his helm. Varons was running up, and Jaclin, running to hlep Crispin, who had managed, using both hands, to tear off his helm. A great gasp, and then a groan ran through the hall, for blood was streaming down one side of Crispin's face.

"He is not badly hurt, I dare say," said Lord Henry. "Such things happen in tourneys . . . . Telfer, I want that lance inspected, to see if the point be blunt or no."

"Joan!" Beata bent over the hysterical woman, and beckoned for help.

Jaclin leaped forward to catch Sir Bertrand a blow on the cheek.

"And that for you . . . now you will have to fight me instead!"

"Sir Jaclin!" Varons had hold of Jaclin's arm, and was trying to restrain him.

"I demand the right to avenge my cousin Crispin!" cried Jaclin, appealing to Lord Henry.

"You cannot refuse him!" The Clerk of the Lists looked from Jaclin to Lord Henry.

"No, I cannot refuse him . . . but I am sure my son is not badly hurt." Lord Henry roused himself, beckoning to Telfer. "The physicians must be sent for at once. The banquet is to go on as arranged. Sir Jaclin will fight Sir Bertrand tomorrow, when the country games are over."

Sir Bertrand was approaching, and saluting them. "My lord, I claim Lord Crispin's horse and armour."

Crispin was being helped to dismount, and laid on a hurdle. At Varons's direction he was borne off the field, his hands to his face.

Elaine smiled down at Jaclin; the first genuine smile she had given them all day. She said, "Cousin Jaclin, you shall wear my favour tomorrow, if you will, and I shall pray that you be the victor in the tourney."

"Impossible," said Lord Henry. "Elaine, you forget that Sir Bertrand is your champion, not Jaclin."

"I forget nothing," said Elaine. "And now, if you please, I will help my sister with Joan."

The banquet was over, the last of the guests had dispersed to their rooms, and the noisy hum that had pervaded the castle was gradually being replaced by silence. Here and there a yawning man-at-arms stood his turn. Lights yet burned in the infirmary, where Anselm tended the sick; in Crispin's chamber, where his doctor and his father's physician argued over their remedies; and in Lord Henry's chamber, where his daughter Beata stood like a chidden child before him.

"I hold you responsible for this," said Lord Henry. "You set them against one another with your lying tales. You incited Crispin to attack a man for whose safety we were responsible not only as an honoured guest, but also as your sister's betrothed. You, and you alone are to blame . . . ."

She blinked, but her wide eyes were tearless, and her mouth set hard.

"If it be so," she said, "then let it be so. I told no lies. I have done nothing of which I should be ashamed in trying to save my sister from a man such as Sir Bertrand. He is a would-be murderer, and a thief of other men's reputations."

"Silence! You anger me. Your childishness is beyond folly. Do you think I did not enquire of the circumstances surrounding the theft at Ware before I invited Sir Bertrand to become my son-in-law? Gervase Escot was brought before a court and convicted of . . . ."

"And what a court! What justice did he have? What justice could he possibly receive when it was in the best interests of the judge to convict him! Oh, if only Crispin had not been wounded! I had a plan to show you the truth of that matter . . . I am sure Lady Escot was behind the theft, and that Sir Bertrand aided her in everything! It was Sir Bertrand who sent men to kill Gervase when he lay in prison at Ware. That at least he can prove! Will you not hear him?"

"Beata, if you say one word more on that subject, tourney or no tourney, guests or no guests, I shall have you whipped and confined to your chamber till I can hand you over to the abbot! Have I not enough to bear? Does Crispin not have enough to bear?"

"At least allow me to nurse Crispin!"

"No, you shall keep well away from him, lest you inflame his fever with your dangerous ideas. The doctors took away his eye – did I tell you?" He had already told her twice. It seemed to oppress his mind, for he kept returning to it.

"If you will only allow me to help nurse him, I promise not to speak of . . . ."

"No, I said! Get you gone to your chamber. It is late, and tomorrow you must sit at my side and watch young Jaclin being torn apart by Sir Bertrand . . . for surely the young cub will be no match for an experienced knight . . . fool that he was to challenge . . . yet I do not think the less of him for it! It was well done, was it not? I did not think the lad had it in him. Well, well. He will be beaten for sure, but I will make it up to him. You and your sister will smile on Sir Bertrand when he wins . . . do you hear? You will smile and give him your golden garlands and, God willing, he will forgive us the insults we have put upon him."

"Is he worth so much to you?" The girl was bitter.

"At least I shall be able to save his marriage to Elaine. There will be that, at least."

Chapter Fifteen

Beata went straight to the infirmary after leaving her father. She told her nurse to wait with Anselm while she made her way to the far end of the cloisters, where a glow showed that a fire had been lit in one of the cells. Varons was sitting with Gervase, in the room which had once been Hamo's. The captain rose with a muttered apology, and left the room when he saw Beata. Gervase drew a stool to the fire for her, and kneeling, chafed her cold hands.

She had fled to him meaning to pour out a complaint of her father to him, to say that she would do it all again if necessary . . . she had had some wild notion of urging him to fly with her, to rape her . . . but at the first touch of his hands, at the first glimpse of his smile she closed her eyes and her hands clasped around his, holding him to her.

She said, "Just once, I wish I could see you dressed as you should be . . . ."

He laughed. He took his hands away from hers, and went

to sit on the far side of the fire from her. He had taken off his caped hood, and his hair gleamed rich and dark in the firelight. He wore the homespun tunic of a peasant, and his woollen stockings had been darned and patched by their previous owner. He had shaved his chin, but left a moustache, whitening it with flour, like his eyebrows.

She said, "Now I know how you will look when you grow old." She felt as if something in her would break if she did not go into his arms. She would have started from her stool to go to him, but he lifted the fingers of one hand. It was the slightest of gestures, but it checked her.

"Varons is watching. And others, maybe. Your nurse of a certainty."

"We are watched? How dare they!" Yet she sank back.

"I always know when I am being watched. And perhaps it is better so. One touch of your hand, one smile . . . it is like wine to a thirsty traveller . . . one step more, one incautious movement, and I am not sure I could hold myself back . . . . "

"Or I," she said.

They sat unmoving, one on either side of the fire. She had had so much to say to him, but everything that came into her mind seemed either too trivial or too weighty to speak of, when this might be – must be – their last meeting.

"I can't believe that it will happen," she told him at last. "That I should never see you grow old, never come to you in bed, never hold your child in my arms . . . . " Her hands made a groping movement, as if holding a small child against her shoulder, with its feet on her lap, setting her cheek against imaginary red curls.

"I had a dream, too. I dreamed of taking you home to Ware, and of your sitting beside me in the hall, and running to meet me when I came in from the hunt and the harvest . . . . "

"Now that I never dreamed," she said. "I always saw you here at Malling in my dreams, in the hall, in my bed, presiding over the court."

His smile was quizzical. "I suppose that is because you have never been anywhere else but Malling. Yet even if everything had been different, you would have had to leave home to live with your husband's people."

"Well, I shall soon be leaving Malling, shall I not? How it will enlarge my experience of life!" She tried to laugh. "Do you know, I keep thinking of the boy who loved nothing better than to roam the woods, and hunt and play with his little dog. And then he was sent to a monastery, never more to hunt and roam. So he used to climb the tower on the gatehouse of the monastery every day, to catch a glimpse of the woods in which he had once been happy . . . . " Her voice broke. He did not speak, but leaned forward to put another log on the fire.

She put her fingers to her temples, pressing on them, forbidding herself to give way. She said, "It was your one-time mistress Anne who put the ring in your wallet, wasn't it? You must have some idea of how it got there; I can think of no-one else whom you would have shielded."

He sighed. "I suppose it was. The ring was wrapped in a fold of paper, and she might not have known what she was putting in my wallet. Once before she put a good-luck charm there – before I went on my third campaign to France – a charm she purchased of a wise woman, intended to bring me luck. I suppose she thought it was some such charm . . . and it is true she did have the opportunity to put it in my wallet, for I did visit her that day. She mended the neck-fastening of my tunic . . . that was her idea, not mine. Yes, I think she put it there, but I doubt she knew what it was when she did so."

"But why did you not call her to give evidence?"

"Why, at first the charge seemed so ridiculous that I thought no-one would believe it. I thought that to have dragged her into the matter would merely bring her into undeserved trouble . . . she might have been accused of stealing it herself, and being a bond-woman, might have suffered dire penalties. Anyway, I had no time for second thoughts. The accusation was made, the ring discovered in my wallet, and I was judged guilty in less time than it takes to drink a mug of ale."

"No jury? No waiting for the travelling judges?" He

laughed, in derision. "Then . . . what will you do now? Father's mind is set against reopening the case."

"I have been discussing the matter with Varons. He believes, and so does Telfer, that your father would be very happy if I could slip away from the castle before he has to hand me over to Sir Bertrand. So I will look out for a chance of leaving in the retinue of one of the visiting knights . . . or slip away with the kitchen hands, when they go out into the villages nearby for provender. We see no great difficulty in arranging that. Afterwards . . . " He shrugged. "Lady Escot is in possession at Ware, and though I am in law entitled to a certain proportion of the property, without influence or money – and as a fugitive from justice – I cannot take what is mine. No, I shall make my way . . . . "

"Not to the monks! I beg you! Is it not enough that one of us must lose his life?"

"Now I do not see it that way. But the answer to your question is 'No'. If I have anything to give, then it is in the world, and not in the cloister. I have heard that there are hospitals in London, founded by this great man and that. I will make my way to one of those, and offer my services. I shall not be unhappy there."

She struck her hands together, and was silent. How was it that he could feel so little, while she was in torment? He had gone beyond her, almost out of reach. When he had been taken from the cage, there had been a look on his face then, as now, of peace. She could not understand it. She did not wish to understand it. She guessed that such peace was attained not by railing against fate, but by accepting it.

"There is no God!" she declared.

"Is it not more comfortable to believe in God, than to deny Him?"

"Everything has gone awry!"

"You are so very like Crispin, and Jaclin. Do you know, I thought I disliked them both, and now that I am come to the point of leaving, I find I have grown to love them. Yes," he said, nodding and smiling. "Even Crispin! And even Jaclin! Men are such odd creatures, and it seems I am even more odd than most . . . . "

Now tears did come to her, but silently. She wiped them away with the back of her hand.

He remarked, as if he had not noticed her tears, "Jaclin said he wanted me to act as his squire. Or so Varons tells me. I think I can trust Jaclin not to give me away if I go to his chamber in the morning, ànd give him what encouragement I may. He issued his challenge in fine style, did he not? Yet Varons says he is now drinking hard, being afraid of meeting Sir Bertrand, and also afraid of showing that he is afraid. Fear is natural enough . . . ."

He talked on, more or less at random, giving her time to recover. Presently they heard footsteps in the cloister.

"So soon?" she asked, hand to throat. Now he let her see how deeply he himself was suffering. "Gervase . . . . " She put out her hand, and it wavered near him, without touching him. Then her nurse stood in the doorway, and behind her nurse stood Varons. Beata and Gervase looked at one another, without smiling.

Then she turned and left him.

A pall of rain fell on the castle, and the sky was dark even though it was not yet noon. In the hall Lord Henry sat, surrounded by his guests, watching the antics of the peasants as they perspired and leaped in rustic games. Lord Henry still smiled, but the lines on his face appeared grey. The two doctors came and went between Crispin's chamber and the hall, and the news from the sick-room was not good. Now Lord Henry sent Father Anthony to lend his skill to that of the doctors, but frowned on Beata, when she petitioned once more to go too.

Beata and Elaine sat on either side of him, stiff in their gold dresses and wreaths. The one smiled little, and the other smiled not at all, for Gervase was not in the hall to watch her.

The weary hours passed at last, and a routine inspection of the sodden tiltyard by the Clerk of the Lists made it clear there would be no mock battle that day, either. The company would eat, and then remove to the tithe barn for the jousting. In the evening there would be the masque at which the two sisters would dance as maidens for the last time, before they were received by their respective bridegrooms.

Lord Henry honoured Sir Bertrand and his cousin Lady Escot with many courtesies and gifts, to show that he bore the man no ill-will for what had happened to Crispin.

Gervase was helping Anselm tend a peasant, who had dislocated his shoulder in the games, when Varons sought him out. With so many extra inhabitants in the castle, there had been a sudden influx of people with accidental sprains, cuts and burns into the infirmary, far more than Anselm could attend to unaided. Gervase had not forgotten his promise to attend on Jaclin, but had lost track of the time in helping the old man with his patients.

"Haste ye!" said Varons, rushing Gervase through the court. "They have finished with the games and are about to leave for the tithe barn and the jousting. There are a couple of bouts before Jaclin is due to go on, but he is far from sober, and we are having difficulty getting him into his armour. Crispin's squire . . . the one whose nose Jaclin bloodied a while back . . . he's attending Jaclin. Not a good choice; though the man seems honest, he bears Jaclin a grudge. Pray God the lad sits straight on his horse's back until Sir Bertrand's lance hits him. He would never live down the disgrace if he fell off, drunk, before he were even touched!"

"Could not someone keep him sober?"

Varons shrugged. Who cared enough about Jaclin to spend so much time and effort on him?

Gervase frowned. "I am sorry for the lad. If I had been free to move about . . . . Well, well. He is over-young and inexperienced for this kind of thing. His first tourney . . . he did well yesterday, did he not? A trifle wild, but that is no bad thing, if the control is there, underneath. A pity he sought to match himself against Sir Bertrand, when he had made such a good start . . . ."

"Haste ye, then! He may pay attention to you."

But they were too late. When they burst into Jaclin's chamber they found Berit, the squire, leaning against the wall with folded arms, while Jaclin snored on the floor at his feet.

Berit shrugged, meeting their accusing eyes. "He sent me for hot water to wash in, and a razor that he might be shaved. When I got back he had a fresh bottle in his hand, almost empty. Then he fell down, trying to tell me how he would beat Sir Bertrand in the lists . . . and he may rot in hell, for all I care."

Varons and Gervase lifted Jaclin to the bed, and tried to revive him, but he was too far gone.

"It is useless," said Berit, not without satisfaction. "The boasts of the bastard brought home to roost . . . ha!"

"I am thinking of his father . . . that Crispin's champion should be too drunk to enter the lists!"

"Poor lad," Gervase looked down on Jaclin. "Perhaps he would never have amounted to much, but this will surely finish him."

"Unless. . .!" said Varons, turning on Gervase.

"I would have liked him to have withstood a couple of charges from Sir Bertrand," said Gervase. "I think he might have managed that, at least . . . though he could never have withstood the man on foot."

"Jaclin said you should have your sword back, if he was vanquished," Varons reminded him.

"So he did. Well, he had forgotten it would have to go to Sir Bertrand, if he lost."

"Here!" Varons seized the bowl of hot water and the razor for which the squire had been sent. "Off with that moustache! Strip! You are taller than Jaclin, of course, but then you are not so broad in the shoulder. Will the mailed mittens fit, that is the question! Move, man! Move!"

Gervase took the razor which had been handed to him, looked at Varons, then at Berit, and put the razor down again. "You want me to take his place in the lists? I could not possibly . . . ."

"Why not? Wearing a closed helm over a chainmail hood, nothing can be seen of your face . . . especially if you take off that moustache. Surely you can withstand a couple of passes on horseback in order that our house be not disgraced . . . and that Crispin, whose ring you wear, be avenged . . . and that your enemy shall learn you are not a cipher!"

"Gerald might . . . ."

"Do you think Gerald would be able to withstand Sir Bertrand? I tell you, you are the only man who can do it, and you are here to hand. Haste, man! At any moment now they will be sending for Jaclin. If you wear his surcoat over your armour . . . Berit here will cover all enquiries, for you must not speak . . . ."

"No, this is folly! Such a deception is not honourable. If Lord Henry knew . . . ."

"There is no time for that!"

A wail from without took them by surprise. Varons and Gervase exchanged startled looks. That wail . . . from Crispin's chamber, which was directly below . . . . Berit dashed to the door and flung it open. They could hear him clattering down the stairs.

"I saw one of the doctors hurry towards the main gate as we came hither," said Gervase. "I thought it odd at the time. Why should he leave, on foot, without a servant . . . . ?"

The woman's wailing increased. Berit cried out, sharply. Then there was silence.

"He went to the village for some herbs – of course!" said Varons, yet his voice lacked conviction.

Berit's feet dragged as he mounted the stairs. He came in and leaned against the wall, his head tipped back . . . he took in great gulps of air, with his eyes closed.

"He's . . . dead?" whispered Varons. "No, never!"

Berit nodded, still beyond speech. His colour was bad. Gervase picked up the almost empty wine bottle, and held it to Berit's mouth. The squire gulped, gagged and then drank. He took the bottle from Gervase, wiped his mouth, and threw his head back.

"You will fight him for me," he said.

"For everyone!" Varons exclaimed.

"There must have been some mishandling of the wound." Gervase sighed. "A man can lose an eye, and be up and about the next day. I have seen it. Why did they not let Beata . . . ?"

"There was talk of a sharpened lance," said Berit.

Gervase shook his head. "I do not think that is Sir

Bertrand's way. He is too proud a man to stoop to underhand means, where he expects to vanquish by strength. You should scotch that rumour. There is always talk of sharpened weapons, if a man is killed in the tourney."

Varons licked his lips. "It was that gold helm. He would have it! I will send for a plain helm for you to wear, Gervase . . . and anything else you require.'

Gervase was silent. Berit moved to the door and went out, calling for a page. He could be heard giving orders, sending for the plain helmet. Then he came back in, lifted the bowl of water and the razor, and took them to Gervase.

"Lord Henry will stop the tourney when he hears the news," said Gervase, but he picked up the razor and began to shave off his moustache.

"If he does; well and good. If he does not, then you will avenge us," said Varons.

"You have a higher opinion of my ability than I have myself," said Gervase.

One doctor – Crispin's – had fled, but the other remained, and although in the absence of his rival the remaining doctor could easily lay all the blame for their noble patient's death on the absconding physician, yet he was in no haste to do so. By the time that Gervase was armed, save for his helm, there was a rumour running through the castle that Lord Crispin was seriously ill or worse, but the physician had not as yet left the sick-room.

The rumour left the keep with Gervase, and ran about the court as he checked the girths on the destrier that was waiting for him, and mounted. He wore a plain helmet . . . the very one he had admired in the armoury. Varons had told him that Lord Henry had been used to wear that helmet in tourneys in his youth. It was not a bad fit, though Gervase would have preferred a larger aperture for vision. Behind Gervase came Berit, carrying three lances and a shield bearing the Malling arms. Varons walked at his side, inspecting the bright but blunted point of Gervase's sword . . . the long sword that had swung at Jaclin's side these last few months.

Within the barn the company waited, growing restive. Two pairs of knights had entered the arena, and given but a poor account of themselves. Now Sir Bertrand sat in his pavilion, waiting for Jaclin to arrive. Sir Bertrand was very confident of himself this morning. He was a healthy, thoughtless animal, was Sir Bertrand; conscious of his good looks and his long-unbroken record of success in the tourney.

Lord Henry addressed his daughters jointly. "You know your duty. You will smile on Sir Bertrand when you give him your ribbons, and you will also be gracious to him when you give him the golden garlands afterwards. We cannot expect Jaclin to run more than one lance, possibly two if he is lucky . . . and then I will announce that honour is satisfied, and we will bring the hour of the masque forward."

"I shall give Jaclin my ribbons," said Beata. "In recognition of his courage in challenging the champion."

"I heard poor Crispin is unconscious," said Elaine. "It seems wrong to be sitting here, enjoying ourselves, when he is so ill."

"Unconscious?" Beata asked, surprised. "I enquired of the doctors at the door of Crispin's chamber this morning, and they said there was no cause for alarm."

"Even if there were," pronounced Lord Henry, who had received later information than either of his daughters, "we should still do our duty. Heaven forbid that either of you should leave your seat before Jaclin is defeated."

"What has heaven got to do with it?" said Beata. Her tone was sullen, for Gervase was nowhere to be seen.

Lord Henry's physician entered the barn and approached the stairs leading to the balcony at the same time as Jaclin's destrier came into view led by Berit, and with Varons in attendance. Sir Bertrand leapt to his feet, calling for his helm and struggling to pull the chainmail mittens which were made all in one with the sleeves, over his hands.

"Jaclin has greatly improved," said Lord Henry. "I had not noticed, before, how well he sits his horse."

"I wish this were over," sighed Beata. She had looked beyond the horseman for Gervase, who must surely have come in with Jaclin, but she could not see him.

The doctor was approaching along the balcony. Sir Bertrand, swearing, mounted his horse with a little difficulty, for he was a big man, and his armour was perhaps something heavier than that normally used for the tourney. The physician stopped beside Telfer, and began to whisper to him. Beata turned her head in an effort to hear what the physician was saying.

"Attend to your duty," said Lord Henry, rapping her on her hand.

The two horsemen approached the centre of the balcony from opposite ends of the lists, but whereas Sir Bertrand still carried his helm under his arm, his opponent was already wearing his.

"Do you hide your face, lest we see how your lip quivers?" jeered Sir Bertrand.

His opponent turned his head slightly to survey Sir Bertrand, and the jibe died on the big knight's lips. Just so had Beata seen someone else turn his head to check an ill-advised remark. She had seen that turn of head used on Crispin when he was in a rage. She had seen it turned on her a dozen times.

She half-rose in her seat, her face white. She feared she might be going to faint, though she never had, before.

Telfer was whispering to Lord Henry, and she heard his words, though Elaine did not – though they were not meant for her to hear.

Crispin was dead. Gervase had taken Jaclin's place to avenge Crispin. Only last night Gervase had said that he had come to love Crispin . . . but what had happened to Jaclin? Had he given up his place to Gervase, as being the better swordsman of the two? Or . . . speculation dissolved into grief and fear, threatening to burst her head apart.

Lord Henry sat as if he were all of one piece, without joints. He retained his smile, but something went out of his eyes . . . and when he came to walk back to the keep later on, it was seen that something had also gone out of his step. Beata waited, half-crouching . . . she waited for her father to give the order to cancel the jousting.

He said, "We are waiting for you, Elaine. Throw Sir Bertrand your ribbons."

Elaine smiled down at Sir Bertrand, and threw the knot of ribbons. This time she threw straight. He caught it with a laugh, kissed it with an extravagant gesture, and wheeled round to return to his end of the lists. Beata dragged at the ribbons on her shoulder, and hesitated. She did not think she were capable of throwing anything straight at that moment. She knew her face was on fire. She leaned forward and threw the ribbons so that they fluttered out and down, and he caught them neatly, gracefully. Chainmail moulded itself to the wearer's form, and the silk surcoat that he wore overall did little to disguise his lean strength.

"He's wearing my old helmet, I see," remarked Lord Henry. "He could do worse, but I must see he's fitted out with a new one. That tunic is barely long enough for him. I suppose the boy has grown while I've been away." The sweat stood out on his brow, but he talked on. "What's that . . . something blue . . . at his throat?"

"Crispin's sapphire ring, I think. Secured in the laces that hold the neck and hood together. Father, why don't you stop the tourney? If Crispin is dead . . . ."

"Crispin would have wished Jaclin to avenge him. I'm glad Jaclin is wearing Crispin's ring. I didn't know Crispin was so fond of the lad."

"He wasn't. Do you mean that Sir Bertrand's lance . . . ."

"Was perhaps not as blunt as it ought to have been . . . though not so sharp as to enable me to bring a case against the man. Let Jaclin do what he can. I have no other heir but him."

She tried to still the trembling of her knees as she re-seated herself. She closed her eyes, her hands clenched. She felt as if she had swayed in her seat. She opened her eyes again. The ceiling of the barn seemed about to descend on her, dark and heavy . . . and that noise . . . the noise was not in her head, but came from the hooves of the two destriers cantering, and now galloping towards one another. He would be killed. She knew it.

"Oh, God! Prevent it!" she prayed. "This is my punishment for denying you! Help me, help him, now! I would give anything for this not to have happened . . . . Crispin's death . . . all my fault . . . I will give . . . ."

Then she knew what she must give, and gave it gladly. She would go willingly into the convent, with a smile. It would be the hardest thing she could do, and she would do it.

It was as if something had burst inside her head, leaving her calm after a long illness.

I can do it, she said to herself . . . and two lances splintered on their opposing shields.

Chapter Sixteen

Both knights recoiled in their saddles, but both kept their seats. Both inspected their shields and threw them away.

"Now this is worth watching!" said the abbot, nearby.

And again, with new shields, crouching behind them . . . and Beata nearly shrieked, for she had remembered that Gervase was left-handed. Surely he could not hold the lance true for long with his right hand, and if he changed to his left, would it not handicap him, riding wide?

The lances splintered true, and Lord Henry said, softly in her ear, "He is better than yesterday. Perhaps his nerves steady, rather than go to pieces, under stress."

"I think it very likely," replied Beata. She thought, it is going to be all right. He did have some experience of tourneys before he went to France . . . I remember now. . . .

The third time, Sir Bertrand became annoyed that a callow boy should have had the power twice to shatter his shield, and so he lifted the point of his lance, as he had done to Crispin. But this time his lance, instead of catching in the helm, scraped over the side of it, as the knight in Malling colours swayed in the saddle . . . and this time Sir Bertrand received a blow on his thigh from a lance which had struck him at a different angle, from a point which had been dropped, instead of raised. Sir Bertrand was nearly jolted from his saddle but cursing, dropping his lance, sawing at the reins, he pulled his horse to a standstill and jumped down. As he turned to face his opponent on the other side of the barrier, Sir Bertrand drew his sword and let out a battle cry.

"A pity I must stop the fight now," said Lord Henry. "But I cannot expect an unseasoned boy to meet Sir Bertrand on foot."

"I believe you might," said Varons, bending over to speak in Lord Henry's ear. "He has learned much from Master William."

Then Berit and Sir Bertrand's esquire came running into the lists, to relieve their knights of shattered lances, and take away the two destriers. Sir Bertrand crashed through the barrier which divided him from his opponent and came forward, swinging his sword with both hands, and bellowing defiance. Sir Bertrand had lost his shield. Now the knight in Malling colours tossed his aside also.

"Folly!" said Lord Henry. "He had the advantage, with his shield!"

"Ah, but now he is free to use both hands," Varons pointed out.

"But he is not wearing mail on his hands!" said Lord Henry. "Varons, you should have seen to it that he was fitted out properly. One cut, and he is finished!"

"He is wearing leather gloves," said Beata, thinking of the damage a spell in the cage had done to Gervase's hands and feet.

"He knows what he is about." Varons rebuked them both for want of faith.

The two knights met with a crash of swords. Loud were the cries from the populace, some urging Sir Bertrand on, and some Sir Jaclin. Of the two men perhaps Sir Bertrand was the more popular with the crowd, for he had a reputation already as a champion in the lists and was about to marry the Lady Elaine. As for Jaclin, his truculence was well-remembered, and those who cried out for him at first were those who remembered only that he was of Malling blood, and was to avenge the spilling of Malling blood.

Swords clashed, disengaged, and clashed again. Sir Bertrand was the more heavily built of the two, and used all his weight as he struck. Gervase was a trifle taller and lighter on his feet. He thought more quickly, and more coolly. His control of his weapon was in every way superior to that of Sir Bertrand's.

Sir Bertrand began to grunt, but Gervase never made a sound as he circled and parried and struck. The first time his sword shot from right to left hand, in order to deliver a blow from an unexpected quarter, Sir Bertrand stared wildly, and gave ground.

"There!" said Beata, pinching her father's hand.

"He has learned his lessons well," agreed Lord Henry.

"And there . . ." whispered Beata, more to herself than to him. Her eyes shone. Her breath was held . . . and released as Gervase swooped . . . and struck and ducked . . . and dodged another great blow. He changed hands again and attacked from a different angle . . . moving lightly around Sir Bertrand, forcing him to turn and change direction . . . turning his mailed head from side to side, beginning to breathe hard and drag his feet.

Then Sir Bertrand bellowed and charged at Gervase, forcing his opponent for once to give ground, back and back, with a fury of blows raining on him until Gervase, giving way a little too quickly, caught his spurred heel on some slight unevenness in the ground, and half-tripped, and half-fell. As he fell he rolled, but not quickly enough to avoid a blow on the back of his left shoulder which tore the silken surcoat apart.

"Christ have mercy!" gasped Beata, clinging to her father's arm.

"I cannot stop them," Lord Henry told her.

"No," said Beata. "I know . . . only . . . oh, Father! Pray for him!"

Sir Bertrand, staggering a little, lifted his sword two-handed to deliver the coup de grâce. But even as his sword descended Gervase was twisting out and away, so that coming up within Sir Bertrand's arm, Gervase threw him off balance. The burly knight staggered, arms flailing, sword flashing.

Now Gervase pounced on Sir Bertrand, delivering blows

here and there, up and to the left . . . down and to the right, changing hands with such bewildering irregularity . . . so flashing the blade, so rapid the blows that it seemed there was an arc of steel before Sir Bertrand's eyes.

Sir Bertrand was driven against the barrier and checked, and in that moment of hesitation the point of Gervase's sword was ripping up and into the rim of his helm, and his cap of steel went spinning off into the air, to fall with a rolling, echoing clang some distance away. The sword dropped from Sir Bertrand's hand.

The knight in Malling colours took his own sword in both hands and raised it high, his arms above his head, the point reaching for Sir Bertrand's unguarded eyes.

"Kill!" said Lord Henry.

A terrible hush lay on the people who watched. The knight in Malling colours brought his arms back, further. . . .

"No" Beata spoke calmly and clearly. "Thou shalt not kill."

The man could not have heard her; he was too far away for that. But he lowered his sword till the point was resting on Sir Bertrand's mailed breast, and leant on it, keeping his opponent pressed against the barrier.

And the crowd stamped and shouted till it seemed the timbers of the building must surely fail, and fall.

Beata was on her feet. By her side Lord Henry sat smiling, with a tinge of colour in his sunken cheeks. Beyond them Elaine, with tears on her face, laughed and clapped her hands. Beata ran round her chair and caught her sister up in her arms.

The cheers died away at last, for it seemed the two knights were having some converse. No-one was near enough to hear what they said. People shushed one another, and nudged and pointed to where Lord Henry was leaning forward, calling for the victor. Then Sir Bertrand, released from his durance, picked up his sword and handed it to the man who had defeated him . . . and walked away down the length of the hall leaving his destrier for the victor.

Gervase did not remove his helmet, even now. He walked slowly to the centre of the stand, and bent his knee to listen to

Lord Henry's congratulations. Then Elaine loosed the garland from her hair, and threw it down to him. He caught it on the tip of Sir Bertrand's sword, and bowed his thanks. And Beata, laughing, put her own garland to her lips before throwing that down, too . . . and this made everyone shout and yell and scream with laughter all over again. Now Gervase had two wreaths, one on either sword. He bowed again, and stepped back.

Berit had brought up the destrier, and gave Gervase a leg up into the saddle. He rode off with the two swords over his arm.

"Who would have thought the lad had it in him?" said Lord Henry. "Well, he is my heir, now. I shall have to acknowledge him . . . have him recognised as my son." Suddenly he was an old man.

Beata stopped smiling. She caught Telfer's eye, and then saw that Varons was also looking at her, and both were worried. In their eyes she saw that they too knew it had not been Jaclin who had fought Sir Bertrand. She looked at Elaine, and Elaine was saying something about going to see how Crispin was. So Elaine had not guessed.

"Why, Father," said Beata. "Jaclin deserves your love, it is true . . . but as to being your heir . . . ."

"Do not be greedy, girl," replied Lord Henry. "The church is satisfied with the dowry I have arranged to give with you, so do not hanker for Crispin's portion as well."

"It is not that, but . . . ."

Telfer said, "My lord is ill?" He came forward to give Lord Henry his arm. Beata looked into her father's face, and was silent. This was no time to deal an old man further blows.

"The masque must be cancelled," said Lord Henry. "When we are returned to the hall . . . I am a little tired, I find. I will go and rest a while. Telfer: make the announcement about my son's death. See to everything . . . he must lie in state in the chapel until such time as . . . ."

"May I suggest that this is no time for weddings, my lord?" Telfer's eyes were going from Beata to Elaine and back to Sir Henry.

"We will postpone Elaine's wedding for a couple of days . . . understandable, in view of family grief." He groped for Beata's arm. "Our guests shall still have their feast tonight, eh? And we shall show them all what we think of young Jaclin . . . hiding his light under a bushel . . . such skill . . . and the only one of you who could stand up to Sir Bertrand, with the exception of Crispin. Crispin . . . ." His smile was back on his face as he began to pass by his guests, bowing here and there, but leaning heavily on Beata's arm. "Crispin would have enjoyed the jousting today, wouldn't he . . .?"

Beata saw her father to his chamber, told her nurse to fetch same salves from the infirmary, and fled downstairs and up again, bursting into Jaclin's room before Varons could prevent her.

"Fool!" she said, forestalling his protest. "Did you think I would not know him?"

Gervase was being helped off with his chainmail and shirt, revealing a bad graze on the back of his left shoulder, and sundry other bruises.

"Show me your hands!" commanded Beata. He held them out, palms up, and she bit her lip. Although he had worn gloves the cuts and grazes inflicted by the bars of the cage had been re-opened in the fight. She swooped on the bowl and towel that Berit was holding, giving the sleeping figure of Jaclin a cursory glance as she set to work on Gervase's hurts.

"Is he sick, or drunk?"

"Drunk," said Varons. "Lady, it is not seemly that you be here . . . ."

"Enough!" said Beata, setting her teeth as she worked on Gervase's hands. "Have I not nursed him before, and no harm befell either of us?"

"I would not agree . . . as to there being no harm done," said Gervases, smiling and wincing. "Yet you need have no fear, Varons."

"No, indeed!" she said. "What is more, Varons, my father wants you in his chamber, to make arrangements for my brother's lying in state in the chapel. The masque is cancelled; there will be no dancing tonight. We shall have to devise some other entertainment for the company."

"I can devise an entertainment, if Varons will assist me," said Gervase. "Berit, too . . . if you have no other pressing duties. First you must see to your master, that goes without saying. But if you will come to me after, in the infirmary . . . ."

"I would take service with you, if I may," Berit suggested.

"Why, Berit!" said Gervase. "I had not thought . . . it might be, I suppose, if . . . . No! You do not know what . . . ."

"Yes, my lord; I do. I know all about it. I caught some of Rocca's whispers a while ago, and then I asked a pedlar who passes through Ware twice a year, and a servant of the wool merchant who buys fleeces from here and from Ware . . . and I soon learned the rest. My lord, you should have killed Sir Bertrand when you had the chance . . . ."

"I nearly did," said Gervase. "Tell me, what was it that you learned from your friends?"

"That you came across your aunt and her cousin in bed one day when your uncle was out hunting, and that they drove you out so that you should not denounce them. The other tale was even better . . . that your aunt climbed into your bed one night, instead of her husband's, and that you threw her out . . . and therefore she plotted revenge. . . ."

"Christ have mercy!" gasped Gervase, growing red in the face.

Varons slapped his thigh. "What, was there some truth in the rumours?"

Beata started to giggle. Berit grinned. "You know, my lord, I didn't believe those stories at first, you were so peaky and quiet . . . but now I'm not so sure!"

"Neither am I," said Beata, openly laughing. Then she sobered, seeing that Gervase was really embarrassed. "However it was, Gervase . . . whether it was simple jealousy on her part, or whatever . . . it is clear that no-one believes you stole that ring. Will you not make a push to recover your inheritance, perhaps by petitioning the King?"

"There might be a way," replied Gervase. "Varons . . . ."

"I must go," said Varons. "But I will return."

Beata spoke urgently. "Quick, before you go! My father must be told it was not Jaclin who performed so well in the lists. I began to tell him, but he checked me, thinking I was jealous of Jaclin. Now Crispin is dead, my father thinks to set Jaclin in Crispin's place as his heir."

"That is his right, surely," said Varons, with a troubled look at the supine figure of Jaclin. "Yet Jaclin will be a difficult master to serve."

"You accept it?" Beata took the salves from her nurse, who now came panting in. "You would let my father continue to believe that it was Jaclin who performed such feats of arms?"

"Lady, I dare not tell him how we have disobeyed his orders . . . or not at present, anyway." He bowed and went out.

"You must have fresh clothes," said Beata, bandaging Gervase's hands.

"I will fetch him whatever he needs from my Lord Crispin's wardrobe," said Berit. "Fear not, he shall have everything he requires."

"Not everything," said Beata, low down. She helped Gervase on with a clean shirt, and then stood back, lacing her hands before her. "Gervase, when you were down there, I prayed to God that you might be saved, and praying, I offered the only thing I had to give – that I would go into the convent willingly."

He gave her his twisted smile. "You will be abbess yet."

"My lady." The nurse pulled at her arm. "Your father has sent pages out to seek you. The abbot wishes to rehearse for your robing on the morrow."

"It is not to be postponed, then?" Her voice was high and thin. "I had hoped for a few days more, in view of Crispin's . . . ah well, now I know how hard it is going to be." She closed her eyes and clenched her fists, raising them to her forehead, shaking her head. "I can do it," she declared, opening her eyes, and lowering her hands. "I will do it."

"With God's help," said Gervase, still smiling that twisted smile.

"Surely I need some help," she agreed.

"My lady . . .!" Again the nurse twitched at her arm.

With a cry Beata leaped forward to be caught up in Gervase's arms. She clung to him, arms round his neck, lifting her face, lip to lip, cheek to cheek, murmuring endearments, her hands in his hair, at the back of his neck, his arms closing around her as if they could never be torn apart . . . both with their eyes closed, breath coming sharply, and as sharply released. One last kiss, slowly, with gentleness . . . .

She smiled. She blinked. Her eyes were shining, but she shed no tears. She took a step back . . . or perhaps it was he that set her from him. He did not smile, but he showed no sign of distress either. Only the watchful care of his eyes belied assumed indifference.

"Surely God will not grudge me one kiss," she said. And then turned and left him.

The afternoon was drawing into dusk when Jaclin woke. He was alone and he felt extremely ill. Presently he was able to pull on some clothes and stagger out. A man-at-arms jumped to attention and saluted the Malling "champion". He had been set there by Varons hours ago to prevent anyone going into Jaclin's room, for it had been decided to keep up the deception as long as possible.

"What's o'clock?" Jaclin screwed up his eyes. "What's that bell tolling?"

"My Lord Crispin died this morning."

Like everyone else in the castle, Jaclin thought first of what this might mean to him personally, and then, because he was not bad at heart, he thought of Lord Henry.

"My Lord Henry ordered that you be taken to him when you woke, to receive his congratulations on defeating Sir Bertrand . . . ."

Jaclin rubbed the back of his neck and frowned. He was trying to remember what it was he had been engaged in before he fell asleep. He was uneasily conscious that he had been about to do something important, but the fog in his brain was so dense that for the life of him he could not recall whether he had actually . . . he shook his head, and groaned. That wine . . . !

He stumbled down the stairs after the man-at-arms. The company were sitting down to meat, but tonight no dancers disported themselves in the body of the hall, nor jesters made merry. Tonight the musicians played doleful airs in minor keys, the drink flowed less freely, and even the conversation was muted. The abbot sat in Crispin's place, and at the end of the high table a cluster of black-clad nuns ate their meal in silence.

Jaclin would have made his way round the side of the hall to the dais, going behind the tables at which the castle retainers and guests' servants sat, but the man-at-arms led him across the hall to stand before the high table. There Lord Henry sat, clad in black, and on either side of him were his daughters, wearing black mantles over their golden gowns, and with filmy black veils attached to the gold fillets around their heads. Joan was not there, but Sir Bertrand was – shifting now and then to ease his bruises – and beyond Sir Bertrand sat Lady Escot, all solicitude for his hurts.

"Welcome!" Thrice Lord Henry clapped his hands, and there was silence as Jaclin collected his wits and bowed. "Welcome, Champion of Malling!"

"My lord jests," stammered Jaclin, going red.

"Indeed he does," said Beata. "For where is our champion's long sword and why does he not wear our golden leaves on his head?"

"I . . . leaves? My sword: well, I did look for it, but it was not in my room."

"And what of Crispin's sapphire?" said Beata. "I do not see that, either."

"Crispin's ring?" His voice rose to a squeak. "I have it not! Am I still asleep . . . ?"

"Asleep?" said Lord Henry, and his voice was sharp.

A fist crashed among the platters. Sir Bertrand pushed back his chair and stood, pointing to Jaclin. "That was not the man I fought. The voice, the hands . . . the height, even . . .!"

There was a buzz around the hall, quickly stilled. Lord Henry's eyelids dropped, as did the corners of his mouth. Jaclin backed away towards the wall, saying, "What the devil is going on?"

Lord Henry's eyes burned. "Beata . . . if it was not Jaclin . . . who was it?"

She laughed. It was a sad little laugh; the laugh of one who finds her victory hollow. "Can you not guess, Father?"

There was a fanfare from the musicians, and the double doors at the far end of the hall were thrown open. A roll on the drums and in the hush that followed Sir Bertrand's destrier appeared, with a tall man seated on his back. The newcomer held his head high, sitting well down in the saddle, guiding his horse at walking pace down the centre of the hall. His dark red hair had been newly cut and washed, short over his forehead, and long over the nape of his neck. It glowed in the candlelight like burnished copper. He wore a fine leather tunic, and over it a silken surcoat of the greenish-blue men call "watchet". On the forefinger of his right hand he wore Crispin's ring, and at his side hung the long sword he had taken from Jaclin. If anyone had further need of identification, it would be satisfied by the sight of two garlands of gold leaves which the newcomer carried on the shaft of his lance, upright in his right hand, with the butt resting on his stirrup.

Beata placed her right hand on her father's left, and felt him start. She looked sideways at the abbot who continued to eat, but whose eyes rolled in her direction, and then fastened again on Gervase. She looked beyond the abbot to where Sir Bertrand was standing with his hands flat on the table before him, his mouth open . . . and behind him to Lady Escot, who had spilt her wine and whose hands trembled as she dabbed at her mouth with a napkin.

Gervase looked neither to right nor left, but held Lord Henry's eyes. He knew that his case would stand or fall by what that dread lord might decide. Eye met eye: black eye and eye of golden yellow, and each eye noted the strength of the other's, taking in the harsh set of lips and the will-power betokened by jut of nose and chin.

Neither seemed to look away from the other, yet both were aware of men-at-arms passing around the hall, singling out a man here and a woman there, and taking them away.

"Has Varons betrayed me, then?" said Lord Henry, speaking to Beata, but continuing to look at Gervase. "Robing or no, you shall be whipped for this."

"Strangely enough," she replied, equally low, "this was not my idea . . . and Varons has certainly not betrayed you."

Gervase stopped before the dais, and lowered the tip of his lance so that the two garlands of gold leaves slid onto the table before Lord Henry.

"I come to claim my prize, Lord Henry!"

"As Champion of Malling you are welcome, Lord Escot," replied Lord Henry. "State what you require by way of guerdon for defending my honour, and you shall have it. You shall have no more and no less than is your due."

Gervase bowed. He set his lance upright once more, and for the first time his eye went along the faces at the high table.

"Then I would ask that you allow me to present a mumming play for your entertainment. It shall tell of love and blood and honour . . . it was a tale in which your son was interested, which he wished to present to you himself. As I wear his ring, I would carry out his wishes."

There was a pause, in which black eyes met golden, and neither would swerve.

"This is no court of law," said Lord Henry at last. "Yet I will not refuse you your wish. You shall set forth your entertainment, and my guests shall choose whether they wish to watch it or no."

At this Lady Escot rose and would have left her place, but that a man-at-arms appeared behind her chair, blocking her way. Another went to stand behind Sir Bertrand, though to give him due, that bold knight had made no attempt to leave.

"This is monstrous!" said Lady Escot, her voice cracking. "Have we not Lord Henry's permission to withdraw?"

"Would you be so discourteous as to leave an entertainment which he presents to his guests?" asked Gervase. "Or have you, perhaps, something to fear if you stay to hear . . . what there is to hear?"

"Why should I be afraid?" retorted Lady Escot, a tinge of colour coming into her cheeks. She re-seated herself, and tossed her head, as if to say that nothing Gervase did was worthy of her attention.

Lord Henry looked at Lady Escot. He looked long and hard. He had presided over many a court in his time, and knew that the woman was lying when she said she was not afraid. It was plain to any man of experience in such matters that Lady Escot had something to hide. Lord Henry reviewed his past conduct, which had assumed Gervase Escot's guilt. He looked at the pale, trembling woman, and he looked at Sir Bertrand who was smiling and cracking nuts – but Sir Bertrand's smile was too fixed to be natural, and his colour a trifle too high. Then Lord Henry looked back at Gervase. At that moment Lord Henry would have given much to have been able to stop the proceedings. Too much, however, had been said . . . he had been outwitted by that implacable man on the destrier. Yes, implacable. Gervase Escot could not be stopped.

Lord Henry said, "You have my permission to proceed."

Gervase shifted in the saddle, and now he was facing Sir Bertrand. "In the lists this morning I bade you, Sir Bertrand, yield yourself my prisoner. This you did, swearing a solemn oath that you would faithfully perform the task I would set you at supper this evening. I call on you now to fulfil that vow. Tell us what you know of the stealing of Lord Escot's ring at Ware, in July this year."

Sir Bertrand rose, and prodded by a man-at-arms, left the dais, and approached Gervase on the floor of the hall. Berit had stepped forward to take the destrier away, and Gervase now faced him, also on foot.

"That man," Sir Bertrand pointed to Gervase, "stole his uncle's ring. He was seen to do it. When challenged, he said he intended to keep it, to revenge himself on his uncle for marrying and cutting him out of the inheritance. I was staying at Ware at the time. Since old Lord Escot was much distressed by the discovery that his nephew was a criminal, I took charge of the proceedings. In fact, the woman who saw him take the ring reported the affair to me, so naturally I felt in honour bound to see the matter through. There was a trial, at which I presided. The evidence was quite clear. The man was convicted and sentenced. Before the sentence could be carried out, however, the felon escaped and vanished. Apparently he came here, and, masquerading under a false identity, wormed his way into the counsels of the late and much lamented Lord Crispin. When I heard the fugitive had been traced, I applied for him to be arrested, so that he might be returned to Ware in chains and duly punished for his crime."

Gervase turned to Lord Henry. "My lord, will you examine Sir Bertrand?"

Lord Henry folded his white hands on the table before him, and turned his head from Gervase to Sir Bertrand.

"Sir Bertrand, it is to your credit that you choose to cooperate in this 'entertainment'. These proceedings are not legal, but since we are here, and under certain obligations to Lord Escot, by all means let us enquire further into the crime of which he was accused and convicted. You were at Ware as a guest of your cousin, I believe?"

"That is so. The hunting was good, but my cousin was not happy because this young man, her husband's nephew, had behaved badly to her – giving rise to gossip of a wounding nature. . . ."

"One moment," said Gervase. "You were on very good terms with Lady Escot. Was not a marriage between you two spoken of at one time?"

"The church frowns on marriages between first cousins," said Sir Bertrand. "Besides, my cousin's first husband left her practically penniless."

"Ah yes. She was a widow when she married my uncle, was she not? I believe her first husband died within a year of their marriage, of a chill?"

"He was elderly," said Sir Bertrand. "And somewhat corpulent."

"As was my uncle," said Gervase. "And he did not live

long after the marriage, either . . . did he?" A ripple of amusement went round the hall.

"He died of a chill, too," said Sir Bertrand, frowning. "I do not see what there is to laugh about in that!"

"Indeed, no," said Lord Henry, in a soothing voice. "Now you went to Ware at your cousin's invitation, to support her in dealing with her husband's nephew, who was at that time also his heir. Is that correct?"

"Yes. I advised her to tell the young man to go from his uncle's house, but she said her husband would not agree to parting with Gervase, because he made himself useful about the estate. Very shortly after this Gervase stole his uncle's ring, so that solved the problem."

"No doubt the witness against Gervase Escot was of unimpeachable integrity?"

"Naturally. A bond-woman called Wanda . . . she has been with my cousin for many a year, and is absolutely trustworthy."

"A bond-woman?" Lord Henry's voice expressed incredulity. "A creature of your cousin's? Surely you are not serious?"

"If it had been her word alone," said Sir Bertrand, shrugging. "But the ring was found in his wallet, you see, and he could not account for how it came to be there."

Chapter Seventeen

Varons pushed two men in servants' dress forward, and stationed himself behind them.

"So much for the crime itself," said Gervase. "I repeat: I did not steal the jewel. It was put in my wallet some time that morning without my knowledge. But we will pass over the trial – and the sentence – and come to an event more strange than anything you have heard till now. There is no gaol at Ware. In times of need we use the innermost of two stone-built storerooms, which lead off the courtyard. The doors are bolted and locked from outside, the windows barred.

While I was lying in one of these cells, someone whispered to me from the window that I must look out for myself. He said he had overheard two men talking in low voices about where they could find a rope long enough to hang a man . . . and discussing whether a certain lock required to be oiled. I will not identify my friend, for fear of possible reprisals. He said he'd attempted to see who it was talking, but by the time he'd got himself to the door the two men had gone. But it had been on his mind, worrying him, for he argued I wasn't the sort to take my own life, and he knew there were certain people in the house who wanted me out of the way. So he took the trouble to find my sword, and drop it through the bars of my prison. And then he fled.

"I could hardly credit that anyone could be so base . . . but then, the whole affair had the proportions of a bad dream. I had not long to wait before I saw a crack of light under the door. The key grated in the lock, and was withdrawn, presumably so that they could oil the lock. Then the door opened and two figures stood there, throwing shadows before them. They had left the candle standing on the floor in the passage. One came in, leaping upon the pile of straw where I had been lying, bringing down a billet of wood, and the other followed, holding a coil of rope. No doubt their eyes were bewildered, coming from the lighted passage into the dark of my cell.

"It took them a moment or two to realise I was behind the door, and to turn on me. I pricked one on the forearm, enough to make him yelp and drop the billet of wood, and the other . . . I put the point of my sword to his throat, through his tunic and cape, and pressed hard enough to make him realise I was in earnest. I could see their faces clearly. I made one man tie his fellow's hands behind his back with the end of the rope they had brought, and then I got them both to lie down and tied the second man to the first. Then I turned the key in the lock, and left them. The candle was where they had set it down in the passage and one of them had dropped a cloak nearby. I took the cloak, kicked the candle out, made my way out into the courtyard, climbed the wall, and took to the forest."

"Devil's brood!" spat one of the accused. "How could you have seen us, seeing as we weren't there?"

Gervase nodded to Varons. "Try pulling up his sleeve."

The second man turned to run, but there was another man-at-arms close behind him. A short struggle, and the two scars were uncovered to prove Gervase's story.

"One of these men," Gervase continued, "came with Lady Escot on her marriage to my uncle. The other," he pointed to the man with the scarred forearm, "is called Choat, and he is in Sir Bertrand's service. I believe he could tell you who sent him to kill me that night."

"I was not there. No-one sent me." The man was sullen, but his eyes shifted to Sir Bertrand's face and then back to the floor.

"If you were not sent by anyone," said Gervase, "then it follows that you two conceived the idea of murdering me yourself, and that you alone can be punished for it."

The man who had gone with Choat into the storeroom now stepped forward. "My lord, I wish to dissociate myself from this fellow Choat." He oozed a smiling complacency. "He came to me, and overbore my scruples, persuading me to accompany him to see if the prisoner were all right. Imagine my astonishment when I discovered Sir Gervase was not only armed, but prepared to turn on those who had come to visit him. I had had no idea, believe me! The depths of depravity to which my friend Choat had sunk had been concealed from me till that moment!"

"What of the coil of rope which you bore?" Gervase's voice was harsh. "Does not that involve you equally with Choat in the conspiracy?"

The man swallowed, sweat on his brow. "My lord, it was his idea, I swear it. I went with him because he said he could trust no-one else. I thought it must be all right, if Sir Bertrand had bid him attend to the prisoner. . . ."

"That I did not!" swore Sir Bertrand. "The man lies if he says I had aught to do with it!"

"But I thought . . . ." The man looked scared. He shifted on his feet.

"Perhaps it was your mistress, Lady Escot, who sent Choat to the cells?" asked Gervase softly.

"Ridiculous!" said Lady Escot. "Why should I have done that? Were you not already discredited?"

"Surely! And I think even that did not satisfy you. Yet if neither of these men can produce a better story, I must ask Lord Henry to hold them for trial for attempted murder."

"Not so!" broke in the second man, his hand to his throat. "I know nothing of who sent Choat, but . . . I do not know if it means anything, but he was close in converse with my lady's tire-woman earlier that day, and I thought . . . as they passed across the yard, she picked up something from the cobbles, and it seemed to me it was my lord's ring . . . ." He licked his lips.

"My uncle's ring? The ring that was supposed to have been in my wallet at that time? The ring for which I was convicted of theft?"

The man nodded, eyes glancing now at the stolid face of Choat, and now at Gervase.

The abbot, who had continued to eat the while, said low down to Beata, "Now Lord Escot must prove complicity . . . if he has not that, he has nothing . . . ."

Gervase frowned at the two witnesses. "How came the ring in the yard?"

"I know not, except that everyone knew my lord had been complaining it had grown loose on his finger. You must have heard him . . . everyone did . . . the woman Wanda must have known whose ring it was! Everyone knew! My lord must have dropped it in the yard as he mounted his horse to go riding. I am sure she knew whose ring it was. Moreover . . . ." He hesitated. "I think it was she who came to let us out of the storeroom after you left. I could not see very well, for my hood had worked round over my face in my struggle to free myself . . . but I heard someone whispering to Choat, someone who had brought a candle into the storeroom . . . and then Choat freed me, and we made ourselves scarce. Whoever it was who freed us had gone before I had a chance to see them. They must have moved very lightly, my lord – like a woman!"

Varons pushed a middle-aged woman into the centre of the hall. She curtseyed, taking her time. She wore the good but plain gown of an upper servant, and had a plump face with knowing eyes. "My lord, if it please you, that man there tells nothing but lies. He is well known for it, and I have often said to my lady that he should be turned off. . . ."

"Why, you . . . !"

"Silence!" said Lord Henry. "Woman, did you pick up a ring from the courtyard that day?"

She hesitated, and then, "Yes, my lord. I found a ring and took it to . . . ." Her eyes flitted in Lady Escot's direction, and then lowered again. "I set it on the chest in my lord's bedroom. Sir Gervase stole it from there."

"And did you go down to the storeroom in the night, to see what had happened to the would-be assassins?"

"Of course not, my lord. I was . . . otherwise occupied." And this time her eyes flicked to Sir Bertrand, and then returned to the floor.

"Is that true, Sir Bertrand?" asked Lord Henry.

Sir Bertrand nodded, and laughed. "My cousin is ever thoughtful of my comfort! Aye, the woman spent the night with me."

"Then," said Gervase, "the two men must hang, as having been unable to prove the plot was anything but their own."

"Not so!" cried the second man, his eyes wild. "Wanda did not go back into the house after she picked up the ring! I watched her, thinking it was a pity it had not been my good luck to discover the ring, for my lord would likely have given me a reward for finding it. She spoke awhile to Choat, and then she saw Sir Bertrand crossing the yard and ran after him, crying that she must speak with him in private."

The woman started, and flushed. "I forgot! Yes, I showed him the ring, and he promised to put it back for me . . . ."

Sir Bertrand strode forward, glaring. "Woman! Did I not give it back to you, though you pressed it in my hand? You said you knew what to do with it. . . ."

"What did you think she meant by that?" said Gervase.

"Why . . . how should I know?"

"But you saw the ring yourself? You recognised it?"

"I . . . yes."

"Yet before noon you had three men come into the buttery and drag me to the ground while you stood over me, shouting that I was a thief – a thief of a ring which you had seen a short while before, in the hands of Wanda – a thief of a ring which you knew very well was not missing?" Sir Bertrand was silent, and his face grew red with anger.

Gervase asked, "Did the woman Wanda suggest that she arrange to have the ring put into my wallet secretly? Did she suggest that you might then have me accused of theft in order to please her mistress, your cousin?"

"I . . . she is a clever piece, Wanda . . . ."

"Did she suggest you misuse your position in my uncle's house to arrest me and try me? Did she suggest that I then be visited in the night by two trusted men, with a rope . . . a rope to hang me with . . . under such circumstances as my uncle might think I had committed suicide?"

"No!" screamed Wanda. Her chubby face was now colourless. "I did not think . . . . I could not have . . . it is true that I arranged for the ring to be put in your wallet, but it was his idea, not mine! I told your one-time bedfellow Anne that it was a good-luck charm, and she promised to put it secretly in your wallet before noon, when I plotted to waylay you, and then accuse you of theft. But of the plot to murder you I knew nothing . . . I swear it!" And she fell on her knees.

"But witnesses have deposed that it was you who came down to the storeroom with a candle in the middle of the night, to see what had become of the murderers?"

"Not I! Not . . . ! No, no! I stayed in bed, I swear it! I did not even hear him leave, for I was asleep . . . I swear it! I only knew he had gone when I woke and found the bed cold! And he told me nothing, even then . . . !"

"Who left you in bed . . . in the night?"

"Him!" She pointed to Sir Bertrand. "Sir Bertrand de Bors. He went down to see that everything had gone as planned. It was his idea! Not mine! Not mine!" She began to work her way to the dais on her knees, sobbing. Sir Bertrand leaped forward, his dagger raised to strike Wanda, but at the same moment Gervase also leaped forward, and the lance he still held in his hand was used as a single-stick to parry the blow, and send the dagger to scatter rushes on the floor.

There was a thick silence. Even Wanda, crouching low, had ceased to sob. The Lady Escot screamed. Hands and mouth trembling, she was suddenly an old woman. Heads turned in her direction. She put her hands over her face, and huddled down in her chair.

"Well, Sir Bertrand?" said Lord Henry. "How much did Lady Escot know?"

Sir Bertrand looked at Lord Henry. He gazed around the hall, with a fair assumption of indifference. He drew himself up to his full height, and laughed. He folded his arms across his chest and stared Lord Henry in the eye. He would say nothing.

Lord Henry rose to his feet, slowly and with dignity. He said, "This was not a court of law. Yet we have heard enough today to justify reopening the case against Lord Escot. Varons: take the three conspirators away to the West Tower and hold them in separate cells for interrogation. Sir Bertrand, you are here as a guest, and will be treated as one. You will return to your quarters but my men will replace your servants, and you will remain confined there until such time as your case can be brought to the attention of the King's Justiciars. I suggest that you consider what damages you can pay Lord Escot for wrongful arrest and slander, which may perhaps provide a mitigating circumstance when the case comes to trial.

"As for you, Lady Escot: nothing has been proved against you, which I think is more than you deserve, for I have little doubt you know exactly what was going on at every stage of the conspiracy. Howsoever, if you will agree to leave Ware and take up residence in some place appointed by Lord Escot, he will, I dare say, allow you sufficient revenues on which to live."

Lady Escot was trying to stand. She was whimpering, like a whipped dog. Two men-at-arms led her away. Sir Bertrand bowed low to Lord Henry and marched out after her, two more men-at-arms falling in behind him. The other conspirators had already been taken from the hall.

Gervase remained, leaning on his lance, still looking at Lord Henry.

Black eyes looked into golden, and neither man smiled.

Lord Henry said, "Lord Escot, you have been greatly wronged, but it shall not be said you sought justice in vain. Rest assured that whatever is in my power to do for you shall be done. Your estates shall be returned to you and you will receive compensation for your sufferings. And now, as your entertainment is over, may I invite you to join us at table?"

Gervase shook his head. "No, my lord. I have served Malling, and you have discharged the debt. Let that be the end of it. I will trespass on your hospitality one night more, and then be on my way."

So saying, he bowed and left the hall.

The abbot said, "You weep, Lady Beata? Did the man mean so much to you?"

Some hours later Telfer was sent to fetch Gervase from the infirmary, to speak with Lord Henry in the green solar.

"You will deal gently with him, I trust," said Telfer, as they went along. "He is much shaken by Crispin's death. He thought at first to place Jaclin in Crispin's stead, but now he has reconsidered. He has had Jaclin with him, talking the matter over, and my lord sees that it will not answer. Provision will be made for the boy, of course, but . . . ." He shrugged.

"He must marry again," said Gervase. "Of his four children, the best is the one he has most neglected, and whom he now intends to throw into the arms of the church."

"That is what I told him. The Lady Beata went further: she said all this had been brought about because he had not paid his debt to the church with his own body."

Gervase gave a short laugh. "The old fox would not see it that way . . . ."

A page threw open the door of the solar and they went in. Beata was standing near the door, waiting for him. Lord Henry sat with Elaine and the abbot by the fire, but Beata had plainly come to greet him, and speak with him before he spoke to the others. She held out her hands to him. He took them. Her dark curls were tousled under a filmy black veil, but she had discarded her black mantle, and her gold dress glimmered with every breath she drew.

She said, "Gervase, you will listen to him . . . promise me you will listen! Swear that you will do as he asks! Believe me, I wish it, too!"

She withdrew her hands abruptly, and walked away. Gervase went slowly to the fireplace, and bowed to Lord Henry. The old man was sitting in a high-backed chair, a fur thrown over his knees. He gestured to Gervase to take a seat beside him.

"Lord Escot, you see before you a man stricken by sorrow, bereft of his heir . . . bereft, too, of the support he had looked for in his daughter's betrothed. I beg you . . ." Lord Henry was so little accustomed to begging that it sounded rather more like a command than a plea, "I beg you to forgive what slights I may unintentionally have put upon you. On this, the eve of Christmas, I wish to be at odds with no man. You refused to eat and drink with me earlier this evening. Will you not reconsider that decision?"

A goblet of wine was handed to Gervase, and it was Telfer who served him. Telfer wanted him to drink. Well, he would do so.

Gervase lifted the goblet to Lord Henry in a toast. "If you will forgive me for abusing your hospitality, at the same time?"

"Indeed," said Lord Henry. "I think myself much in your debt. You have a talent for handling affairs, it seems. You will be glad to hear that the man Rocca has been laid by the heels, and a search of his house revealed a large amount of money for which he seems – at the moment – unable to account."

"I am delighted to hear it," said Gervase. He thought, and now he will come to the point. . . .

"In other matters, too," said Lord Henry, "I believe I have much to thank you. Your attitude to my daughters has been most honourable . . . may I say chivalrous? Yes, I believe I may say chivalrous. It reflects great credit upon you . . ."

" . . . and upon them." Gervase bowed.

"Of course, to a man your background – and wealth – these girls must seem insignificant little creatures?"

Where was the trap? Gervase could sense there was one, and yet he could not see it. He said, "Surely they both deserve the title Queen of Beauty."

"You are something of a flatterer, I fear. Yet a large dowry will often compensate for other shortcomings, and she is still young, and would bear you healthy children . . . ."

A pulse began to leap in Gervase's throat. He could not believe what he was hearing . . . there was a gathering dread . . . and then the words came, and they were terrible in his ears.

"All things considered, I believe we could both do worse than return to the arrangement whereby you were to wed my daughter Elaine. More wine for Lord Escot, Telfer."

Elaine had turned her head away from him, and was looking into the fire. Now she put up a hand to cover her eyes.

Gervase rose, but there at his elbow was Beata. She said, "I wish it. I beg of you, think! You must marry and have children. Can I rest quiet in the cloister, knowing that you lie alone at night? Grief passes, they say. It must be so, or we would all die when we are taken with this sickness. I am sick, but I suppose I shall be well in time, and all the quicker for knowing you are wed to my sister."

Elaine said, "I do not think he will . . . although it would make me very happy to . . . ." She pressed her hands to her mouth, and shook her head.

"She is a good girl," said Lord Henry. "I am lucky in having such dutiful children, am I not? Yet I think there is something more than duty in Elaine's agreement to marry you."

Gervase looked at the abbot, to find that cleric nodding and smiling. He looked beyond the abbot to where Telfer stood with bright eyes, also nodding and smiling. He looked at Lord Henry, and noted the tired lines around his eyes, and the effort he was making to hold himself straight in his chair. He felt Beata's hands close around his forearm, and heard her whisper, "I beg of you . . . ."

"You do me too much honour," he said, and his voice seemed to come from a long way away. "The Lady Elaine would grace any king's court, and I am but a humble knight, occupied with matters of hedging and ditching. I am too coarse a robe for her to wear."

Now Lord Henry's eyes began to burn, and his fingers to shift along the arm of his chair. He said, "Elaine, Lord Escot requires assurance that you will be a loving wife to him. Walk with him by the windows, and talk with him awhile. He needs to be convinced of your good faith."

Elaine walked away to the window, and after a moment Gervase followed her, stroking his chin. Elaine did not look at him, but tugged at a tress of her hair and spoke softly, her eyes lowered.

"My lord, I know you do not love me, yet it is true that I have learned to care for you."

"Hush, lady. Do not say the words. Surely you will wish them unsaid tomorrow."

"I realise it will take time for you to recover from . . . I know that you love my sister. I would not have urged this . . . or not so soon. My father is too hasty. It was Beata's idea to speak with you now. She wanted this settled, that she might leave, knowing we were both provided with . . . . In six months, or a year, perhaps . . . ."

He did not know what caused him to look round, but he was just in time to see Beata put her hand to her forehead, and close her eyes. It was only for a moment, and then she straightened up – with an effort – and bent to pull the fur higher over her father's knees. And now she was smiling.

He turned back to Elaine. She was looking at him, and beyond him . . . and now Elaine was smiling, too. She said, "I understand. You would look at me and think of her, always. There is something between you, I have seen it happen so many times . . . she does not have to speak to pull you to her, nor you, to turn her in your direction."

"Lady, I wish it were not so, for all our sakes."

"Yes. Gervase. . . ." It was the first and last time that she called him by his name. "Do not lose heart. . . ."

He bowed over her hand. "Lady, if you ever need a friend . . . ."

"I have a better one in mind," she said. Then she walked past him, and left the room.

Gervase bowed to Lord Henry, and followed her example.

Morning came at last. Gervase had spent most of the night sitting motionless by the fire in his cell at the infirmary, dozing, thinking, praying. He had been so chilled, despite the fire, that he had pulled a blanket over his shoulders, in addition to the cloak Berit had found for him.

"Burial of one kind today," said the squire, helping Gervase to don the sky-blue surcoat. "And of another kind tomorrow. Robing today . . . not to be postponed under any circumstances, apparently. Burial tomorrow of my lord Crispin . . . then everyone's to go . . . and Malling will be so quiet . . . !"

"I suppose I should wait to see Crispin buried," said Gervase. He plunged his face into cold water, trying to wake himself up. He felt numb with grief.

"Captain Varons said he would come to fetch you for the robing . . . instructions to give you a good position, where you can see it all."

Gervase winced. "Did he think I would run away? Though I confess that now it comes to it, I wish I had not promised to attend." Yet she would not run away. And she would expect to see him there.

Varons came at last, his snapping eyes telling of the strain of recent weeks. "No swords in the chapel . . . that's right. You've to stand at the front. There's a chair set for Lord Henry, but for no-one else. The place will be packed. What a way to spend a feast day!"

The chapel was crowded with noble company, and few of the servants had been able to find a place to stand. Some of the pages had climbed up the pillars, and clung to the rafters, in order to get a good view. Beata was popular and they were sad to see her go. The air was heavy with the greasy smoke of countless candles and of incense. Rushes had been freshly laid on the floor, to take the chill from the stone flags.

Varons led Gervase to a pillar under the rood, at the point where the nave of the chapel joined the chancel. It was a somewhat exposed position, and Gervase would willingly have drawn back into the crowd, but that Varons remained at his side.

Then his eyes were taken with the sight of the black-draped coffin on the bier before them. It might be Christmas

Day, but Crispin dominated the castle, in death as in life. Beata would have to pass by the coffin on her way to the altar to be robed.

He clenched his hands on his belt, and began to pray for her.

They were coming . . . a susurration of rich fabrics, a sigh or two from the congregation, and Lord Henry came into view with his daughters, one steadying him on either side. The abbot and his retinue, the cross and its bearer . . . the black-robed nuns . . . nothing was lacking by way of ceremony. The boys' voices swung high, in arcs of sound, and the bases echoed them below.

Elaine and Beata were still wearing their gold dresses, but one wore a filmy veil of black, and the other had her head and shoulders swathed in folds of white linen. Then Lord Henry was sinking into his chair, and the abbot was speaking, in a voice surprisingly sonorous for one so small of stature. He told once more of the vow Lord Henry had made, of how its fulfilment had been deferred, and of how it was now to be redeemed.

Then the girl in the white, all-concealing veil stepped forward, and the abbot spoke to her, and she was received up into the chancel, among the nuns and the clergy, to take her vows.

But Gervase continued to look at the girl who stood on the far side of Lord Henry's chair, the girl in the filmy black veil, with the short dark curls, with the broad yet delicate face and dark eyes that blinked to hold back tears . . . lips soft yet full, that smiled at him over her father's head. At Beata, his love, his all . . . Beata, still standing beside her father . . . not gone into the arms of the church.

Eventually it was done, and the new nun, her sweet face joyful within the close cap and hood, was kissed by her family for the last time and withdrew from the world.

Then Lord Henry, trying to rise from his chair, found he needed more assistance than Beata could give him. Gervase stepped forward, took the old man's right arm, and helped him to his feet.

Gervase walked with Beata in the moonlight, beneath the

cloisters. Tomorrow Crispin would be buried . . . tomorrow many of the guests would depart from the castle . . . tomorrow Gervase was to move into Crispin's old apartments, and the following day he was to be formally betrothed to Beata.

But now they spoke of Elaine as they walked close together, with his right arm around her, and her left hand in his.

" . . . for it was not my idea," Beata was saying. "Even if I had thought of it, I could never have suggested it, because I had sworn to go willingly into the convent."

"Perhaps it was because she saw you could make the ultimate sacrifice that she found the courage to do it," said Gervase, putting her hand to his lips. How nearly he had lost her!

"No, I cannot take the credit, for she said she had been thinking of it for some time. Since that poor ostler was blinded . . . you remember? She said it was brought home to her then what a feeble sort of creature she was. She said she wanted to change, but needed help . . . help which she did not feel she would obtain in her marriage to Sir Bertrand. She said it was only a step from that to thinking of how peaceful it would be in the convent, and to long for it. Only she did not think Father would allow both of us to go into the convent, and of course he would not have done so. Then she began to see how much I had changed, and how I hated the thought of becoming a nun. She said she could not understand why I dreaded something that she wanted so badly."

Gervase frowned. He did not speak, but she picked up his moment of doubt, and answered it. "Yes, she did love you, I think . . . not as I do, not with every thought, but quietly and gently. If she had been able to marry you, instead of Sir Bertrand, if you had not shown her so clearly that you could not be happy in such a marriage . . . then I think she would not have dared to oppose Father's wishes." She pulled his arm across her, and stood still, cradled in his embrace. She said, "I thought I would die with the pain, when you went with her last night to the window, and I saw she was pleading with you . . . I could not see how you could resist her, and it hurt . . . though indeed, I would have gone with a smile if . . . ."

He turned her to him, and kissed her.

Presently they continued their stroll, up and down. "I went after her, last night, and found she had cut off all her lovely hair. She was laughing and crying, both at the same time, and saying she couldn't marry anyone now . . . ."

"The abbot took your part?"

"Yes. He had seen everything. He is a wise man. He went to talk to her, and then he talked to me, and made me confess that I loved you, and that I thought you loved me, although you had never said so . . . ."

"Had I not?" said Gervase, his lips on her hair. "Now I quite thought I had, once or twice . . . or ten times."

"Or twenty." She shuddered, and his arm tightened about her once again. "It was so close . . . I can still hardly believe it . . . even though all these years I never really thought it would happen! Marry me quickly, Gervase! I am so afraid something will go wrong! Father has changed his mind once too often about Elaine's marriage, even though he has now consented to ours. . . ."

"I will carry you off over my saddle-bow, if necessary. But will you be satisfied with Ware, after this?"

"Ware?" She pushed away from him, searching his face by the fitful light of a cresset set in the corner of the cloisters. "Ware . . . ." She looked about her. "I never thought to leave Malling. Yet if that is what you wish . . . ." She nodded.

"My lady of Ware!" He kissed her, and in that same moment was filled with doubt. Ware was a small place. Perhaps she might be content there, if she were lucky enough to produce a child straight away, but he . . . ? After Malling, what would Ware seem like to him? Then, like a lion which had been kept locked for too long in a cage, the responsibilites that went with the position of steward of Malling leaped onto his shoulders. The burghers in the Midlands, seeking remission of taxes: someone should ride up there up there at once . . . the poverty Rocca had created among the peasantry hereabouts . . . the new corn-mill . . . the dozens of men awaiting trial in the West

Tower . . . Telfer, and Varons . . . all his friends here . . . .

While thoughts like this passed through his mind, Beata's nurse came to take her away, and Gervase was left to pace the coisters by himself. Although the hour was late, he did not feel that the day was over – yet he could not think what it was he had left undone that he ought to have done. He went out into the great courtyard, and looked up at the keep. There were torches alight on the ramp, and a dog and a man descending. Flash jumped up at Gervase, barked, and ran back to the ramp.

"They await you in the solar, my lord," said Thomas. His writing implements were under his arm.

Gervase went with Thomas up into the keep, across the hall, up more stairs and into the solar. There, where he had first seen Crispin at the head of the table, Lord Henry now sat in state. He was lapped in furs, and a pile of documents lay under his hand. Telfer sat on his right, and Varons on his left. Thomas brushed past Gervase to take a seat at a desk, a little to one side. There was a vacant chair at the foot of the table. It would have been Hamo's chair once, completing the circle.

In that moment Gervase saw that Lord Henry would never let him go back to Ware, save perhaps on a short visit. He saw that he could marry Beata whenever he wished. He also saw that if he took that vacant chair, he would be tied to an old man's whims all over again, that his days would be filled with work from dawn to dusk, and that there would always be a threat held over him that if he did not please his master, Lord Henry would take another wife. . . .

He looked into Lord Henry's eyes, and saw there an appeal for understanding; more . . . he saw that the old man was to be trusted.

Everything he had ever wanted was within his grasp.

He took a deep breath, and sat in the vacant chair.

"Now," said Lord Henry, "we can begin. . . ."